THE HUNT

The first they took were a pair of campers, young men surf-casting for their breakfast and too busy to notice the figures moving toward them through the fog until there was only time to turn and recognize, as in a nightmare, the sharp stick skewering the neck of the teenage boy, the trailing entrails of the Greek, the charred black face of the thin young woman dressed in rags—time only for that before the big man with the open, festering shoulder wound sunk his fingers into the eyes and mouth of the nearer one and pulled him down into the foaming sea, breaking his neck as he fell, while the others moved over his friend with open, hungry mouths.

The big man watched them die.

Then, later, watched them slowly rise . . .

SHE WAKES
Jack Ketchum

"KETCHUM KNOWS HOW TO SET UP SUSPENSEFUL SITUATIONS, IS ABLE TO CREATE IMMEDIATELY RECOGNIZABLE CHARACTERS—AND MOST IMPORTANTLY—POSSESSES THAT SPECIAL ABILITY TO MAKE THE READER KEEP TURNING TO THE NEXT PAGE!"

—*Fangoria*

SHE WAKES

JACK KETCHUM

BERKLEY BOOKS, NEW YORK

SHE WAKES

A Berkley Book/published by arrangement with
the author

PRINTING HISTORY
Berkley edition/March 1989

ISBN: 0-425-11453-8

A BERKLEY BOOK ® 757,375
Berkley Books are published by the Berkley Publishing Group,
200 Madison Avenue, New York, N.Y. 10016
The name "BERKLEY" and the "B" logo
are trademarks belonging to Berkley Corporation.

PRINTED IN THE UNITED STATES OF AMERICA

10 9 8 7 6 5 4 3 2 1

Thanks to Susan Allison, Ellen Antoville,
Carole Bates, Dean Kaltzas, Tasos Moutzouris,
Alice Martell, Marjorie Shepatin, and
Evangelina Siriandu for their help on this one.

For Paula White,
who got me to the islands.

SHE
WAKES

PROLOGUE

THE SPHINX

"There are no covenants between
sheep and wolves."

—The Iliad

LELIA

SANTORINI

There was always flesh . . .

She stepped back across the cool concrete floor, trying to see herself head to thigh in the small bathroom mirror. She was standing in the middle of the bedroom before she could. Beside her on the bed her clothes were neatly stacked, the better items already in the closet. By contrast the other girl's pack looked like an open wound, its gaudy contents spilling out over the bedspread and pillow of the second bed and trailing to the floor like the entrails of some headless, legless, armless beast.

She could not remember the girl's name. Ula or Mia. Something Swedish. The girl had been traveling a long time. Her whites were a tired sallow color. She ought to have found a washing machine. Even in Greece they had them.

She looked away in distaste, back to the mirror.

Even naked she still smelled of donkey.

There were five hundred sixty-six steps from the harbor up into the town. In the midday heat the animals had sweated and struggled. The driver would allow them to slow down only so much and then he'd whip the flanks of the last in line and that one would bolt, which would spook the others.

She liked the feel of riding, the quick jump of the muscles beneath her. She would reach out and touch the neck. It was hard and hot and wet. She could feel the animal's pain, its effort.

No matter how hard and strong the body, she thought, there was always flesh. Something too soft and yielding.

Here.

She pinched together the pale thin skin between waist and hip.

And here.

Under the arm, where the breast began.

She looked over to her bed. The sewing kit was there, open.

She pinched the flesh of her inner thigh.

And here, she thought. The skin tingled.

Her roommate was on the terrace, three floors up, taking in the view down the mountain in the waning sunlight. Lelia knew what the girl was seeing; a bay seven miles long and five miles wide, the mouth of a dormant volcano, sparkling with light. Blue sky and blue sea on an infinite horizon. From that height it was spectacular and it would keep her there awhile. And this would not take long. It never did.

In the sewing kit she found a needle. Also a ball of cotton. She put the needle between her teeth. In the side compartment of her travel bag she found a pack of matches, the name of a Paris restaurant on the cover. She returned to the mirror.

It was something she had taught herself to do and it had not been easy at first, but that was years ago and long since there had been satisfaction in it, and finally there was pleasure. She struck a match and held it to the needle. The tip went black with carbon. She smelled sulfur. She wiped the needle with the cotton.

She pinched the skin of her inner thigh and pulled it safely away from the muscle beneath, then pressed the needle to it and slowly pressed it home to half its length. Eyes closed, aware of the needle slowly displacing the layers of skin, the cells committing to its long foreign shape.

Her eyes flicked back and forth under the closed lids. Inside the thigh she felt a throbbing, a bruised feeling. On the outside, a sensation of burning.

Slowly she withdrew the needle, concentrating, focusing on the feeling of closure as millimeter by millimeter the flesh moved together again, as she was whole again.

Whole but not so, she thought. The cells protested. Her lip, her breasts, her belly glistened in the mirror.

Indestructible—but not exactly. Illusion.

The pain receded. She exhaled deeply.

She stared into her own pale blue eyes, alight and beautiful.

There was always flesh . . .

Something to be conquered, beaten.

JORDAN THAYER CHASE

MYKENE

He had walked nearly a mile uphill by now and he could see the ruins of the fortified city high above in the distance, a splash of honey-colored rock against the lush green mountains. The town lay behind him; the restaurants and bars named Agamemnon and Menelaos and Klitemnistra, the tourist shops and hotels, the teenage boys in designer-jean jackets roaring by on mopeds, revving them like hogs; he was glad to leave it behind.

Beside the road he passed two crypt sites where excavation had begun. Cypress trees grew in the valley along with century plants and frail red poppies. The sun was not too hot. The silence admitted only the wind. He could see it blowing the skirts of tourist women and snatching at sun visors as he got closer to the ruins.

To his right a herd of goats and sheep milled through the long wild grass. He stopped and watched for a while until the herdsman pulled off his cap and stared at him. He gazed across the field at the man.

He read him. The man was open.

It was easy.

Flashes of anger under tight control. Anger and moral outrage.

He saw why. The images that came to him were vivid. Three days ago a group of boys, tourists, had stood here drunk and pelted the man's flock with garbage. Cans, bottles, and a half-eaten feta cheese sandwich. He saw it exactly as the man had then, startled, running toward the boys, waving his cap and shouting. He saw them laugh and point and then run away.

He felt the man's pain and anger.

One goat still walked with a limp. One of the boys had hit him squarely on the shin with a bottle. Chase picked the goat easily out of the flock. There. The young one. The man's favorite, directly in front of him.

Now the man was wary.

Chase walked away.

The road was steep. His breath came hard now. Forty-five years and too many cigarettes and too much single-malt whiskey. He liked the exertion, though. A man his size needed work or else he got soft. Lately he got much too little. The belly was flat and his shoulders thick as they had always been but the legs had softened some. I'll have to work on the legs, he thought. When I get back.

If I do.

It struck him like a snake, the second time that day.

I might die here.

To hell with that, he thought. Just keep going.

To his left lay a narrow dirt road marked by a wooden sign that read TREASURY OF ATRAEUS.

There was a buzzing in his head like an angry swarm of insects. His hands trembled.

Yes, he thought. *Right here.*

He wiped his forehead. Mild as the day was he was over-dressed for the weather. Already the gray suit jacket looked wilted. The rich leather shoes were covered with dust.

Elaine warned you, he thought. Back home before you left for the airport. But you were in a hurry.

You're not prepared for this, he thought.

Of course you're not.

• • •

It always happened that way. He was always unprepared to one degree or another. Like the shepherd before, reading him.

Or being drawn here.

Suddenly, inexplicably, two days ago he was sitting in a conference room in New York across from his board of directors and Mykene had simply *spoken* to him.

I have to go see Tasos, he'd told Elaine. Check on the export deal.

She knew him well by now, knew his gift and knew enough not to question him, though it was as clear to her as to him that the deal could be checked by phone in a matter of minutes. That was the excuse, not the point. Made for her benefit, so she wouldn't worry. She understood that.

So far he'd not even phoned Tasos.

He couldn't have if he'd wanted to.

He barely remembered stepping off the plane, buying his bus ticket here.

Mykene had him now. He gave himself over.

It had happened to him before but never quite like this.

He'd be visiting a place and suddenly it would just reach out to him. Always someplace of some antiquity. Something alive and ancient there touched him, something always deeply moving. Each touch was dangerous. Yet each had changed him somehow. Thus far, he felt, for the better.

This was different.

This had been more in the nature of marching orders. He felt some strong, firm hand pulling the strings. Get your ass to Greece, Chase.

He knew better than to resist. To resist was madness.

He obeyed.

And now he blinked into the sunlight and wished for dark glasses.

Back home there were a few thousand people depending on him in one way or another, in companies with names like

Laserlab and Ampcomp and JTC Imports. To them this was foolishness, irresponsible.

It didn't matter.

And he wasn't exactly a kid anymore, burrowing through the ruins of Tenochtitlán in the blazing Mexican sun.

That didn't matter either.

He had the feeling he'd never done anything so important in his life. If he was a little old for it, so be it.

He'd learned to trust these things. There wasn't much to do but trust them.

He climbed the road through a copse of trees. There was a chain-link gate and an admissions shack and a small dark man wearing sunglasses inside it. He handed the man seventy drachmas and received a ticket. He kept climbing.

The trail veered off left and when he rounded the corner he found himself alone at the base of the *dromos*, a passageway about twelve feet wide and a hundred feet long, cut into the mountain, flanked with stones and fitted with mortar. Huge stones. Cyclopean. The term was right. An immense hand here.

The mountain sloped gently down around him, speckled with brown and green grasses, the entrance to the tomb like a great forty-foot dagger-thrust into the heart of it, cruel and magnificent too, big enough to thwart the sense of distance. He could see why the ancient Greeks had confused the shapes of gods and men. Who could say which had built this place?

Agamemnon's tomb.

Agamemnon.

The king who led the Greeks to Troy. Heir to the curse of the House of Atreus, which began somewhere in unrecorded time with brother feeding brother the flesh of his own children. King to a rough Bronze Age people sixteen centuries before Christ whose gods and goddesses were of earth and harvest—not the pacific sky gods of Olympus.

Agamemnon. Murderer of his daughter. Killed by his wife and queen.

The male, generative principle. Sacrificed to the female, reproductive principle.

It happened again and again, whenever the earth was starved and needy. There probably was such a man, thought Chase. Sacrificed, like many kings before him when they grew old—their judgment questionable or their power spent—to the goddess earth, to replenish it and begin the cycle anew.

These were the people who had built this place.

A gust of wind cuffed his thin brown hair and he pushed it back over his forehead, wiped a line of sweat off the stubble at his chin.

The tomb was still vigorous, still magnetic. Even standing out here he felt it.

He stood at the entrance and looked in. It was empty. He'd beaten the tourists here. They would still be at the fortified city on the mountain.

Good.

He felt excited, receptive, almost passive. Open to whatever was inside, the adrenaline gently flowing. Exactly as it should be.

Go on, he thought.

He stepped inside.

At first footfall the place began to sing to him.

Physically sing.

He heard the droning of bees—from where? He could see none. Mud daubers probably, in the niches between the stones. And then the chattering of birds, dozens of birds, sparrows, growing louder and louder as he moved inward, scolding from their nests and swooping through the circular beehive chamber constructed so that with each footfall the entire room seemed to shudder with short sudden tremblings of echo. He walked to the center of the chamber.

He stood gazing at the walls blackened by shepherds' fires, at the great stones of the base cut smaller and smaller as they ascended the wall until they were only brick size, set in concentric circles at the top. Soon the birds subsided. The air inside was cool and still. The single bright shaft of sunlight from the entrance washed him with gold.

He emptied himself, lay open.

Not quite, he thought.

He felt a sense of past but not of power. The power was elsewhere. But near. Very near.

There.

To the right was a doorway maybe six and a half feet high—a smaller, man-sized version of the gigantic entranceway he'd just come through. He was sure he was right.

This place.

The sparrows protested as he crossed the floor and stood in the doorway, its massive lintel only inches from the top of his head. He looked inside.

Perhaps in the morning there was some spill of light into the chamber, but not now.

He peered blindly into a deep rich darkness.

His eyes would not adjust. He felt the dark like a physical shock.

He raised an arm, held it straight in front of him.

From the elbow on it disappeared entirely.

He strained to see, closing his eyes and a moment later opening them. There was nothing. Fingers, wrist, forearm–all were completely gone. Something shivered across his spine.

He raised his other arm and started forward.

It was not like night. It was not like closing his eyes. It was not like both together.

It was deeper than that, much deeper, like the bottom of a pit that had never seen the light. He could feel his pupils dilating rapidly, trying to accommodate to this impossible environment.

He inched along, working forward in a direct line from the doorway. The air was cooler here, much cooler, and damp. But there was no musty smell—just the smell of earth, of something clean and hard. He felt sure he was in nothing man had made now. It was a cave—a natural chamber deep in the belly of the mountain. He was wary of breaks and pitfalls. He scuffled forward groping like a blind man. Ten feet. Twenty. Twenty-five.

Still there was only darkness. He did not look back.

He could hear nothing but the sound of his feet on the rough pitted floor and his own breathing. Even the birds were silent.

He wondered if he was alone.

Then finally his fingers and hands found the cool sweating stone.

Its touch was electric. He felt something race inside him—a strong, wonderful presence here. So strong he almost spoke to it—*Yes. I hear you. Yes.*

He turned his back to the wall and stared toward the entrance, its honey glow, the muscles of his back relaxing, relieved to finally see again. He felt the scrape of rough stone across his shoulders.

And then he froze there.

He shook his head in disbelief.

He'd been walking though the dark. Swimming through it.

Yet ten feet back on either side, spaced evenly apart and resting on slabs of stone, a pair of candles stood burning. Birthday candles. Very small, illuminating only a tiny space of floor.

But *burning*.

LELIA

SANTORINI

It was late by the time she got rid of the Greek boy at the bar and then walked home, and her roommate, the Swedish girl, was already sleeping.

Cow, she thought.

• • •

The girl slept nude, and though the night had started out cold
it was milder now, so the sheet and blanket were down around
her waist. She lay to one side, one hand beneath the pillow and
the other arm draped over it, mouth slightly open. Her
shoulders and back were brown and firmly muscled, the breast
flesh very pale by comparison.

She knelt beside the girl's bed and blew gently into her face.
The eyelids fluttered.

"Hello? Are you awake now?"

The girl slept on.

She watched her, thinking of the Greek boy as he'd tried to
hold her, thinking how easy it was to get rid of him once she'd
wanted to. *You know what Greek boys like, don't you?* she'd
said, deadpan, and the boy thought he understood so he smiled
knowingly and laughed and watched her as she nodded toward
his friend at the table, who smiled too, and then she said,
Ass-fucking. Go fuck yourselves, sonny.

She smiled now. There wasn't much worse you could say to
a Greek. He'd wanted very much to hit her but he hadn't. He
hadn't dared.

The Swedish girl's breathing was shallow and even. She slept
deeply. Lelia did not and was glad of it. What if someone came
to you in the night? Robbed you? Touched you?

Like this.

She pressed her forefinger to the girl's shoulder, rested it
lightly there for a moment, then drew it down behind the
shoulder blade to the rib cage and finally to the base of her
breast. Then she stopped and looked at her. The face registered
nothing.

She turned her hand palm upward and gently moved it down
with the back of her hand against the mattress and drew the
breast out toward her so that the weight of it rested in her palm.
It was warm and slightly damp. The girl hadn't moved. She
looked at the nipple. It was large, a pale brown color, soft now.
She wondered how long it would get.

She moved her thumb and forefinger together and gently turned. She felt the skin wither and tighten.

It got long. Very long.

There was a tiny sound, almost a purring in the girl's throat, and she saw the eyelids move and the side-to-side motion that told her the girl was dreaming. Lelia almost laughed aloud. The Swedish girl was having a little dream. And she bet it was a nice dream. She moved in closer so the girl could smell the scent of her, the fine dusting of expensive perfume.

Maybe she should lick it. Or bite. See how it tasted.

But no.

Leave something, she thought, *for tomorrow.*

JORDAN THAYER CHASE

Mykene

"Paracalo."

He called the waiter and ordered another Metaxa, draining the glass in front of him. *"Meh pagakia?"* asked the man. With ice? *"Sketoh,"* said Chase. Add nothing.

There was a white elastic strip around the tablecloth holding it down against the evening wind, and somebody had penciled in TOO MANY FOREIGNERS IN GREECE along the front of it. That was true enough, thought Chase, though whoever had written it was probably a tourist himself—the English was just too perfect. The sign above him, for instance, read RESTAURANT BAR HOMER. HERE WE HAVE GREEK SERVICE. ALL GRILLDED.

That was more like it.

He watched the waiter move off to the bar.

He was drinking more than he should, he knew, three empty

glasses lined up now in front of him, and he didn't know why except that he needed it; he always did. The power of a place took a while to roll off you. Sometimes a long while.

He kept coming back to the candles.

He presumed they were left by an earlier tour group, but that only explained the least interesting thing about them.

How could he have missed *fire*?

He'd read somewhere that black holes in space had the capacity to suck in light like a vacuum cleaner but that was space and this was a cave in the countryside of Greece.

So how could he have missed them?

By the time they'd guttered out and his eyes finally adjusted to the dark he'd found himself alone in what turned out to be a roughly circular cavern about twenty-five feet deep by twenty feet wide with high pale limestone walls. For a while he'd inhabited the silence like a ghost.

But like a very humble ghost. Because there was awesome power in the place.

It calmed him.

Then it frightened him.

He'd felt it before. In Mexico once, and once in England. And worst of all on a foggy New England afternoon, the very last day of his childhood. Times he didn't like to remember and wouldn't remember now.

He felt too much. Too often.

Murder in the eyes of a man in the streets of Toronto. A hotel fire in San Francisco that killed two children and a fireman. The imminent deaths of his aunt, a teacher in the eighth grade, his father.

Stop it, he thought.

It was always the same but always different too in the way that anything elemental was, like water in a stream or like fire. You recognized the familiar power. It was the configurations that surprised you.

He recognized the feelings too—the tuning-fork intensity, the sense of having access for a moment to some impossible vantage point where you could see worlds turning, growing green or barren, imploding or exploding, mountains formed and seas going dry. It was wonderful and terrifying. And it was meant to be watched with humility if it was meant to be watched at all.

Even the elation of it, even the joy, was painful. It could drive you crazy if you let it.

You had to lighten it, make it livable.

Like you are now, he thought.

So that in a way he'd been glad when the tourists arrived.

They couldn't see him. They'd stood in the post-and-lintel doorway and held their matches and lighters inside but they wouldn't go in. Instead they'd done the sensible thing and gotten the hell out of there. He'd sat back on his heels and watched them, feeling like a spook, feeling almost like laughing out loud—and they'd dissipated his tension. He was, glad for that but he'd resented them too. Nothing spoke to them. Nothing ever would. He was alone in that. There was room to love this gift of his but room to hate it too. It defined him and made him one of a kind, and lonely.

There was another reason for resenting them too. The cave had broken off with him once they'd arrived. It had stopped communicating. He was jealous of that communication. It was what had called him here.

And now he'd have to go back again.

Which, he thought, is the main reason you are drinking.

The waiter set down his Metaxa. Chase thanked him and raised the glass. The waiter nodded. The amber liquid felt hot and smooth.

He thought about going back in.

There were only two options really. One was to wait until morning and beat the tourists again, but beat them early this time so that he'd have at least an hour or so before they arrived. It might be enough time.

The other was better, and more threatening. Even a little embarrassing. Something a kid might do.

He could go tonight and jump the fence.

If he did he wouldn't have to worry about tourists, just the police—but from what he'd seen the police were in short supply here. He hadn't seen a single uniform since arriving.

Still it was risky.

He supposed a Greek jail could be nasty. But his connections were international. So that even in a worst-case scenario jail wouldn't keep him long. It wasn't that. It was something much simpler.

It was night.

He'd be jumping the fence at night, walking the *dromos* alone, entering the tomb. The prospect worried him. Places got stronger at night; they often did. And in daylight this one was strong enough.

He heard it humming like the droning of thousands of bees.

He'd see.

He'd have another Metaxa. Then he'd see.

You should call Elaine, he thought.

But you won't. Not now. Not yet.

He lifted his drink and, impassively, watched his hand tremble. It wasn't much to speak of, just a slight tremble, sending honey-colored ripples in concentric circles over the surface of the brandy. It was enough to remind him, though, and to intrigue him. And he thought he knew what his decision would be.

LELIA

SANTORINI

She slept in the sun on the black beach and dreamed that she was not one woman, but three.

The first woman that she was stood first in a cornfield and then in the woods beneath a cypress tree, and there were deer beside her and wild goats, and in the tree above a lynx or a lion, and all these things—cornfield, tree, animals—she blessed, and they blessed her.

The second lay peaceful and naked in full moonlight.

The third woman that she was stood at a crossroads at dark of the moon and howling dogs surrounded her. She walked with the souls of the dead.

And blessed nothing.

JORDAN THAYER CHASE

MYKENE

He paid the bill and walked up through the quiet town into the hills. There was a half moon and plenty of stars, leaching color from the landscape, turning it gray and white. The wind was gone. He heard only his own breathing and the scrape of shoe leather and the hiss of fabric on fabric—reassuring, personal sounds. He walked mechanically, thoughtlessly, his mind open and empty of fears and speculation.

To the left of the gate there was a gap between the fence and the road big enough for him to pass under. He wriggled through. He felt composed and ready. He dusted himself off, walked up the trail and turned, and ahead of him was the long wide passageway and beyond that the mountain and the tomb. All of it pale and glowing.

For a moment he felt a sense of *push* and *pull* in equal measure, washing out from somewhere inside the mountain. He was excited now, eager to take what was given, all his earlier ambivalence put aside. He felt the energy of the place feeding him, searching him out and giving him instructions. *Move slowly. Do not presume.*

He stepped out onto the passageway.

The sounds began.

Low at first, building.

Finally, an electric jolt up his spine.

• • •

At first he thought of bats—then birds, the ones he'd seen this
afternoon. But neither was right. Because birds just chattered
and bats—what did bats do? Well, they did not do this. This
was *one* voice, a single sound. And he couldn't place it. He
couldn't link it to bird or animal. There was something of both.
And he kept thinking *bats, bats,* ridiculously, because he knew
it was not bats yet thinking that it was was all that allowed him
to go on because he wasn't afraid of bats and he was afraid of
this.

This hissing. Howling. Screeching.

All of them together and building. Building continuously as
he walked slowly forward, slowly and without wanting to but
without wanting to stop, either, because the sound was so
obviously a warning yet it was calling to him too. It beckoned.

He felt privileged, powerful, terrified.

Farther.

And now he did hear birds, but only the usual bright chirp of
birds. Not this bizarre unearthly shrieking.

Then it was back, jarring him, blotting out all sounds not its
own, louder and more violent the closer he came, like the
hissing of a snake, the snarling of a huge cat, wildly feminine
somehow though he knew the tomb was a man's. In the still
night air it seemed impossibly loud, and he was trembling, the
fear in him boiling swiftly to the surface.

Go back to sleep, he thought. Please. Whatever you are.

And then he was standing at the entrance, eyes probing the
darkness, while the screeching rose higher. *Warnings,* he
thought. *Portents. Signs.* His throat was dry, his stomach
churning. I must be crazy, he thought. *There are no gods. No
gods awake.* He felt a white-hot flash of pure superstitious
terror. He willed his legs to move. He took a single step inside.

And got his final warning.

The scream broke over him like an angry fist, a naked rush
of power. He flinched. Then ducked, cringing. Because out of
the darkness something flew at him, he felt wings brush his
forehead, graze his cheek. He stood frozen while claws and
feathers swirled around him. Sparrows. Tiny sparrows at the

call of something huge and inhuman that commanded him now to *go*, commanded him imperiously to go *now* so that he turned and did go, the screeching voice behind him driving him back, burning at him like a cattle prod while the birds flew away over his head and he asked himself *Why? why?* until finally he stood at the entrance to the *dromos*, where he had begun.

He turned and looked back, breathing hard, thinking *Whatever you want, brother*—and something washed gently over him, one finally heavy wave of understanding. He dropped to his knees.

In the shrieking dark, all sounds stopped together.

Yes, he thought. *I see.*

He closed his eyes. The calm was more than calm. It was something like peace.

In the dark behind his eyes an image skittered into focus.

A man. Himself. Climbing a mountain. Glowing with an inner light. There were ruins at the top of the mountain and ruins all around him. *Delos*, he thought, though he had never been there and did not know the place.

The image changed.

It was a woman, or something half woman, something amorphous and cruel, like a scaled, winged lion with the breasts and face of a woman. The contours of the face almost blank, hazy, shapeless, yet vaguely familiar to him.

It shimmered and changed again.

The face remained the same but now the body was black and wholly female except that where the hair would be—on the head, in the armpits, between the legs—snakes writhed and hissed. He shuddered.

The woman's eyes dripped blood.

The image changed again.

Now the body was pale and soft and beautiful. It reached up naked for him out of a churning sea. He felt a pure cold blast of hatred buffet him like a foul wind and knew that this was the cruelest image of all, and heard his own voice whisper *You will die here*. The image faded.

He opened his eyes.

It was over.

From where he stood he could feel the air inside the tomb quiver like the wings of bees, pulsing outward.

He stood and walked to the gate. He did not look back. A breeze was up and the night was cool and lovely.

• • •

At the bottom of the mountain there were dogs barking.

Farther along cats hissed in a closed and silent taverna. He registered them merely as sounds, familiar and unimportant.

Days later he would realize that they were neither.

LELIA

SANTORINI

Ula or Mia—whatever her name was—was tied securely to the bed.

Naked.

It would be that much more distressing for her when, eventually, they found her.

She wondered how long that would be. A day or two, probably. Plenty of time.

She walked to the dresser where—finally—the Swedish girl had put away some of her clothes, opened the top drawer and pawed through the T-shirts and panties until she found what she was looking for. The girl was vain. The glasses were there but she refused to wear them. She was also, in her way, orderly. She had tucked the rent money for the two of them into her eyeglass case so that neither would be tempted to spend it. A child's idea of order. Ultimately, very silly.

And very stupid to tell her about it.

So stupid that she almost *had* to steal it. It was almost a point of honor.

She threw the glasses to the floor and heard them crack against the smooth concrete. She dug out the money and counted it. The girl was honest. It was all there—two thousand four hundred drachmas for three nights in the room, about twenty-four dollars American. It wasn't much but that was not the point.

The point was that the girl was unbearably dumb. She'd decided that—and decided to steal from her—the day before yesterday at the black-sand beach at Perissa. The girl had allowed two German men to sit with them and buy them beers and the men were boring, stupid. They spoke no Swedish and little English. Yet the girl hadn't bothered to discourage them.

Lelia had, but it hadn't taken. How many times could you snub a man, ignore him, laugh at him even, before he got the message? Finally she could stand it no longer. She got up and said she was going for a walk, and when the one with the bump on his nose and the languid smile had said *Perhaps I too go with you* she'd turned and said *Perhaps you die* and that was the last she'd seen them. And that was when she'd decided to take the girl's money.

There wasn't much risk involved. The landlady had asked for only one passport and the Swedish girl had offered hers. The Swedish girl was very generous, very thoughtful, very nice to people.

Lelia had met virtually no one on the island and no one had her address or even her full name. Even the girl knew her only as Lelia. So there would be no tracing her. By the time they found the girl trussed and gagged her ship would be long gone—the landlady only came to clean every other day or so—and nobody was going to try to find her for twenty-four dollars anyway. Nobody cared about that kind of money.

Except the Swedish girl.

She knew that the girl would care because the girl had confided in her. She was nearly broke. And she was going to try to find work on the island. Unfortunately she had no papers. It was hard to find work unless you had papers because it was illegal for a Greek to hire you, but it could be done. The girl was young and she guessed that to some she was attractive and given a little time, some bar or restaurant would probably hire her. High season was approaching and the police tended to ·look the other way when the islands were mobbed with tourists—it was too much trouble not to—and so as long as you kept a low profile and did not attract attention, they left you alone.

Too bad. The girl was going to attract a lot of attention.

Tied to a bed stark naked with eight hundred drachmas in the pockets of her dirty jeans, less than ten dollars. Less than the bill for the room.

A lot of attention.

Her stay in Greece was going to be a short one.

Little girl, she thought, you should pick your friends more carefully.

She was staring now, following her around the room as Lelia packed up the last of her things, dark eyes blazing. Lelia ignored her. There was a dirty sock in her mouth and two more tied together for a gag. She could scream all day at the top of her lungs and nobody would hear her. Her wrists and ankles were already badly chafed from struggling against the nylons that spread-eagled her on the bed. She'd done her worst in that area; she'd tried and failed. Obviously they'd hold.

Lelia zipped her shoulder bag and went to her, tugging at a lock of long blond hair, pulling her forward so she could examine the lump on the side of her head. It wasn't bad. The blood was matted dry. She'd done more damage to the wall than the wall had done to her, but it had been necessary to subdue her.

Funny how quiet they got when you bashed them against the wall a couple of times.

She reached down and stroked the girl's body.

"I touched these at night, you know," she said.

"This too."

The girl squirmed, trying to get away from her. She laughed.

"And here I thought you enjoyed it. Well, you live and learn."

She hoisted the shoulder bag and moved toward the door.

And then at the door she stopped and turned. Her handsome light blue eyes went suddenly wide, the amusement in them gone. She stared seriously at the girl, her face strangely open and expressionless.

Frightened, the girl looked back.

She twisted the doorknob and opened the door a crack.

Her body shuddered. It was the dream again. The dream of power. Sliding over her vision like a second snakeskin membrane of reality.

"Dream of me," she said.

And was gone.

. . . AND ELSEWHERE

. . . the islands drowsed and dreamed. They lay in a hazy stupor of impending summer. Work was done, but slowly. There was not yet any need to hurry. Tourists came and went while the islanders waited for them to arrive in more serious numbers so they could begin to take some profit from the season. They sat in open doorways and waited over rich dark coffee and talked until evening. Breezes were cool and even, the days long and warm, nights just cold enough so that sleep was restful. It was a good time of year, perhaps the best time of year, when flowers were beginning to bloom in the fields and there was a sense of fullness and regeneration.

Greece dreamed easily and waited to awaken.

On the island of Delos something slept no longer. Indeed it had awakened days and weeks before. Yet it waited too, gazing off to Mykonos hungry-eyed and ancient as the spring. Watching for the shell of itself and for its consort. And it was patient, knowing, avid.

Alive again.

PART ONE

CIRCE

"It does not matter whether or not
you meant to brush the web of things . . .
what happens always happens and there
is the spider, bearded black and with
his great faceted eyes glittering like
mirrors in the sun, or like God's eye,
and the fangs dripping."

—Robert Penn Warren

"I'm okay
You're so-so."

—David Bowie

DODGSON

MATALA, CRETE

He and Danny were dressing for dinner, even being a little careful about it—because though there was nothing about Matala that called for anything special, the women did.

Dodgson had stopped through Matala six years before and it was a quiet place then, prosperous and hospitable. Now the paint was chipped and flaking off the tables in every taverna in town. There were too many cars, trucks, mopeds. Red Beach was strewn with garbage. Except for Andreas the people had gone sour.

The town stunk of fast money, made and gone.

Were it not for the women he'd have left it.

But as it was he guessed he'd stay a little while.

He walked to the bathroom and looked over Danny's shoulder into the mirror. Surprisingly the Scotch last night didn't show at all. A miracle of Greek sun.

Danny was shaving, singing a little tune from *Oklahoma*!. He'd changed the words some.

> "Chicks 'n ducks 'n geese better scurry . . .
> When I eat you down where yer furry• . . ."

It caught him off guard and he had to laugh.

Sometimes he thought Danny had seen Belushi in *Animal House* one too many times. There was even some physical resemblance there.

Danny laughed too but kept shaving.

"You like that, huh?"

He shaved the way he seemed to do everything else—with abandon. Long, dangerous strokes of the razor. In constant motion. If he wasn't singing he was talking nonstop, moving like a fighter on his short bandy legs, his thick wrestler's body leaning into the mirror like he was about to bust its jaw.

"Hey. Hey, asshole, I'm *talking* to you! What do you think? Are we going to have a time tonight or aren't we. Button your shirt. That woman really likes you, you know? I can tell. I'm not kidding. You see what Michelle did to me last night? You *see* that? She's got her hand here, see, and she's feeding me *kalamaris* with one hand and she's grabbing my balls with the other. I couldn't *believe* that! I like that woman. I really do."

The guy was halfway crazy and hyper as hell, but he made Dodgson laugh and that was something nowadays. He enjoyed Danny. He liked the recklessness about the way he dealt with people, the mix of take-me-as-I-am-or-leave-me-be and in-sight, even sensitivity. He'd seen the guy loosen people up in a matter of seconds. It was a nice talent. Maybe it had to do with having family money, the easy confidence that could come with that. Maybe it was just that he was younger—at twenty-three, ten years younger than Dodgson. He didn't know.

He would never have anticipated Danny. They were poles apart, really. But he wasn't a bad roommate. Not bad at all. In fact he was a tonic.

He had his face submerged in the sink now, gurgling through the rinse water. Dodgson tapped him on the shoulder. The head dripped up at him, blinking.

"You think we can get out of here by high season?"

Danny reached for a towel, wiped his face and tossed it on the bed.

"Sure. Just let me get my shirt on, will you? I paid a hundred twenty bucks for the thing; I'm not going out without it. Look at that, pure cotton."

"Very nice."

"I'm very glad you like it, Robert."

"Ready?"

"Just about. I look good, right?"

"Right."

"What do you think, shoes or sandals?"

"Shoes. Chilly out."

"Okay. Now step into my office and I'll tell you something. You want to learn to relax, Rob. You don't relax the woman's going to think you're needy. Think like you *want* her or something."

"God forbid."

"Right. Never hurry. It's death. Relax. You got that?"

"I got it."

"Good."

He liked the role reversal. Dodgson the green kid. Danny the philosopher.

"How do I look? Great, right?"

"Great."

He patted Dodgson's cheek. "Thanks, Skippy."

They went out the door and across the whitewashed terrace and down the steps of the Pension Romantica. Danny took the steps two at a time.

Never hurry, thought Dodgson. Sure.

Andreas, their landlord, sat with his wife under the shade tree off the kitchen, beside him the tall bright flowers blooming. He was sipping coffee. Dodgson saw them there often and usually stopped to talk awhile. They were good people and a handsome couple, always very friendly. Six years ago the Romantica had been the best place to stay in town and it still was.

"*Yassas.*" Andreas's voice was lazy. A long day. He smiled and waved at them.

"*Kalisperassas.*" Dodgson waved back. He had maybe a hundred words of Greek and was slowly learning more.

It was something worth doing, anyway. Something.

The short walk to town was good when the cars weren't roaring by. They passed a field of bamboo and a grove of olive trees.

By the side of the road something shifted in a dry wash. A goat. Bedraggled chickens scratched along beside it.

They walked the long wide valley that always seemed to Dodgson like the pincers of a great limestone crab, one claw just next to the road to the left and the other far off to the right. Every now and then he'd be walking along and he'd hear the pounding of hooves above and a sound like heavy rain falling, and a herd of goats would come rolling off the high steep incline, crapping their little round goat turds all the way.

It was nearly sunset now and the sky was taking color. They passed a pair of German boys, very young, smelling of dope and sweat. Their clothes were threadbare. He doubted there was a dollar between them. And that was part of the problem with the place, he thought.

In six years the tourists had gotten much younger and much, much poorer. Now things were bad enough so that sometimes he thought the only Greeks making money here were the guy who sold thirty-drachma souvlaki on a stick and the man who ran the campground, and maybe a couple of purveyors of cheap Attic beer. Kids sat around in the tavernas playing cards all day. It was cheap but it was sad too. You came to paradise and all you could think to do was cut the deck. While the town bled slowly dry.

They came to the square.

The women were sitting at a table outside the taverna. Michelle looked up and smiled and waved to Danny. Danny waved back and turned to Dodgson.

"They don't look like they've been saying much, do they?"

He was right. Something about the body language wasn't all that friendly. Dodgson had noticed it too.

Of course they had little in common.

Michelle was a teacher from Paris. Dodgson thought she had a nice professional poise and lovely eyes and an equally lovely body. She seemed to tend to seriousness, unless she was with Danny. Alone with Dodgson she'd talked about her job and the Special Ed kids she handled and even French politics, such as they were, and even when her English faltered she was smart and good to listen to. He'd found that out two days ago on Red Beach, and after a while he'd even forgotten about her nude brown body lying next to him on the wicker mat.

Lelia, though.
Lelia was something else.

The way she looked at him.

He was not exactly unattractive and over the years he'd had his share of interested sidelong glances. This, though, was different from the onset, a matter of degree and kind.

It was as though she were constantly hungry.

It was as though she'd been waiting for him, waiting a long time, and now that he'd arrived they were going to play, and play hard.

That was the message he got from her. Got from her all the time.

He didn't know much about her. Her name was Lelia Narkisos and on her father's side she was Greek, on her mother's French, and she'd grown up in Canada near Quebec. From her father, she said, she'd inherited the dark wavy hair and the Mediterranean coloring. From her mother came the strange wide pale blue eyes, the generous mouth, the good nose and high cheekbones, and the wide set to the eyes that in Dodgson's view made her look both innocent and extremely distant, distracted from the everyday comings and goings of ordinary mortals. Worldly.

How she got by he didn't know. She told him that in Santorini she'd seen a boy by the side of the road holding a sign that said JUST DRIFTING.

"I'm like that," she said. "Permanently."

She had an economics degree from McGill. She hated economics.

She was thirty.

And that was all he knew.

They'd met on the beach that day. They agreed that fat people should not go nude in public. He'd discovered in her a tendency toward the sardonic.

And he saw that she loved to be looked at.

He'd stared shamelessly.

He could not imagine a woman more to his tastes. She was slim and long-legged. Willowy—but not soft. There was a wiry tension to her as though she were held together not so much by muscle as by ligaments and tendons; you could see them in the neck, in the line between shoulder and breast, behind the knees. Her skin was tight and golden brown, lightly freckled across the chest. There was no tan line. Her breasts were small and lovely, the nipples nearly the color of the breasts themselves and disproportionally large. Her pubic hair was bleached to a light blonde-brown by the sun. Her ass was tight and a lot more boyish than Dodgson's.

She made him a little crazy.

And half the time as he stared at her she would meet his eyes and hold them, so he knew she was enjoying herself and had permission. The wide full lips held just the trace of a smile.

And the eyes were . . . hungry.

He'd feel himself start to rise.

It was a problem on a nude beach. He'd spent most of the day on his belly.

And looking at her now in the white linen dress, hair still damp from the shower, he could feel it again. The woman carried a major sexual wallop. It made him feel slightly giddy—because she was his tonight if he wanted her. She'd made that clear on the beach today in a hundred little ways. A touch. A glance.

He was old enough to read for god's sake.

And he did want her. He was sure of that already. That was what Danny had been responding to when he'd told him to relax. But it was hard to relax entirely and he suspected Danny knew it.

It was not just Lelia.

Lately sex was the drug and he was the user.

Though of course it was Lelia too.

They were close enough now so that Danny had to whisper.

"Look at that Michelle," he said. "Isn't she pretty? I could dive right down under that table now, you know that?"

"Go ahead. I'll order drinks."

"Don't you tempt me. And jesus! look at what's-'er-name. That is a fabulous woman, Skippy. You better not screw up. I almost envy you."

"Almost?"

"Hey. I'm a faithful man."

"Right. Sorry."

They sat down and Michelle kissed Danny long and hard. He whispered something and they laughed.

Lelia stared at him, smiling, and he felt the promise between them again rich and humid and strong. For a moment it felt wonderful; he basked in the heat of her gaze—and then suddenly it was all ashes. The world turned in on him, exploded.

Why? he thought. *Why?*

The memories flooded back.

For the billionth time he damned Margot Perrone for dying. He damned the voice on the telephone, the scratchy metallic-sounding tape on the answering machine that had told him *This is Margot. I can't come to the phone right now but leave a message and I'll get back to you. I promise. Wait for the beep, please.*

He'd left his message.

And then found out that she was dead two days by then, bled to death in a bathtub full of tepid water.

I promise. Wait for the beep, please.

And Lelia, it seemed, missed nothing. "What's wrong?" she said.

He essayed what he hoped was a smile and shook his head. "Too much sun. No food. I better drink."

She laughed. Danny began joking with the waiter. Dodgson ordered a double Scotch on the rocks with plenty of ice. Lelia's ouzo sat in front of her. Cloudy, untouched.

Just for something to say he asked her "How was the shower?"

She shrugged. "Naked. Wet."

And that was better. That gleam in the eye.

"Hot or cold?"

"Oh, quite hot."

She smiled. Dodgson thought it a wonderful smile. Wicked.
Like her eyes it held evanescent flashes of promise. Her mouth
was probably the finest and most erotic orifice he'd ever seen
in his life. He resolved to make her smile as often as possible.
It would be good for both of them.

Margot, go away.

But she wouldn't. Not just yet.

He saw himself in a Honolulu bar, silent, drunk, a deep blue
twilight folding in over the sea, while after all those months of
manly fortitude something finally broke in him and he slumped
down onto the bar and began to cry.

A waitress came over. Sobs racked his body.

What's wrong?

Lelia was studying him now, head tilted slightly forward as
though evaluating something. Had he shown again? Sure he
had. She moved slightly toward him and put her arm across his
shoulder. He could smell her light perfume, the clean fresh
smell of her hair.

"Come here," she whispered. "What is it?"

"Honestly, nothing." He smiled again. "Crazy with the
heat."

She looked at him. Her proximity was dizzying. The pale
blue eyes were wide. Then he guessed she decided to believe
him. The eyes seemed to flicker and he sensed there was
laughter in them. Was she laughing at him?

No. Her gaze was steady now. The pressure of her arm on
his shoulder gentle but firm.

It was very strange. It was probably remembering Margot.
But for just half a second or so he'd felt . . .

. . . *trapped.*

She pulled him closer.

"Good. I'm glad you're all right."

She glanced from his eyes to his mouth and then back again. Her tongue slid lightly across her upper lip.

"Tell me," she whispered, "so I'll know."

"Tell you what?"

"Just tell me."

He laughed and glanced at Danny and Michelle. They were whispering too, oblivious. "Okay. Sure. Only what?"

She moved closer. The pressure across his shoulder grew greater. He could feel her breast warm and soft against his arm.

"Tell me everything you'd like to do to me, Dodgson."

And now he did feel dizzy. The light musky smell of her still-damp hair, the delicate spice of perfume.

"Tell me everything. And then we'll do it. I promise."

I promise, he thought. *Margot.* I didn't do it. It's not my fault.

Get off me.

It rang a very nasty bell deep within him for a moment and then he thought, impossible, forget that. You heard what she said. *Everything.*

He told her.

LELIA

She had taken one look at him on the beach and thought, oh, you are just fine.

She pulled a cigarette from her pack and walked to where he sat with the other two, the man and the girl, and stood over him naked so he had to look up at everything she had and she asked him for a light. And he was impressed all right, she could see that, but all the same he moved with a control that she liked; he was no child, no boy, and it didn't matter that it was the oldest ploy in the book because he lit her cigarette and smiled politely and she didn't try to take it any further than that though she knew he was watching as she walked away. And she wondered if he'd find some pretext to come and join her but did not look back at him again; it was up to him now, and when he did come over it was without any pretext at all. He simply said, May I join you, and she said of course and that was that.

If he'd asked her she'd have fucked him right there on the beach.

But he hadn't.

He wasn't shy. It wasn't that. He was not a man who was shy with women. She looked at his face and read pain, and a reticence to face more of it or even to bother, a kind of weariness there, and she knew that even though he was interested he was basically just going through the motions with her so that she would have to sink the hook fast and deep, and she did not wonder how or why he had come to be in pain but only how she could escape its consequences in him and have him now, because he was a beautiful thing and halfway hers already; and he did not even know what pain was. Not really.

DODGSON

The taverna overlooking the bay was operating on Greek time so the food was late. The first bottle of wine was gone by the time they ordered. The second disappeared with dinner and half the third as well. When that was gone they ordered a fourth out of sheer bravado and nursed the stuff.

The night was young.

From Danny's and Michelle's corner there was laughter and maneuverings under the table. From theirs a quiet heat. The wine augmented both. It was a rule of thumb in Greece that the wine did not depress. It elevated. Why that should be so nobody knew. Dodgson had heard it attributed to the heat, the food, the light, even to bouzouki music. His own theory was that if any place was depression-proof it was Greece. Even his own had relented—somewhat.

When finally ten o'clock rolled around the town's sole surviving disco was open so they walked there and ordered cognac. Dodgson and Lelia watched and talked while the others danced. He thought Danny was a lousy dancer. When the cognacs were gone she squeezed his hand and they quietly slipped away.

They walked to the beach.

The night was warm, the moon waning but very nearly full. They were both a little drunk. It was impossible to fall in step together.

The beach at Matala was shaped like a horseshoe and on the left prong of the shoe was town, on the right the limestone caves high up in the cliffs that had been crypts in ancient times and then later, during the sixties, makeshift homes for globe-trotting hippies. Behind them lay the campground. They could still hear music from town so they walked away toward the cliffs. They took off their shoes and followed the tideline.

When they were far enough away from the noise and town he turned and kissed her.

He thought her mouth was wonderful.

There was art there and fire in something like equal measure, and even as he felt himself rising toward her he saw that they had this in common; that neither would wholly let go just yet. That was why the art was there. It banked the fires with illusion. It teased, promised much, intimated what full aban-don would be like between them. He opened his eyes and saw that hers were open too, staring not at him but at the caves, shadowed holes in the blond moonlit rock.

Their bodies ground together. He tasted cognac. He didn't mind.

She stepped away.

The eyes looked smoky; the heavy lips smiled.

"Do you swim?"

She walked up the beach a ways and dropped her shoes in the sand. She turned to face him, moonlight drowning the pale irises so that for a moment her eyes had no color—pinpricks of ice pointed at him.

"Sure, I do."

Linen hissed once longingly against flesh. Under the dress she was naked. He'd known she would be. She dropped it in the sand. Then she waited for him.

He undressed. He went to her and they walked side by side into the water, not touching, and he felt the cold glide of waves across his thighs, the air warm, the water cold, her pale nipples tight and darker now, smaller, gnomic pyramids crowning the gently swaying flesh. His head felt clearer. By the time the water reached his waist he was ready for her, the heat of his erection strangely alien in the drifting chill.

She turned and wrapped her strong thin arms around his waist. They moved sideways together until the water was chest-high. She slid her hands down to his buttocks, caressing him and pressing him forward, capturing him suddenly between her legs and then moving back and forth gently.

She laughed, thin music on the still night air. She released him, grasped his shoulders and lifted herself smoothly onto him. She was warm inside and soft as velvet. He gasped at her sudden heat. Her eyes flashed at the sound and she stopped it with her mouth, tongue driving deep, lips crushing his until he thought he would taste her blood.

Inside her something tightened as she drew back over him and then slid forward again, sinking him deep, then lifted away and pumped at him, opening wide this time, pumping hard, and he met her strokes while a bright delicious fog fell over him so that all the art was gone in the drugged heat of bodies and cold water and swirling white waves around them, the slide growing smoother and smoother, the woman suspended in his arms raking his shoulders with blunt hard nails—until finally her neck snapped back and he felt the sudden flush of her skin and the slide go wide and soft and she grunted once, twice, mouth frozen for a moment in a wide unspoken scream that drew the lips back over her teeth and rolled the eyes while convulsions seized her. Drawing out of her completely he plunged back in again and flooded her with sperm and seawater, and then he shuddered too.

He rested. His erection would not subside.

She pressed her cheek to his shoulder and held him tightly. He closed his eyes.

For a moment they were almost tender.

When they drew away they were trembling, gooseflesh covering their bodies. He saw faint blue veins in her temples and in her breasts. They walked slowly from the water. He handed her his shirt and watched her use it to pat herself dry.

She put on the white linen dress. He put on his pants. They sat in the sand and soon they were lying there staring at the moon and stars. Her head rested lightly on his shoulder. The sand was fine and soft beneath him.

He felt the liquor again. A good sensation. An exhausted drifting.

He fell asleep.

And the last thing he remembered was that she turned to him, the eyes their own true color now this close to him, and said, "You'll pay for this, you know."

He smiled and said yes.

Yes I know. Yes I will.

And when he woke up she was gone.

So was the moon. It was colder, getting on to dawn.

He called her as loudly as he dared without waking the campers on the hill. He got no answer. With the clouds drifting over the moon it was hard to see. The beach was a gray thin streak along a glittering black sea. He walked slowly, looking first to the town and then back toward the cliffs.

He couldn't find her.

He felt the beginnings of a headache.

Okay, he thought. We fell asleep. At least I did. But what about her?

Yes, she'd been sleeping too. He remembered the pressure on his arm. There was still a stiffness there in the shoulder muscles. So she must have stayed awhile.

He wondered what time it was.

No matter how he thought about it, it made no sense. If she'd gotten cold she could have told him. He'd have gone too. Why not wake him? Why just disappear?

It was damn disorienting. As though he'd dreamed the whole thing—the walk along the beach, making love, everything. He wasn't angry—just puzzled.

He walked back to the Romantica, turning it over in his mind.

What the *hell*?

He opened the door to his room and there was Danny asleep with Michelle in the far bed, the sheets twisted around them like snakes. He moved silently into the bathroom and took off his clothes and hung his shirt over the door to dry. He tiptoed across the floor to the bed and slipped between the covers. He rolled over and slept a second time that night.

He slept late.

It was noon before he was out the door. By that time all the questions were amusing. He knew it wasn't anything he'd done or said that had made her go. So he wondered what she was up to. *Lelia? What's the story, Lelia? Where are you?*

He found Danny and Michelle drinking sweet Greek coffee in the square, sitting with a pair of German girls he knew vaguely from the beach. To Dodgson it looked like Danny was into some serious flirting but Michelle didn't seem to mind. Confident of him, he guessed.

They waved him over.

"Hey, Sparky. I hear you were a bitch last night."

"You do?"

"Sure. Lelia was by."

"Un-huh. And?"

"She's one angry woman, man. Says the two of you fell out

on the beach awhile, then she woke up and you weren't there, Sparks. You'd skipped on her. How come?"

"Me?"

He couldn't believe it.

"*I'd* skipped on her?"

"Yeah, you."

Michelle smiled. She shook her head. "I don't expect this of you, Robert. Him, maybe. Him of course. But . . ."

Danny poked her.

"This is really too weird. I didn't leave her. It was the other way around. I woke up and *she* was gone."

"Oh yeah?"

He rolled his eyes as though Dodgson were slipping, and everybody laughed. Everybody but Dodgson. It was too damned early in the morning.

"She really told you that?"

"Sure. Stood right there and said you'd deserted her. Am I right, ladies? Am I lying?"

The German girls nodded. It occurred to Dodgson that he might have introduced them.

"And you say she was pissed? Really angry?"

"I'd say she'd like to stuff you in a blender and shake up some piña coladas. A woman scorned and all."

"Jesus."

"You going to the beach?"

"I was planning on it."

He nodded. "Man of Steel. Actually, I'd think about hanging around down here with us if I was you."

He needed a cup of coffee. The headache was back. It really was too early in the morning for this shit.

"Danny, how drunk was I last night?"

He shrugged. "Light to medium. I've seen you worse. It really didn't happen that way? You're sure?"

"I swear it."

"That's a strange lady, then. You better have some coffee. Maybe a beer or two."

He thought about it.

"No, I think I'll go to the beach. See what I didn't do last night. You're positive she wasn't putting you on?"

"She was serious," said Michelle.

"She sure looked serious. She has nice flary nostrils, know that?"

He turned to go. "See you later," he said.

He started walking, then heard Danny shout behind him: *"Hey, Skippy! Don't worry. She'll forgive you!"* Then there was laughter.

"I forgive you," she said.

He looked at her.

"You're kidding."

"No. I do."

"For what?"

"For leaving."

"I didn't leave, Lelia."

"Don't be silly."

"Silly? I woke and you were gone. I looked for you. I called you. I couldn't find you. Anywhere."

"Now you're being irritating."

"Huh?"

"Look. We fell asleep. I woke up. *You weren't there.* I had to find my own way back from the beach alone. And I was still a little drunk, too. I was angry. I'm not anymore."

"That's it, then."

"What's it?"

"You were drunk."

"I said a little. You weren't."

"Well, maybe some. Not enough to—"

"Robert. Let's not make a thing of it. I've long since forgiven you. I told you that."

"You have?"

"Of course. The rest of it was lovely, wasn't it?"

"Yes it was."

"Well then."

He sat down on the sand. It's some sort of silly game, he

thought. And if she has to win it then I suppose she has to win it.

He looked at her lying on her back, eyes closed against the sun, at the lovely easy nudity, and he couldn't figure it. He felt the first uneasy stirrings of doubt about her.

I don't like games, he thought.

I hope she isn't into that.

Or it's going to be a short relationship.

Yet the rest of the day passed pleasantly.

There was no more mention of the night before. The sun and sand worked on them and Dodgson relaxed again. They talked about very little. She asked about his books and he told her. A serious and flawed first novel that had somehow after three long years found a publisher, and which everyone—quite rightly in Dodgson's estimation—ignored. Followed by a cynical commercial thriller that had found a home easily and, surprisingly, sold even fewer copies than the first book had. He spoke of them without regret or anger.

Which was something.

"There are a few . . . perks, I guess you'd call them. I still have some of the advance money on the thriller, for one thing. It got me here. And then I suppose there's some cachet to being a published novelist. People figure you're probably bright enough, possibly talented. So you're accepted into circles you wouldn't be, ordinarily. That's sort of interesting for a while."

"Fashionable circles, you mean?"

"Some, yes."

"You're handsome, you know. Your looks can't hurt you much either."

He shrugged.

"Anyway, *I* accept you."

"Are you . . . fashionable?"

"You mean am I *rich*. Obviously I'm fashionable."

"Obviously."

He wondered if she was. If so that would leave him the poor relation again. Michelle had private money and so did Danny. He'd inherited his father's pharmaceutical company. It ran itself, he said. Working it was hardly more than a hobby for him at the moment.

He wondered if he gave a damn. He didn't think so. He worried, sometimes, what would happen after the money ran out. He doubted that there was another book left in him—except for the one about Margot. And he wasn't writing that one, not ever.

He'd probably wind up teaching.

And for a moment the depression was on him again, perched like a vulture.

You're a bore, he thought. Cut it out.

He lay back on the sand and baked awhile, and the depression lifted. Here, eventually, it always did. So much of Greece was purely physical—it was his own particular brand of Zen. Oh, there were ruins, museums, monasteries. But Greece reached Dodgson through sun and sand and sea, through the senses, through good light eating and clean air, through women, through nude bodies and hot dry days and breezy nights, through the wine and liquor and the taste of clear fresh water. If there was struggle at all it was only for more of what was good—more comfort, more wine, more long cool nights.

Greece was benevolent. It abetted his side for a change. It was not arrayed against him.

Even the smokes are good, he thought. They'd make you cough like hell in the long run—they were strong—but the sinuses drained. You could breathe with them.

He lit one. Smoke drifted.

They swam later and the sea was calm. He watched her dive and surface, the water rolling off her oiled naked body. She was beautiful. She swam and you could see the strength hidden in the slim graceful body, the strong shoulder muscles, the thighs, the long slender arms.

He couldn't keep up with her. He didn't try.

He lay back at the tide line and let the waves curl over his ankles and watched her.

She's a little strange, he thought. So what. Maybe she'd got the message now that games were out. He hoped so.

Seawater stung his eyes, trickling from his hair. He wiped them as he watched her dive again.

Time to towel off, he thought. He got up and walked to the wicker mats. Behind him he heard her splashing. She swims like a seal does, he thought. Mostly underwater. He dried his hair. He brushed the sand off his legs and sat down on the mat.

At first he couldn't see her. There was too much glare off the water.

Then he did.

And it must have stopped his heart for a moment.

She was floating.

She floated faceup, buoyant with the high salt content of the water, calves and forearms dangling limp, arms and legs spread wide so that the waves lapped over them and tossed her gently. Her head lay back, the hair completely under, completely submerged. And for a moment he thought, *Dead. She's dead*. My god, she's drowned herself. *How long have I not been watching?*

Long enough.

He got to his feet. *Impossible*, he thought. And then he thought, no, it's not.

He started forward, moving fast. Then stopped.

He saw her left hand rise and brush a long dark lock of hair off her cheek.

He laughed. It wasn't pleasant laughter.

He stood there feeling foolish and relieved, feeling his heartbeat slow down, the blood in his face recede. Dodgson, he thought, you're an ass. He kicked at the sand in front of him. He watched her.

Now that he knew she was okay it was very sexy, what she was doing out there. Quite sexy indeed. The languor. The wide-open spread to the arms and legs—he could see the waves lap gently at her pubic hair; it glistened wet in the sun. She wore a look of submission to the elements, to the air and water. He could see her body rise and fall as she breathed, lungs and liquids keeping the heavy bones afloat. And he imagined what it felt like—the air warming her upper body, buttocks and legs and genitals colder, caressed by the cold as the body sank and rose and sank again.

He remembered what they called it now.

Dead man's float. Or was that facedown? Whatever.

It was just a little too apt and for a moment it scared him again. He thought of Margot in a tubful of bloody water.

He looked at her and he couldn't help it—he pictured her dead.

Lelia dead.

Sickeningly, the sight of her still aroused him.

You're crazy, he thought.

She turned in the water and saw him watching, got to her feet and came splashing out to him on a run. He must have showed, though. Because she stopped then in front of him and said "What? What's the matter."

"Nothing."

"Come on. What?"

She stared at him, and then smiled. Comprehension lit her face.

"You were worried about me, weren't you?"

"A little. For a moment there."

She laughed. "You fool. That's wonderful!"

"You think so?"

"Of course I do." She touched his face. Her hand was cold and wet, clammy.

"You thought I'd drowned out there."

"For a second or two, yes."

"That's lovely. You're a sweet man, Robert."

"Am I?"

"Yes, you are." She reached for the towel, dried her hair, draped it over her shoulders and looked at him.

"But I think you worry, Robert. I don't know what about. I know you've been hurt somehow and you're very gloomy sometimes. It's all right. It really is. I can take care of you."

She kissed him. She tasted like the sea.

"Trust me. I can take care of you."

She kissed him again more deeply this time, and people were

there close by and he felt an erection growing—but her mouth was fine.

And still in his imagination he saw her there, floating. The dead man's float.

He thought: *The dead would float higher, wouldn't they? Gases in the body. But the caress would be the same, the caress of cold seawater, the heat above.*

He kissed her.

Forget the dead, he thought.

Forget whoever's watching. The erection was insistent now and her mouth was nearly everything.

He took her hand and led her back into the water.

LELIA

What belonged to her was hers alone and now she could feel the sudden white-hot anger choking her inside like an imploding star, turning in upon itself, pulling into her silent rage the entire table full of them, even the entire island. Just to see him smiling at her, another woman, a stranger. While she, Lelia, had given him her body twice now, in the sea, *had come beneath him, had bathed his prick in the pale living blood of her uterus.*

Who is this bitch? How dare he?

It was dinnertime and Lelia was a little angry.

They sat at the taverna at the farthest edge of town, overlooking the bay. Danny, Michelle, the German girls, Lelia, Dodgson and now this other one. It was the best place in town for fish and Lelia saw that the cats knew it too, probably better than the tourists did. They prowled the floor searching for morsels of food, a bit of *kalamari* here, a flake of swordfish there. Over a dozen of them. She'd had to shove one away in order to pull out her chair and sit down, a mangy little tabby cat that looked at her hopefully now, creeping close, as though it *knew*.

Cats.

That was what the bitch was saying.

"I don't like 'em."

Sitting right next to him, a pretty green-eyed blonde, Dodgson listening as though he could care. As though he could actually give a damn.

Her face was burning. She bathed it in a cold inner control.

Billie. A man's name. Billie Durant. From England, Danny said.

"Cornwall, *acshually*."

You little cunt.

Lelia forced herself to talk to her. *Make her face you. Yes.*

"You have a problem with the cats?"

"Well, yes. When I was a child, you see, six or seven, I got between a pair of them. It was very stupid. They were fighting."

She laughed. Her teeth were very white and even.

"Little bugger left me with some very pretty scars. Here . . . "

She indicated a long curved line on her left calf. A good calf, thought Lelia, golden brown. No doubt she was a real blonde, too.

". . . and here."

There were two smaller scars at her collarbone.

"And here." She poked at her thin blue dress just above the left breast. She laughed again.

"Climbed me like a tree."

"You're lucky," said Dodgson. He pointed to the scars at her collarbone. He was right, of course. They were only inches from the jugular.

"I suppose I am. They had to pull her off me, you know. I still don't care for cats much."

Noted, thought Lelia. The tabby at her feet nudged her ankle with a wet pink nose.

"You must be . . . uncomfortable," she said. She swept the cats with her gaze and then fixed upon the girl, who met and held her eyes.

"A little. Perhaps."

There was just enough reserve in her voice so that Lelia knew the girl had heard her, had heard subtext as well as text, and was resolved to tough it out. All right. Dare me, she thought. Go ahead.

"Shame," she said.

And hugged her rage like a lover.

BILLIE

They had moved from pussycats to accidents to murder. Their conversation had. In this case, it was not an inappropriate progression.

Billie thought that Dodgson was handsome and rather nice too, and might have been wholly glad that Danny'd found her on the beach and introduced her were he not so obviously a previously claimed territory. But of course he was and that was that. She had no intention of moving in on someone else's man. It was not her style at all. She wished someone would tell that to Lelia.

If looks could kill . . . she thought.

But she also had to wonder why he was there with her. The woman was beautiful, certainly. But such possessiveness! Such high-handedness. She'd been jealous as a cat the moment she sat down.

He didn't seem the sort to put up with it.

And perhaps he wasn't.

The conversation had taken a fairly unpleasant turn at the moment and Dodgson was looking at her with less than indulgence.

"Manson didn't kill anyone," Lelia was saying. "All he did was move others to kill people. And that's their problem, isn't it? Their weakness?"

"Weakness isn't the point," said Michelle. "Responsibility is. If I am a general and I lose the battle, this is my responsibility, correct? Not only the soldiers'."

"Yes. But Charles Manson isn't a general. He's a private citizen the same as you and I are. If I tell you, or Danny tells you, to jump out a window, do you jump?"

"No. Of course not."

"Of course not. Because he holds no power over you. He's not a god, he's not a general, he's just a man. He holds no authority at all."

"Authority can be delegated," said Michelle.

"Who'd delegate authority to Charlie Manson?" said Danny. "Some asshole desert rat with dirty hair and a beard and a couple of old Beatles records?"

"They did," said Michelle.

Lelia settled back in her chair and looked at Dodgson, spoke directly to him. "He had very good eyes," she said dreamily. "Very sexy, I thought. I might have considered him."

For a moment everybody just sat there.

"Oh, right," said Danny. "Good point there. I kinda like Nixon's chin but I'm a pervert."

The German girls laughed.

But it was meant as a goad to Dodgson and it was clear to Billie that he got the message, because the silence lengthened while they just stared at one another and Michelle moved some food around on her plate in an embarrassed kind of way and then he said "Excuse me" and quietly left the table, walking toward the WC.

She liked his control.

Lelia and the others turned to their dinners in silence as she watched him walk away.

It was really too bad, she thought, that she was leaving

tomorrow. Because while it was a rule of hers not to move on another woman's man she had no such scruples governing her behavior once a relationship was over. She couldn't see this lasting much longer between them.

Forget it, she thought. You are a waitress in a pub on a two-week vacation—no—you are a painter, a student anyway, on a two-week vacation and the point is to study the ancient Greeks. He on the other hand is a published novelist and she is probably a model and who knows how such people think. For all you know it will get uglier before it's over, much uglier, and you don't need to be around to see it. Go study. Go off and lie in the sun. Either or both. Alone.

Because you don't want to start with a man now anyway. Not yet.

And for a moment she saw the doctor's hands on her through the thick haze of fever, dark hands against her pale naked thighs. She smelled the stink of her own illness in her mouth and the hospital smells and the cigarettes on his breath as he leaned over, as the oily hands moved up and up. . . .

No, she thought. Not yet by a long shot.

So which will it be? Mykonos or Santorini?

Dodgson returned to the table and she watched him and Lelia finish their dinners in hostile silence. Danny was talking with Michelle and the German girls, all of whom seemed very nice. She tried to pick up the conversation, something about a pharmaceutical company back in the United States. But Dodgson and Lelia continued to distract her.

She felt something brush against her leg.

Damn these cats! she thought.

They'll be the death of me.

DODGSON

"I just want to know one thing," she said, leaning toward him, whispering. "Which of us are you going home with tonight?"

"What?"

The question was right out of nowhere. He'd made no moves on the British girl at all. None. In fact he'd arranged with Andreas at the Romantica to have a second room there, just to be alone with her. But she was serious. Her voice like a nice quiet bludgeon.

"Lelia . . ."

"I just want to know."

"Lelia, I just met her. She's Danny's friend."

"Aren't we all."

"What's that mean?"

"You all share a room together. Don't tell me you haven't fucked Michelle. How is she, by the way? Is she good? Is she as good as Danny seems to think she is?"

"Cut it out, Lelia."

"Maybe I should fuck her myself and see."

It was all he could do to hold on to the whisper through the rising anger. Games again. He saw Billie watching. The last thing he wanted was some childish scene but she seemed bent on that.

"I don't give a damn what you do with them, really," she said. "I just want to know who you intend to take home tonight. Presuming you've made up your mind."

He'd had enough.

"Look. I'll answer your question for you. The room is

waiting. It seemed a good idea at the time for us to be together. Now I'm not so sure. You keep this up and you can take a walk on the beach, you understand me?"

She started to say something but he cut her off.

"No. You understand me? Just shut the hell up, all right?"

And she did.

He didn't need it. She was beautiful, intelligent, and as sensual a woman as he'd ever met. But mostly she was maddening. And he didn't need it. He didn't need the mind-fucking, not last night, not this afternoon, and not now.

Good god. Charles *Manson*.

He found himself wondering the best way to leave her.

He had the feeling it wasn't going to be easy.

LELIA

I can wait, thought Lelia.

You bastard. You green-eyed bitch.

I can wait.

For both of you.

DODGSON

Dodgson, Lelia, Danny and Michelle were the last to leave. Billie and the German girls had been as graceful as possible about it, given the lethal silences.

They walked home through town and into the long wide valley, the limestone cliffs like open shears glowing in the moonlight. The night was clear and there were so many stars in the sky, the breeze felt so good, the stillness was so complete and perfect that it was hard to stay angry at anyone: he felt himself softening toward her, and what remained was disappointment, a sadness.

Another whirlwind romance, he thought. Another bad choice on his part. One of many. He knew that the rest of tonight would be merely saying good-bye to her. Matala was too small a town for them to remain there together without bumping into each other continually and that was no good, so one or the other of them would be leaving on the bus tomorrow; he was sure of that. And he felt some sympathy toward her now. The woman was troubled.

He tried to explain to her.

"You just can't do that," he said, "not to me and certainly not in front of people. Hell, I wouldn't do it to you. It's too . . . possessive. We hardly know each other. It doesn't make sense. It's a holiday, for god's sake. We're supposed to be having a good time here. Nothing happened with that woman but that's beside the point. The point is you come to a place like this expecting a certain freedom. Freedom to be open, relaxed, to make friends, to be yourself. Without the freedom there's hardly any reason to be here, is there? A tan you can get anywhere."

"Freedom lies," she said.

And then they walked in silence.

BILLIE

She was sitting on her terrace when she saw them go by, the floor lamp burning behind her, a glass of red wine in her hand and the heavy paperback art book she'd lugged all the way from London lying open on her lap. She hoped they wouldn't see her and was glad when they passed by.

He was a nice man. It was too bad.

She'd decided on Mykonos. From there you could get day trips to Delos and the ruins on Delos were supposed to be spectacular, tile floor mosaics in excellent shape and a colonnade of lions leading from the old port into the city; then, high atop the island's summit, ruins of temples to Apollo and Artemis who, according to legend, both were born there. She was looking at one of the mosaics now—Apollo riding an enormous lioness, taming her.

She glanced down to the street.

Quite a package, she thought.

They were yards away by now but even at a distance there was something in the way Lelia walked beside him that suggested much—the hands clenched into fists; the precise, calculated step; an attitude in the slim stylish body of something held tight and dear that was somehow animal and aggressive and . . . yes, *predatory.*

She shuddered.

She looked down at the snarling lioness.

She presumed he would be taking her to his bed tonight. She hoped he knew what he was doing.

She sighed, finished the wine, and closed the book.

Tomorrow there would be Mykonos.

DODGSON

He looked at his watch. It was twenty after three in the morning. They sat around the table on the terrace, the brandy nearly gone.

Danny was talking quietly so as not to wake the neighbors, and meanwhile they were pushing back the Metaxa, trying to pour something light into the evening. And that was all right because it gave him some time to think about Lelia, about what to do with her exactly, about how to let her know that he wasn't going to sleep with her again—tonight or ever.

Danny was talking about a Fowles book called *The Magus*. You saw it in all the kiosks here. He hadn't read it.

". . . so this teacher is trespassing and making excuses and this Conchis guy turns to him and says, 'Hey, cut the shit. *You came here to meet me. Please. Life is short.*' And it's supposed to be very mystical because how does Conchis *know* that—but *I'm* thinking, wow! what a terrific pickup line. That's actually what it *is!* A pickup line. 'You have come here to meet me. Please. Life is short.' So I tried it."

Dodgson drained his glass. "What happened?"

"I scored." He poured Dodgson some more. "Then I got the clap."

They laughed.

"And life is too fucking short for *that*, let me tell you."

There was more laughter and then a silence while Michelle

poured out the last of the Metaxa. Danny uncorked the wine and set it on the table. Lelia went for it immediately. There was still some brandy left in her glass. She took a long pull of wine directly from the bottle, swallowed, and kept the bottle, holding it tightly in her lap.

"I had that once," she said.

It was the first she'd spoken since they sat down. Her voice was quiet, casual-sounding. Her eyes pegged a star in the western sky.

It was a moment before she continued. They let her take her time.

"I waited awhile before I went to the doctor. It seemed like an opportunity to me. There was a man I didn't like. So I waited. And then I went to the doctor."

She filled her glass, the wine on top of the brandy. She put down the bottle. She looked at each of them. Her eyes were hard and narrow.

"Jesus Christ," whispered Danny. He shook his head.

They heard night birds in the distance.

"You carrying now?" he said. "I mean, I worry about my friend here."

"Fuck you," said Lelia.

And for a moment he thought Danny would hit her. He leaned across the table and his face was white with anger and Dodgson thought, This is enough, enough; this is too much.

"Danny," he said.

"Fuck *you*, Lelia."

Michelle put her hand on his arm. "Danny . . ." He shrugged it off.

"No!" He turned to Dodgson.

"I'm sorry, old buddy," he said. "But this is one beautiful piece of shit you got here. She's really fucking gorgeous."

And Dodgson felt a kind of sickness in the pit of his stomach. Because she'd done this all so neatly. Waited and struck.

Danny was never violent, never angry.

She likes this, he thought. Actually enjoys it. Messing up people's minds. She's crazy. I should have known this morning. The business about the beach the night before. *You weren't there.*

He'd been a fool to try to explain himself to her.

When are you going to grow up? he thought. How can your judgment always be so miserable?

It all went through his mind in an instant and he was about to reach across the table and say *Easy Danny, relax, it doesn't matter* when beside him there was a sudden movement and Lelia was on her feet, face contorted, sneering at both of them, her chair heaved back away from her so hard that it fell and clattered loudly against the wall and then dropped to the concrete floor. She moved fast across the terrace and then flung open the door to Dodgson's room and then slammed it shut.

To Dodgson it was like gunshots on the still air.

Two doors down from Danny's room a light went on.

"Damn!" whispered Dodgson.

They sat astonished, silent.

Soon the light went out again. There was an elderly couple in there, he remembered. British.

There was no sound at all from his room.

Danny poured them some wine.

"I was out of line there," he said. "Sorry." "

"No you weren't," said Dodgson. "She was. Very." He thought for a moment. "How'd you like to see another island?"

"Sure, Sparks. Why not?"

"Michelle?"

"I have one more week." She smiled. It was an understanding smile and Dodgson was grateful for it. "Yes, I think that would be nice."

Danny shook his head. "Guess you never know about people, do you."

"I guess you don't."

He drank the wine.

LELIA

She took off her clothes in the dark and, naked, wrapped herself in one of the coarse linen sheets. She heard metal scrape against concrete outside and looked out the window.

Danny and Michele were getting up to go to bed. Evidently Dodgson was staying awhile.

She supposed there was something left in the bottle.

I know you, Robert, she thought.

He was acting like a child. In fact all she'd done was break up their ridiculous, boring little party. Done what it was necessary to do. In order to have him. And have him the way she wanted him. Now.

She wrapped the sheet around her tightly and opened the door, and then stepped out onto the terrace.

DODGSON

He'd half expected her.

Nor was the bed sheet surprising.

What was a little surprising was when she opened it.

At first he was aware only of her nudity. Nature had given her something formidable and fine. So he looked at her.

Then she let go of the sheet and he stooped to retrieve it, to cover her, cognizant at once of the sleeping strangers in the rooms that lined the terrace, of the hour and of the whole long exhausting night with her—when he felt her hands on his shoulders and heard her say "No. I want to do it here. Right here. Let me show you I'm sorry."

"Don't be . . . get inside, will you please?"

"No! *Here*, Robert."

"I mean it, Lelia."

"Let me show you. Let me *help* you, Robert."

"Dammit, Lelia!"

He wrapped the sheet around her.

She stepped outside his grasp and he'd forgotten how strong she was—she broke away easily—and laughing, let the sheet fall again from her shoulders. She ran naked to the door where the lights had come on before and then whirled to face him. He moved toward her.

"Stop!" she said.

And he did stop. Something *made* him stop, something that was almost physical. It slid suddenly into her eyes clear and dangerous as a snake, cold and mad and god! *it was erotic too,* suffusing the beautiful features and turning them almost ugly, inhuman.

"Stop there, Dodgson," she said, *"while I get these people out to play."*

She turned to the window beside the old couple's door and he heard someone moving inside, something rising slowly, painfully out of bed—and all at once he felt frightened for them, scared of what she'd do. He saw her hands go up to cup her breasts and heard her crooning *Come out, come out, come play with me,* and heard it obscene as they would hear it, obscene and seductive too, and something snapped in Dodgson that moved him across the terrace like some great angry beast and he grabbed her and slapped her hard, pulled her back across the terrace while she laughed and gasped in amazement.

He shoved her into the room and flung her on the bed. With a control that was almost eerie to him he quietly closed the door.

"Bastard!" she hissed, crouching there. "Bastard!"

"Shut up." He was trembling now. "Just shut your mouth or so help me I'll . . ."

"You'll *what*, Robert? Kill me?" She laughed. "Oh yes. Try it, Robert. Try to kill me. I want you to. I dare you."

Someone knocked at the door.

"You all right in there?"

Danny.

"Go to bed, okay? We're fine."

"You sure?"

"Yes. Go back to bed."

He heard him move away. He looked at her.

"*Are* you sure?" she said.

She lifted herself up on the bed. Hands in her hair, posed like a pinup. Her smile was pure cold hatred for him.

Admit it, he thought. You're afraid of her. You are.

The pale eyes glittered.

"Are you absolutely sure? *Maybe you ought to be careful going to sleep tonight.*"

Like a slap in the face it sobered him.

"Get out," he said.

"Like this?" She laughed. "Oh, no."

"Get your clothes and get out of here."

"It's not that easy, Robert."

"I said get out!"

The smile broadened, horrible now. "If you want me out you'll have to throw me out, Robert, and you'll have to fucking gag me when you do. Because I don't care, Robert. I don't care at all. I'll wake the whole fucking town and I won't bat an eyelash. But you'll care, won't you. Poor baby."

He moved toward her.

"Come on," she said. "Come on. Try to throw me out. Try to kill me. Try it, you bastard! I want you to. Come on and kill me. Fuck me! Make me *scream*!"

She lunged, slapped him, and Dodgson almost fell she hit him so hard; then before he could recover she hit him again, her fist closed this time, the blow ringing in his ear, and he felt her going for his eyes, her fingernails tearing at him. He twisted away but she was on him again in an instant, gouging him. He felt one eye tear up and blur his vision, felt blood roll down his cheek. Pain and rage surged through him and he hit her, not openhanded as before but the way you hit a man, to stop him, hit her in the stomach and heard the breath whoosh out of her. She fell back on the bed, gasping, then came at him again, fists flailing.

He grabbed at her wrists, held them and forced her down onto the bed, his full weight pressing on top of her. She rolled and bucked, sweat streaming off her face and body. She lurched at him, trying to use her teeth on his arms and neck. He kept them away from her. He held her.

And finally she subsided.

"Enough?"

"Yes."

"Don't lie to me."

"All right."

"Enough, then?"

"No."

"You want me to hit you again?"

"Yes."

"Is that it?"

"Yes."

"You want that?"

"Yes."

She rolled beneath him. Her hips pressed up to him. The blue eyes burned; the bruised moist lips hung open.

"You're crazy."

"Fine."

"Stop it."

"Give me your hand."

"No."

"Give me your hand, Robert."

"Stop it. I'm telling you."

"I'll fight you all night long, Robert. I'm strong. You know that. *I'll do anything.* Now give me your hand, you son of a bitch!"

He stared at her. Then he released her. He pushed himself up away from her, leaning back. Her hips continued to writhe beneath him.

He extended his left hand.

She spread his fingers wide and pressed them to her breasts. She seemed to flush with the contact. The breasts were slick with sweat.

It was a dream, erotic and awful. He would awaken, he knew, feeling as though he had slept with the dead.

"Hurt me," she said. "Hurt me badly."

And because he wanted to, he did.

Afterward he lay awake, only pretending to sleep.

There were two good reasons for that.

He felt as though he had crossed a threshold now and wondered if it was even still possible to go back. His guilt was not only guilt but knowledge. She had goaded him, yes, angered him right to his limits and beyond, but after that the crossing was mutual. They had not made love, they'd made combat. He'd hurt her all right—but hurt her because he needed to as much as because of anything she'd said or done. Only a part of him could plead insanity. The other part knew it was not her at all but had more to do with the death of a woman far away in New York and the empty, angry years that followed, the nursed and curdled anger that could no longer reach her, the question that tormented him useless on his lips, to remain unanswered now forever—*Why, Margot? What did I do? And why have you done this thing to me?*

That was one good reason to stay awake.

The other was fear.

He remembered what she'd said.

"*Maybe you ought to be careful going to sleep tonight.*"

His guilt hadn't numbed his sense of her, his fear.

And he wondered—just how crazy was she? Did it only run

to rough, punishing sex or was she capable of more? And worse?

Hurt me. Kill me. I dare you.

He had his guilt, his knowledge.
  But he also had someone in his bed.

He looked at her. She looked very peaceful now, her face composed and tranquil.
  Jesus, he thought. Who is she?
  What have I done?
  He lay still and silent, watching her, and waited for sunrise.

JORDAN THAYER CHASE

SKIATHOS

Chase sat in the harbor where the tour boats departed for the grottoes and waited for Tasos, "Koonelee Tasos" to his friends—because at the age of seven he'd stolen a rabbit, skinned and dressed, from his father, and tried to exchange it at the local grocery store for a liter of wine which he then intended to peddle elsewhere at a cut-rate price. In Greece a nickname tended to stick with you. So Tasos was forever doomed to have the word for rabbit prefixed to his name. Even at age forty-eight, a successful businessman, the memory of that first aborted deal walked with him.

  Beside him men in overalls were painting chairs bright green, gearing up for the influx of tourists over Easter and then high season to follow.

  A hook-nosed old man in a light brown three-piece suit moved among the tables, his orange worry beads held loosely behind his back. His suit was cheap but impeccably pressed and tailored to his withered frame.

He stopped behind Chase's chair. He could feel the man staring. He turned around.

"*Yassas,*" he said.

The man didn't answer. His watery eyes seemed just short of hostile. Chase felt he'd been judged and found wanting. *All of us*, he thought.

As the man walked by he imagined what it would be like to see the harbor through eighty-year-old Greek eyes. Boys zooming by on their Hondas. The tourists sweaty and half-naked off Kokonares or Banana Beach. The middle-aged sons sitting lazy in the shade, sipping Nescafé frappés instead of hot Greek coffee, rattling their newspapers and staring at the halter-topped women.

It's disappearing so quickly here, he thought.

Even down to the man himself. Ancient worry beads and a three-piece suit. The country was experiencing a massive identity crisis on every level. The old looked at the new with fascination and horror, with both jealousy and dismay.

"*Yasu,* Chase! *Tikanes? Kala?*"

Tasos stood over him, reached down and pumped his hand.

"Hell, Tasos," he said. "I always get by."

He hasn't changed, thought Chase. The same round weathered face, the same hard handshake, the gold-toothed smile. He was suddenly very glad to see him.

Three years is a long time for friends to remain apart, he thought. He and Tasos went all the way back to college together. There had been a deal for a tract of land just outside Athens almost as soon as they were out, and then other deals that moved them into shipping—but mostly they worked together by phone now. Chase realized he'd missed him.

He sat, grinning, and Chase looked him over. He looked good—slim and fit. The clothes, he knew, were from Paris. Most of the Greeks who could afford them seemed to prefer Paris shops to London.

"It's good to see you, my friend."

"It's good to see you too, Tasos. How's Annalouka?"

"Fine, fine. She sends her love. And Elaine?"

"Fine. At least I think she is. I haven't called her yet."

Tasos frowned. "Why not? You're not having trouble, Chase."

"No. No trouble. Things are just a little bit complicated at the moment, that's all. I'll call. How's the baby?"

"A baby no longer, Chase. A four-year-old *meltemi!* With shoulders like this!"

"Like his dad."

"Like his dad, yes."

"So fatherhood agrees with you?"

Tasos smiled. "I was *born* a father. You should try it sometime."

"Yes. Sometime."

Tasos leaned forward. "You look a little tired, I think."

"No. I'm fine."

"You'll stay awhile in Greece? Take a vacation maybe, stay with us?"

"We'll see. Have you been in touch with Yannis lately?"

"Yes. He says there is no problem. The growers are eager to supply us, and they expect the wine to be superb this season."

"My people have orders in excess of 5.5 million now. Up .6 million in just ten days. We project another 2.5 million as the cutoff, for this year anyway."

"Excellent! We will put Santorini wine on the map, my friend. You'll see. They'll be begging for it in America a year from now. As usual your timing is perfect, Chase—your instincts, perfect. I am a lucky man to do business with you."

Chase smiled. "And I with you."

"Bah! I am a shopkeeper compared with you. So I own a few businesses. So what? We must not bullshit one another. Few men have what you have, *feelo.*"

"Few men, I think, would want it."

Tasos studied him.

"You do look tired," he said. "Tired and more."

"Maybe."

"And not Elaine?"

"No."

"So what is it? We are old friends, eh? So speak to Koonelee Tasos. He is a shopkeeper but his ears are very good."

"It's nothing, Tasos."

"With you it's never nothing, Chase."

He hesitated. He didn't know why. It would be a relief to tell somebody. An immense relief. And Tasos knew all about him, as much as anybody knew. Ever since Chase had moved them into shipping together and they'd made their first fortune, Tasos had known. If he could help, he would.

But Chase was wary of involving him. He was as much the captive of this thing now as he had been kneeling humbly at the entrance to the *dromos*. Something told him he was supposed to be going this alone. That, more than anything, was why he hadn't phoned Elaine.

What could he tell her that wasn't a lie? What could he say that wouldn't involve her somehow?

The warm, intelligent eyes were waiting.

He made his decision.

"All right," he said. "Let me order something. Have you got about an hour or so?"

"I have a lifetime, my friend."

He called the waiter over and started talking.

When he was finished Tasos looked at him and said, "It reminds me of a story they tell here.

"Two fishermen met a priest along the path to the sea in the middle of the night. Naturally they were surprised to see him there, alone, at such a late hour. So they asked him, where are you going, *papas?*

"'I am looking for a light,' the priest answered. And the fishermen, they didn't know what to think. Perhaps the priest is crazy. Because he was *carrying* a lantern, and it was lit, and the light was bright.

"You see? I think you already have the answers to your questions, Chase. Like the priest, you carry your own light."

"I don't know, Tasos."

It was late now. The wine they'd ordered was nearly gone.

"Listen to me, my friend. You say you hear a voice that tells

you you may die here. If that is to be so, then it will be so.
There are many worse places to die. We Greeks are fatalists.
But we are pragmatists too. You cannot undo this thing that has
happened to you. You say that something commands you—
then you must listen. And do what it tells you to do. And save
your life if you can."

"And if I can't?"

"Then you must give it up."

"You believe that?"

"I do."

He sighed. "I just keep wishing I were drunk or dreaming or
some damn thing."

Tasos smiled. "Were you drunk or dreaming those times you
told me of in Mexico, or in England, or when you were a child
in . . . where was it? Maine? You were not.

"You remind me of Our Lord, Chase—at Gethsemane. 'My
Father, if it is possible, let this cup pass from me.' But the cup
never passes. You were born with this gift, and it has been
good to you. It has made you a rich and—am I wrong?—a not
unhappy man. But now perhaps you must pay it back. And it
may ask much of you."

There was a silence. They watched the gulls in the harbor.

When at last Chase spoke, his voice was thick with emotion,
surprising him.

"Where *are* they, Tasos? *Who* are they? Do you believe in
God?"

Tasos shook his head. "I don't know, my friend. Since our
talks so many years ago I have made a little study, I confess.
I have read all the books about people like you, but I still don't
know. I have feelings, and my feelings tell me you are very
special, that sometimes you hear the voices of others coming
from deep inside themselves, and sometimes you hear the
future happening. And sometimes, maybe, you hear the earth
itself—which we call gods, or the voices of gods. Perhaps it is
the earth, speaking to you."

They drank the wine in silence. It was not as good as the
Santorino wine but it would do.

"I'm supposed to go to Delos," he said. "I don't know why I know that but I do."

"Delos?"

"Yes."

Tasos frowned and thought a moment. "Like Mykene, Delos is a place of great power in the ancient world. Pilgrims went there for healing. In our legend it is the birthplace of Apollo and his sister Artemis, or Hecate. Once it was the holiest place in all of Greece."

"I know. I've done a little homework. I get there by boat from Mykonos, right?"

"Yes. Ferries run each morning if the weather is good."

"And Mykonos?"

He shrugged. "Ships leave daily from Piraeus, or you can fly there from Athens. You mean all these times you've come to Greece, you've never been to Mykonos?"

Chase shook his head. "I've never been to Mykene, either, up to now."

"Ah, but that's different. Mykonos! It is our jewel!"

"I come to see you, Tasos."

He smiled. "We are good friends, no?"

"Of course we are."

"Then let me come with you. I would like to."

"No."

"I think I should, Chase. For one thing I am very good company."

"No. You take care of business for us, and of Anna and the boy. As you say, this cup's mine."

"Any cup can be shared, Chase."

"Not this one."

And he thought, *Nothing speaks to you*. But there was no bitterness to it now.

Mykonos, he thought. *Our jewel*.

All right. Whoever you are.

He drained the wine.

I'm coming.

BILLIE

MYKONOS

She was sitting at a café by the harbor only two hours off the plane, barely showered and changed, when the Frenchman walked by, saw her, stopped, turned, and headed for her table.

Oh, no. This I can do without, she thought.

His hair was long, blond, and none too clean, the teeth very white and oddly pointed. I wonder if he files them? she thought. It was not a delightful smile.

He was tall and built to scale. His tan was a deep nut brown. His shoulders were absolutely massive, the arms long and simian. His hands were big too and there were tiny scars along the ridge of knuckles.

A brawler. Wonderful.

She felt the queasiness again. It happened a lot these days when a man approached her. She rallied against it.

All right, she thought, let's make this as fast as possible.

He stood there grinning at her, and the grin tugged at the too-sharp nose and sharpened it further, squinted the small gray eyes.

"You speak French?" he asked her.

"No."

"English, eh?"

"Yes."

He looks like a monkey, she thought. A very large monkey. With a pointed nose. A dangerous monkey. He shifted from one foot to the other and the long, threadbare silk shirt swayed back and forth over the dusty jeans. Stop smiling, she thought. For god's sake go away and leave me in peace.

"I've just come back from India," he said. "Is very good there, I think. Very spiritual."

"That's nice."

"We learned many things, my friends and I. You would like to hear? I think you should."

The smile was an open leer now.

"I don't think so."

Enough, she thought. You are probably what? twenty-one? And all very latter-day hippie. I bet you've a good stash of pot in your backpack. Beyond that, not a shilling. In 1967 you weren't even born yet. You're ridiculous. And threatening. Please go away.

"You're a very pretty woman."

"Thank you. Good-bye. Have a nice day."

He looked at her.

"You have a cigarette for me?"

She couldn't help it. He infuriated her. Threat and swagger and now he wanted handouts. She drew hard on her cigarette and blew the smoke out away from him.

"I haven't any."

The smile disappeared. But the man said nothing.

"Nor do I have any money for you. So good-bye."

"No money."

"No. And no cigarettes."

"So, give me that one."

"No."

"Why not? You don't need it."

"How is your English?"

"Eh?"

"I said how is your English? I said good-bye to you. Twice. Do you understand the word 'good-bye'?"

Bug eyes, she thought. Dead bug eyes. There's nothing in them.

"You're a bitch, you know that."

"Yes, I know that."

He turned abruptly and walked away. He made a fist and jerked his arm into the air. He did not look back. She could feel his anger, his violence, pass over her, rippling away from him like waves off a stone dropped into quiet water.

Very spiritual, she thought. I have fears for the spirit these days.

She stubbed out the cigarette and called the waiter for another ouzo.

SADLIER

The Frenchman, whose name was Gerard Sadlier, was very cross with her.

Once before, in Pakistan over a year ago, a man had made him cross in a different sort of matter—a problem over hashish and money. So he had filled a flight bag with ice, which was very rare and expensive there, and tied the man to the flyblown four-poster bed in his cheap hotel room and smothered him with the bag of ice while Dulac and Ruth walked across his ribs.

It would be overreacting to do that here.

Still he thought he might be seeing her again.

Everyone deserved a second chance.

DODGSON

HERAKLION, CRETE

He'd said good-bye to Andreas, his landlord, and they'd shook hands and Andreas had said, "Well, do you think you will be back this way again, my friend?" And Dodgson said, "I don't know, Andreas. Matala has changed."

And the handsome old man nodded sadly. "I know," he said. *There is a saying.* The earth is only sleeping. And you will have to pray for us when she rises.

Lelia, he thought, had taken it very well.

They'd breakfasted alone. He talked and she listened, and then when it was over she said, "You want me to leave?" and he said No, it wasn't necessary, because he and Danny and Michelle had had enough of Matala anyway.

She nodded.

He was shocked. He'd expected a scene. What he got was understatement.

"I'm not too easy to get along with sometimes," she said. "I know that. I'm sorry. I'm really very sorry about last night. Sometimes I get . . . out of hand, you know?"

He knew.

But she seemed so sincere and looked so unhappy that despite himself he started feeling sorry for her and tried to make it easier for her, joking and drinking *lemonada* with her until the bus arrived. When they boarded he'd kissed her on the cheek and it was as though they were a pair of friends parting, and he had that strange feeling of unreality again, the same as

73

he'd felt when he awoke on the beach to find her gone. As though his perceptions were out of whack somehow.

All told, he figured he'd got off easy.

He knew he had when Danny leaned back in the seat and said, "Whew! good-bye *Matala*!"

And then he knew what this was.

This was escape.

There was one last flight to Mykonos tonight. They'd be on it.

Meantime they sat in the square nursing Amstel beers, waiting for the eight o'clock Olympic shuttlebus to come and take them to the airport and watching the beginnings of the *volta*—a sort of nightly fashion show cum meat market, as people paraded by in their evening best, on the lookout for friends, lovers, and pickups. Heraklion was a big sprawling town by Greek standards and it was refreshing after Matala to be somewhere so cosmopolitan. Girls in white strolled arm in arm together, smiling into the rows upon rows of café tables. Boys cruised by in threes and pairs, denims crisply pressed, arms draped over one another's shoulders in macho solidarity. Young mothers wheeled along pretty wide-eyed babies in carriages.

They sipped their beers and nibbled their *mezes*.

"You know," said Danny, "I've always hated this town more than any town in Greece next to Athens. But right now it doesn't look too bad at all, buddy."

Dodgson translated: *No madwomen.*

He nodded.

It was amazing how little thought he'd given her once they'd pulled away. Past was past, right? Sure it was. Yet it bothered him. Because this was a pattern of his. You screwed up. Then you forgot about it, buried it. You drank too much, wrote too little, and before too long you chose the wrong woman again. Always the wrong woman. Sure the world was full of neurotics but it was a special talent of his to keep on finding them. He'd met lesser versions of Lelia before, less fierce certainly, far less extreme, but a little unhinged just the same. Passive/aggressive types. Drinkers. Cokeheads. Paranoids.

And then there was Margot.

That had lasted three long years.

And who was to say that Margot, who had taken her own life after all, was any less crazy than Lelia?

You got what you looked for, didn't you? What you were ready for? What you wanted? So where was his own mental health in all this?

Gone fishing, he thought. Looking, maybe, for a line into or out of that bloody bathtub.

To strain a metaphor.

The *volta* moved past him. The girls in white paraded.

His mind did what it damn well wanted to do and slipped Lelia Narkisos away for a while, maybe a good long while.

Maybe forever.

Tonight he'd be in Mykonos and a tiny, toothless woman dressed in black would rent him a room. He knew the woman and he knew the rooms. The woman was in permanent mourning for somebody. The rooms were good and clean and cheap. He knew just where to find her.

They'd bring in the bags and then go out to the Harlequin or Pierro's or Anna's Bar for drinks. He knew people in all those places. The people would be well dressed and handsome. Some even glamorous. You could forget anything inside. You were supposed to.

He pinched an olive off the plate of *mezes*. It had a rich dark taste, the flavor of earth. He moved it around inside his mouth and scraped it with his teeth until the pit was clean. Then he spat it out.

A girl walked by and looked at him. A slim Greek girl not more than seventeen.

Greek women were getting bolder.

He turned to Danny. "Mykonos will be a whole lot better," he said.

Danny nodded agreement. "You bet. No bears there, Sparky."

"You promise?"

The Greek girl moved away, her hips a gentle tide to Dodgson.

"I promise. Nothing with teeth. Honest, Sparks. You got it made now. I promise."

LELIA

MATALA

"Excuse me."

The shopkeeper's eyes were furtive. They moved over her, then away, then moved back again.

It was nothing new. It was difficult for most men to look directly at a beautiful woman. Men were weak. Men were idiots.

Dodgson hadn't found it difficult. Not yet, anyway. It was one thing she'd liked about him.

Dodgson.

"What time's the bus to Heraklion?"

The man's eyes darted. *I could put them out for you.*

"You are leaving us?"

"Yes, I'm leaving you."

"That is a shame. You go somewhere else?"

"Yes."

He waited for more. *Of course I'm going somewhere else, you asshole.* But she thought she might as well tell him.

"I'm going to Mykonos."

The man smiled. There was something furtive in the smile too, as though she'd told him she were fucking half the island.

"Mykonos!" he said.

"The bus. Just tell me about the goddamn bus, will you?"

Or I will pull off your cock and stuff it into your goddamn ugly mouth.

I'm coming, Dodgson.

The man told her.

PART TWO

ARTEMIS, THE HUNTRESS

"What reasons do you need to die?"

—Boomtown Rats

DREAMERS . . .

On Delos the shepherd Dinos Siriandu dreamed he caught a chicken in his yard for dinner. The chicken had led him a merry chase. He cornered it, finally, against a bale of wire by the side of his hut.

The chicken did not die right.

He put the bird to the block and beheaded it with a single short stroke of his axe. The head fell away.

Normally the body trembled, the legs tried to run. It was a while before the chicken knew it was dead.

But this bird did nothing. It just *stopped*.

Normally, there was blood.

This chicken had no blood.

In his dream Siriandu was repulsed. He threw the bird off the block. He crossed himself. He kicked away the carcass.

The carcass struggled to its feet and calmly walked away.

He woke, listening to what his wife called Hecate's wind howling off the mountain.

Tasos Katsimbalis lay sleeping in his bedroom in Athens dreaming of his friend Jordan Thayer Chase.

He saw an island rising out of a dark starlit ocean, rising to a single peak. At its summit, by torchlight, a group of ecstatic naked women—Greek women, young and lithe—slaughtered a huge black tethered bull with their bare hands. By sheer weight of number they pulled it to the ground. They tore it open. They drank its blood and ate handfuls of its living flesh. The bull bellowed. Tasos watched them carry pieces of it away with them and dance down the mountain.

The bull rose up bloody and maimed on its hind legs, its intestines dangling, steaming, and slowly became a man. And the man was Jordan Chase. Tasos waved to him, and Chase waved back. And faded.

In Heraklion Lelia Narkisos dreamed herself lying naked in a driving wind, a brutal stinging sandstorm, and impassively watched the force of it tear at her and the hot winds crumble her to dust.

And then she was suddenly whole again. Lying in a dark sudden silence. In a hotel room in Heraklion and on an unknown mountain all at once.

Powerful. Cruel.

Inevitable.

DODGSON

MYKONOS

They sat at the Sunset Bar in Little Venice, listening to the lapping waves in the gentle heat of evening. Above his head an octopus dangled from a clothesline, drying. He could smell them cooking over charcoal fires. He could smell the ocean too a few feet away.

The night would be neither cool nor hot. The sun burned down the horizon. The music from the big outdoor speakers poured sweeping and romantic over the sea.

In the distance he could hear the flower man. "*Tee oreo-anthi oanthopolis!*" It was a cry that anyone who came to Mykonos got to know by heart and it made Dodgson feel at home here. In a moment or two he'd round the corner, a stooped old man with powerful shoulders, white hair, and a huge wicker basket of flowers on his back. Some tourist would photograph him while he beamed into the camera. Apart from the windmills and the pelicans in the harbor he was the most photographed thing in town, and the effortless grin was always there. He was a man who seemed to love his work. Half the time he'd give his flowers away. Dodgson envied him.

Dodgson was amazed that so little had changed here.

Long ago the international types, the jet-setters, had discovered the island and money had come pouring in—big money and from a very few hands only, and they held it that way as a sort of private preserve for quite a while before the crowds descended, and maybe because of that, change had come more gradually than on other islands.

There were hotels now where there hadn't been six years ago but not too many, and people like the flower man still existed, there were still the fishermen who went out to their boats every morning and had their own private bar to repair to, still the old women who met the produce wagons mornings and then sat knitting every afternoon in the narrow winding fieldstone streets, still the farmers and donkey men, and it seemed to Dodgson that while the new world had arrived here in force the old one had managed to hold on, at least for now.

After Matala it was good to see. For all its chic shops and glitzy bars, the place still had character. It was not what you'd call the "old" Greece—you had to go out to the countryside for that—but it was not all pollution and mopeds either. The scent of decay had not reached here, he thought.

Or had it.

"Jesus!" said Danny.

He was looking at a big dirty bear of a man walking toward them through the tables. Another smaller man and a woman walked behind him. The big man was dressed in silks but they didn't hang right. He looked like a glacier draped in a schooner sail. There was just too much of him.

The girl might have been pretty if you cleaned her up, washed the stringy hair and fed her now and then. She and the other man were little more than ragged skeletons. It was like watching a small social group of predatory animals, the big man dominant—so much so that the others were starving in the face of his appetites. Even the female. Strange, he thought, the groupings that make people happy.

They walked past them and disappeared into the streets, heading toward the harbor.

"Where do you figure they're from?" said Danny.

"Got me," said Dodgson.

"French," said Michelle. "They're countrymen." From her tone she might have said *weasels*.

"Thought I smelled Gauloises," said Danny.

"It is very fashionable," said Michelle, "to go very far away and come home dirty. Especially to go east. For that I think we must blame the Beatles. The silks were Indian."

"Ugly little bunch," said Danny.

Over by the rocks two fishermen were working on the day's catch of octopuses, holding them by one tentacle, swinging them high over their heads and then whacking them hard against the rocks, a sound like the slap of wet leather. Was it to tenderize the flesh or get the insides out? Dodgson wondered. Two mongrel dogs stood watching.

A pair of hands slipped over his eyes.

"*O singrafeas!* My writer!"

He knew that voice—rough, Greek and feminine.

"Xenia."

"So turn around and give me a kiss, Robert Dodgson."

He turned to familiar bright gray eyes, a familiar crooked smile, the smile lines webbing her broad scarred face. He put his hand into her thick mane of jet-black hair and kissed her.

She smiled. "You are back."

"For a while."

"So how come you not tell me? Bastard."

"We just got here."

"Good. Okay. These are your friends?"

"Michelle Favre, Danny Hicks. This is Xenia Milioris. Best kiss on the island." They shook hands.

"You are here for a while?"

"A week or so, yes."

"Good. You come to the bar tonight?"

"Of course."

"Okay, good. I have to run. I got to put my boat in the water." Predictably, she was suddenly fierce. "These assholes at the dock, they don't know *shit* how to do it. *I* got to show them. Tomorrow we go to Delos. Eduardo, me—a bunch of us. We have a picnic. You like to come? All of you. If the weather is nice."

"Sounds good."

"Okay. We'll talk about it tonight, all right? I'll tell Eduardo, Dimitris, the rest of those bastards, you're here. All right? I kiss you, darling!"

"I kiss you, Xenia."

She moved quickly away. Her gait was almost a man's. He watched her.

Sometimes Dodgson thought she was the only person in Greece who was always on the run, a single locomotive in a world full of strollers. At the bar where she worked she was amazing, weaving through the thick crowd of dancers with her tray held high over her head, her policeman's whistle shrill over the pounding music, darting around with uncanny accuracy and nerve-racking speed.

Like the flower man she was essential to the place for Dodgson, part of the landscape. Six years ago they'd hit it off immediately and he figured he was lucky. You wouldn't want to get on the wrong side of Xenia. He'd seen her break a beer bottle over some witless Irish kid's skull one night. Once she decided he deserved it she hadn't hesitated an instant. More than that, though. If you got on the wrong side of her you'd have missed something.

The others were looking at him.

"Just friends," he said.

"An interesting lady," said Danny. "A bit two-fisted, I think."

"She is. Xenia was born and raised here. She works in a bar and takes home whoever she likes in a country where most of the women stay in the house all night sewing and wouldn't be caught dead in a bar, and where the men damn well keep them there. It's a small island. She's tough."

"I get you."

"It's just as well she's two-fisted. Otherwise they'd crush her."

"Tee oreo-anthi oanthopolis!"

The flower man turned the corner.

"Watch this," he said. "God, I love this place."

The flower man posed and smiled.

Flashbulbs popped in the gathering dusk.

LELIA

AT SEA

The Greek was a sailor with the merchant marine and he'd trotted out his limited opening gambits the moment she sat down. But it was easy to discourage him.

It was easier every day now.

Why was that?

The sailor sat beside her a discreet distance away, reading a book.

Lelia leaned against the rail and watched the sea roll by. The lower deck was crowded, mostly with Greeks bound for Tinos or Síros. They were noisy and dirty. Their children ran around like Indians and there were plastic bags dripping bread and cheese and fruit everywhere. *Overripe. It's all so overripe*, she thought. The only problem with Greece was Greeks.

And one of them was staring at her.

A skinny old hag of a woman dressed in black.

Go to hell, thought Lelia.

She looked back across the railing and watched the gulls scavenge the sides of the boat.

When she got bored with that the woman was still staring.

Her face was expressionless but her gaze was hard and steady. And now two middle-aged women were watching her too. The hag was fingering a blue bead hanging from a chain around her neck.

The sailor looked up from his book.

What the fuck is this? A show? Who do you think you're staring at?

She stood up.

Abruptly the woman turned her head and spat.

Lelia stood rooted there. Surprise and anger boiled in her. *Why, you dirty old bitch.*

She started forward.

The woman saw her move and turned her head away again, spread the fingers of her left hand and shoved the hand palm outward toward her.

"Nah!" she barked.

And suddenly the sailor was on his feet, rattling off some unintelligible Greek to the woman and at the same time stepping toward Lelia, stepping between them to hold her back. The woman answered angrily and then it was a shouting match between them, the old woman and the sailor, with everybody on the lower deck watching.

She didn't understand a word of it.

She damn well didn't like it either.

The woman was pointing at her, yelling. The sailor shouted back, red-faced, gesticulating wildly.

Finally the old hag snatched up her plastic bag and repeated the palm-outward shove in Lelia's direction. *"Arpa!"* she said.

She pulled the shawl up over her shoulders and walked stiffly away.

Lelia and the sailor looked at each other.

"Do you mind telling me . . . ?"

The man looked sheepish. Forty-five, she guessed, and acting like a ten-year-old. *Greeks.*

"I am very sorry. I apologize for her. Very stupid old

woman, very . . . insulting. I am sorry. She is old, you see, and these old peoples, they have stupid thoughts. She says you have the evil eye. I am sorry."

He grinned, embarrassed.

"She gave you a *moondza*."

"Moondza?"

"A bad word. How you say? A *curse*. Yes, a curse. A swearing word. That is the spreading of the fingers, you see. '*Arpa!*' she say. Catch! You catch the moondza. You see? Is old foolishness. I apologize for her."

Lelia sat down. So did the sailor. She could see how embarrassed he was, how much he wanted to return to his book.

Not yet, she thought.

Something swirled in her. Something wonderful. Just outside her consciousness.

"And the bead? What was the blue bead she was fingering? She wore it around her neck."

"Ah! To preserve her from the evil eye. You understand, we are new country now, but we are old country too, and many peoples still believe in this . . . this evil eye. So they carry the bead. And you have blue eyes, you see. Very blue."

"So?"

"Is the thought, the belief, that the woman with blue eyes is best to give the evil eye. Is stupid, no?"

Lelia said nothing.

"But she will not trouble you now."

"She'd better not."

"Don't worry. I have told her."

"Thank you."

"Is fine."

The man went back to his book, his face still flushed with excitement. She wondered if he was really reading.

Now and then the two middle-aged women would glance nervously in her direction.

She lit a cigarette.

"What if it were true?" she said quietly.

"Eh?"

"What if I could cast the evil eye. You'd have been very wrong then, wouldn't you? To have helped me."

The man stared at her, forgetting it was impolite, forgetting himself completely for a moment. He gawked.

Then he grinned.

"But you are a tourist," he said. "Are you not?"

"Yes."

He spread his hands and shrugged.

"How can tourist have the evil eye?"

How indeed, thought Lelia.

DODGSON

MYKONOS

"Hey, Skippy. Look who's here."

He looked where Danny pointed and saw another ferry full with passengers pulling in to Paradise Beach, scraping bottom in the shallow water. Climbing off the ladder, carrying a towel and beach mat, was Billie Durant, looking tanned and fine in a black one-piece bathing suit slit high along the thighs.

He stood and brushed off the sand and was about to call her over.

"No. Hold on a minute. See where she goes."

There was a taverna up the beach and a small store next to it where they sold paperbacks and tanning lotion. They saw her head for that.

"Come on. Let's go."

Michelle lay beside them sleeping in the sun. They didn't wake her.

They slipped on their trunks and walked up the beach. It

occurred to Dodgson that they'd almost missed her. Had they gone to Delos as planned, if Xenia's boat hadn't developed leaks, they wouldn't be on the beach today. The leaks were no longer disappointing.

She was paying for a pack of cigarettes. Danny slipped up behind her. He whispered in her ear.

"Before we begin. Do you have loud orgasms?"

She whirled and he saw fury in her face before she recognized them. Then she began to laugh.

"Why you pair of rats! You gave me a turn!"

"So how are you, English?"

"I'm fine. Even better now you're here."

"Well, of course you are."

"When did you arrive?" she asked Dodgson.

"Just yesterday."

"Lelia and Michelle?"

"Lelia we left home," said Danny. "Michelle's down at the beach. Come on. We'll surprise her."

"Wonderful. Just let me pay for this."

The man behind the counter took her thirty drachmas. She slipped the cigarettes into her bag and took Dodgson's arm as though she belonged there. It was noon and the sun was hot, but the breeze was still good and strong. The beach was crowded. They walked past naked bodies browning in the sun.

He liked her on his arm. She felt good there.

At the mats the two women greeted each other like old friends and Dodgson thought how quickly an intimacy could spring up in this place.

He thought of Xenia.

They'd known each other a mere three weeks and that had been six years ago, yet last night at the bar it was as though it were only a matter of days and they'd been friends forever.

She'd taken a break and they'd talked.

"Listen," she'd said to him, "this is my home and probably it will always be, but it gets no easier, Dodgson. Too damn many peasants here. You know what I mean, *peasants?* Especially the women."

"You're strong. You can handle it."

"I am a *sonovabitch*, Dodgson. But who knows if that is enough? You know?"

He understood. She was breaking all the rules, and in all the Greek community of Mykonos she was alone at it. Much as he admired the old ways and worried about the new he thought she had courage, and was glad of this intimacy with her.

And now he was glad to see Billie too.

He felt safer, surrounded by friends, people who wished him well.

Though with Billie it was already just a little different.

Christ! he thought. Haven't you had enough? After Lelia?

No.

Because that was the whole point. After Lelia, getting interested again was almost a necessity. You had to keep going or maybe you'd get to thinking that the only way it could be was bad or crazy, that it would keep on being that way with women forever, one more Lelia—or worse, one more Margot—after another. And if that happened all the friends in the world weren't going to help any.

He watched her peel off her swimsuit. It was the first he'd seen her naked. He liked what he saw. The slightest bit soft in the belly—as he was—but barely noticeable. But she had long shapely legs and her neck was lovely, her body tanned a light golden color, probably, he thought, about as dark as she got. There was no tan line.

She was not in Lelia's class physically but few women were, and the important thing was that she carried her nudity without the slightest hint of self-consciousness or immodesty, with a nice easy grace. No coy seductiveness and no parade. What you had here was a straightforward girl with all parts intact, he thought. Mind and body.

And I bet her orgasms are deafening.

He realized she was talking to him.

"What happened? I mean with Lelia? If you don't mind my asking."

"You don't want to know, really."

She nodded. "I had a feeling that would be a hard one."

"It was."

"I saw you go by that night. I was sitting on my terrace. She looked . . . very determined about something."

"She was determined, all right."

"She worried me. I thought at the time . . ."

"Go on."

"I thought she looked . . . *ferocious*. Honestly. That's the word that comes to mind. Isn't that amazing?"

"Less than you'd think. I'll tell you about it sometime."

"I didn't mean to pry."

"You're not prying."

"You're sure?"

"Yes."

She smiled. "In that case I'll let you tell me. Sometime. Care for a swim?"

"Sure."

They stood up. They used their sandals to weigh down their mats against the gusty breeze.

"Did you make any plans for dinner tonight?"

He had a sudden urge to lock her into something—into that much, at least. She looked at him and smiled again.

"Of course. I'm eating with your lot, aren't I?"

He laughed. "Yes."

"Good, it's settled then. Last one in!"

She bolted away.

God knows I've been wrong before, he thought. I may be wrong again. But I think this one's healthy.

He glanced at Danny, who was looking at him, nodding.

LELIA

When she got off the boat the first one she saw was the Frenchman, big and crude-looking.

Good, she thought.

Very good.

Right after Dodgson.

BILLIE

She found herself wondering how his kiss would be.

And wondering that surprised her.

Now and then, as they walked, the trail over the hill moved through rough terrain and Dodgson would take her hand. It was meaningless, the gesture of a gentleman and nothing more. But the hand was smooth and warm and dry—soft, the way she supposed a writer's hands ought to be. They pleased her. And that surprised her too.

Because the other man's hands had been soft as well, she remembered them vividly, lying in a hospital bed in Spain half-unconscious at first with amebic dysentery and then slowly awakening to the shameful, terrible fact that the attendant's hands had been on her frequently through her days of fever, stroking her, invading her cruelly, invading her everywhere, and then one final nightmare day of full awareness, of seeing and feeling all he did to her with utter clarity, too weak to stop him.

The authorities' response had amounted to a smug dismissal. It had taken her a good long time even to think of a man again.

Precisely, it had taken her until now.

They stopped for a breather. It was four but the sun was still hot. There was no one about. The beach was far behind them. Away in the distance she heard the tin-can tinkle of a goat bell. That was all. Only that fine peace, that familiar Greek stillness.

The trail was bare and rocky. She looked around.

"Do you suppose there are snakes about?"

He shook his head. "I doubt it. Too late in the day. The only poisonous snake in Greece is the viper anyway. And they're no problem if you're careful. Sometimes you see them sunning themselves on paths like these but you're not likely to step on them if you watch where you're going. They're pretty big. Why? Afraid of snakes? I thought it was pussycats." He smiled.

"Not me. Michelle. She says she's so scared of them she's been staying off all the trails and rocky bits."

He pointed to a series of low stone walls running parallel to the trail a few yards away.

"See those? They build them to catch and hold rainwater along the hillsides. That's where you'd see a snake or two most likely. So if you're climbing in there, say, around midday, I'd be careful. Otherwise you're fine. I'll mention it to her."

They continued walking. She was glad they'd decided to take the trail back from the beach rather than the ferry with Michelle and Danny. It gave her time to be alone with him, and time to digest all he'd told her about Lelia after their swim. It must have been gruesome for him, harrowing. No doubt he'd be shy of aggressive women for a while—maybe of the opposite sex in general.

She knew how that felt.

But he had her hand in his again and she thought she'd like

that kiss; she really, surprisingly did. She felt such quiet warmth from him.

Damn!

The path opened up. There was room for them to walk two abreast now and the trail was worn straight and smooth. Yet he kept her hand. She glanced at him and smiled, and he returned it.

It was all downhill from here and soon the dock was in sight and the bus stop beyond it—the bus that would take them back to town. So that in a way she felt it was now or never.

"Could we try something?" she said. She stopped and faced him.

He looked at her, puzzled for a moment. Then he understood.

"Yes, I think we can."

"And then if it doesn't work particularly, we can just . . ."

He smiled. "Just a guess, but I think it'll work."

She moved into his arms. His lips, his hands on her back—all the sensations were smooth and enveloping and wonderful.

"You're so gentle!" she said, and heard the surprise in her voice.

They kissed again.

Sometimes they can be, she thought.

Sometimes they can.

SADLIER

Twenty minutes later Gerard Sadlier watched them get off the bus.

"That one," he said. "The blonde. The Brit." Dulac nodded.

Their table was angled uphill at some distance from the bus stop so the British woman and the American didn't notice them.

Dulac kept nodding knowingly. Dulac was a fool. Ruth sucked the last few drops of *lemonada* up into her straw. Her deep-set eyes squinted at the woman.

"Bah! She is not so pretty I think."

"Pretty enough," said Sadlier.

"*Him* I like."

Ruth smiled. He didn't like it when Ruth smiled. Her teeth were bad. He didn't like to see them.

"You like the American?"

"He's very pretty."

"He would not even look at you."

"He would look at me if he had to."

He shrugged. He was not at all interested in the American. He would not involve himself for Ruth's sake.

But the girl. She owed him a cigarette. And more.

Tonight would be good to be collecting.

LELIA

It was evening and she dressed for him slowly, facing into the mirror—and it was like a camera lens opening and shutting, opening and shutting, bright flashes of light pouring in through the darkness and then only darkness again, but she took her time and didn't mind.

Her fingernails raked shallow furrows of blood in the soft sweet-smelling earth of her skin, her thighs, her breasts.

She plowed and furrowed for him in the darkness.

DODGSON

The Harlequin Bar was as it always was: packed. Packed with bodies throughout the narrow front room along the bar, packed through the back room, packed along the terrace and down the stone steps, spilling out to six or eight deep between the steps and the outdoor tables in the courtyard. The tables were packed too and people stood between them. The seamless music thrummed and blasted.

Inside they danced on the tables pushed back to the wall, danced to the bar, danced out the door with drinks in hand. It was the only way to move, to get from one place to another. Outside, men cruised men and men cruised women. Lovers were being born there on the terrace while above them on the balcony of the bar upstairs a Victor/Victoria party was in progress and women spilled champagne over their tuxedo jackets. The choreographer for the Crazy Horse in Paris reached down to pet his black Afghan hound, a Brazilian chorus girl on each arm. A British rock star ambled through the crowd looking as conspicuous as possible in black leather jacket and shades and flanked by a pair of pink-and-blue-haired gofers. Dimitris, the club's owner, sipped wine with a Ford Agency model whose blonde, swimsuited body had adorned *The New York Times* magazine section just last Sunday. A videotape was being made nearby and the redheaded Danish photographer was easily as beautiful as the model. Dimitris's eyes kept wandering.

Their own party had the best seats in the house, from a table on the terrace with a good view through the window into the bar and the best possible overview of the crowd below. These complements of old friends—Dimitris, Eduardo and Xenia. It was the best place to be seen as well so they'd dressed for it. Billie, in white, and Michelle, in black—they swore they hadn't planned it that way—looked stunning.

It wasn't the champagne. But Dodgson's grin just kept on spreading.

He saw Xenia in the doorway, sliding through the crowd like a knife through butter, her police whistle shrill above the drums and synthesizers. She's having a bad night, he thought. She looked tired, the strain showing. It occurred to him that she'd probably been fasting. Greek Orthodox Easter was only two days away.

She threw them a smile but it had no real backbone in it.

A few steps behind her Eduardo came through with another tray and the difference between them was obvious. A slim, sandy-haired man in his late twenties, a native Portuguese, he looked fresh, unruffled and calm. He and Xenia had lived together once when he was barely twenty. They were the talk of the island then but it hadn't worked out for long. Xenia was a fighter. She had to be. Eduardo, a lover, was easy as the island breezes. But they had remained fast friends.

Eduardo acknowledged them too.

"Come sit down!"

He pushed past a man in a soft cream Stetson. The hat was probably worth as much as everything Dodgson was wearing.

"Soon!"

He watched them disappear into the crowd. He saw the big ratty Frenchman from the Sunset Bar who Billie said had been bothering her the night before sitting with a pair of blondes at one of the tables in the courtyard. His two scrawny friends weren't with him. Then the crowd closed up and Dodgson lost sight of him.

Had he imagined the man was watching them?

The music halted for the first time that night and Dodgson checked his watch. One o'clock. Time for the floor show.

"Have a look," he told Billie.

Through the window they saw the spots come up on the wiry little chunk of a man standing on the bar, wearing black lace mantilla, glossy lipstick and a red sequined dress. He held a single candle, burning, in each hand.

The song was "Don't Cry for Me, Argentina" and the man—Dodgson wished he could remember his name now, it was the same guy as six years before—the man was lip-synching it, looking like a sailor's drunken dream of a Spanish whore, emoting like crazy during the first slow torchy part, then peeling down to a red maillot and black stockings as the Europop started, beginning to strut and bump and kick, all razzle-dazzle and Broadway glitz, and the crowd howled, loved it. The guy could even dance.

Billie, Danny and Michelle looked happy as kids in a candy-store window.

By the time he was finished, rolls of toilet paper strewn like streamers into the hooting, dancing crowd, even the rock star had his shades pushed up on his forehead and was watching and grinning. The man with the Stetson waved it, whistling. Onstage the dancer took his bows happily amid wild applause and accepted a rose from a young man at his feet. He blew kisses to the audience as the lights went to black and the music started up again.

"I love this town!" said Dodgson.

Across the courtyard an old Greek woman closed her upstairs window. Somewhat belatedly, thought Dodgson.

Xenia came to their table and they ordered drinks. "When I come back, I sit with you," she said. They watched her plummet back into the bar like a bird of prey.

An expensively dressed but overweight young woman leaned over the railing to Danny. There was too much perfume to tell if that was expensive too.

"Excuse me," she said. "I don't know you."

Danny looked at her, puzzled, and laughed. "Hey, I don't know you either."

"No. I mean, are you anybody?"

"Anybody?"

"You *know* . . ."

Dodgson got the feeling she was new at this.

"Well *certainly!*"

"See, we're making a film here . . ." She pointed to the willowy redhead with the video portapak.

"Oh. Are we in it? Is this fiction or nonfiction?"

"Nonf . . . it's a documentary."

"And of course you want people who are somebody."

"Yes. Right."

"As opposed to nobody."

"That's right."

Dodgson had to laugh. He had her on the run now.

"Well for god's sake *he's* somebody. Robert 'Fast Eddie' Dodgson, author of . . . what were those books again, Sparky? Oh yeah, *Small Woods* and *The Killing Season.*"

Dodgson was astonished. "You read them?"

"I read *Small Woods.* Pretentious as hell."

"It was."

"But talented."

He turned to the girl again. "That's my buddy here," he said, "pretentious but talented. So you should get him in. As for me . . ."

"Yes?"

"You really don't know me? You're sure?"

"I'm sorry. No."

"Well shit, that's really refreshing, you know?"

"Untalented," said Michelle. "Just pretentious."

The girl looked at her.

"She's kidding," said Danny. He put out his hand. "I'm Daniel Morgan Hicks. Hicks Pharmaceuticals. Now you know me, right?"

"Uh . . . no."

"We make Arafat."

"Arafat?"

"It's a feminine hygiene spray; smells like the PLO. No. I'm kidding. More like apricots, really. I designed it myself. My dad loves it. Hey, I could send you some. Give me your address." He pulled out a pocket notepad and the stub of a pencil. "We got *crates* of the stuff."

"No, that's— "

"And you need to know about the women."

"The women? Thanks, no. Maybe later."

"They're very beautiful, don't you think?"

"Yes. Very."

"This one here, her name's Michelle. She loves me. Used to be the mistress of Idi Amin. It's true! Now she's a speech therapist. And this one here . . ."

But the girl had backed away and disappeared into the crowd.

"I think you lost me the interview," said Dodgson.

"That's okay. Your books are out of print anyway."

"Morgan? Daniel *Morgan* Hicks?"

He shrugged. "Everybody ought to have a Morgan in the family, don't you think?"

Xenia arrived with the drinks. She served them, then took one herself and sat down next to Dodgson. Cognac. She swirled it in the glass.

"What a night!" She smiled at Billie across the table. "Excuse me," she said. "I don't know you."

Everyone laughed.

"What? What's funny?"

"We just got that line, in a very different context," said Dodgson. "You had to have been there."

Billie reached across the table.

"Billie Durant," she said. "And you're Xenia. Robert's told me quite a little about you."

Xenia took her hand, smiled, and looked knowingly from her to Dodgson and then back again. "Robert, eh? Did he tell you I was a jealous woman? Did I hear you say you *leave* tomorrow?" They laughed. "No. I'm joking. Welcome to Mykonos."

"Thank you."

"Your first time?"

"Yes."

"You like it?"

"I love it here."

"I get you some more champagne. You love it even more. Where's Eduardo?"

She turned to Dodgson.

"I think I like this one. Much better than the last one. What was her name?"

"Margot."

"Margot, yes."

"She's dead, Xenia."

"Dead?"

"Almost two years now."

"Jesus! How . . . ?"

"A razor. A bathtub full of water."

"My god. And what about you? You were still with her then?"

"Off and on. Mostly off."

"I'm sorry. I really am. I shoot my mouth off again."

"It's all right."

"She must have been . . ."

"Crazy. Yes. Well, I guess she was a bit. There were a lot of pills . . . she'd lost her job. And we . . . we weren't getting along at all. There were other women, other men . . ."

"You mourn her. You still do. I can smell it on you."

He smiled. "You have a very good nose, Xenia."

"Xenia has the best damn nose in Mykonos. And it's not right that you do this. You go with this one here now. Have a good time, eh?"

"The best nose and the best kiss, Xenia."

"The best kiss, yes."

Her scarred, weary face moved toward him and she did have a fine kiss, warm and friendly as it had always been.

There was a commotion in the crowd.

He looked down the terrace steps and saw that it was more than the usual jostling and shoving. Someone was plowing through fast toward them, head down.

A pair of boys stumbled against each other, spilling their

drinks. A tall blonde woman was pushed aside and then the man with the big cream-colored Stetson, who started swearing. The figure—he could see now that it was a woman–swung her head around and shouted something back to him.

And Dodgson suddenly knew her.

Some knowledge of the body even from behind, of the harsh voice driving beyond the angry, unintelligible words.

The crowd parted for her. As though it *knew.*

His blood seemed to rush to his head as he rose and for an instant he was afraid he was going to black out—it was the adrenaline—and something cold ran the length of his spine as he thought, *It can't be. She can't have followed me. Impossible.*

People just don't do that.

Then she stood on the landing, glaring at him. A cigarette in her hand, legs spread wide apart. Breathing hard, glaring.

The night went suddenly dark and bleak and cold.

Yes. *Lelia.*

LELIA

. . . inside her the winds blew hot and dry and wild, and they were fearsome, awesome, magnificent. Blood sang in her ears. Dogs howled. She did not think; she just pressed on, some great wide hand propelling her through the stricken crowd, and they were there together, Dodgson and the other one and the three women, and the dark one had his lips, she had them for a second, had his mouth, which was Lelia's, and she saw the heads turn and all eyes on hers, the eyes of his English whore as well, her eyes; but she knew that the way to kill the Hydra was one head at a time so she walked to the dark one who had put her mouth on him and she jabbed the cigarette into her chin, pushed it into flesh and made it sizzle.

BILLIE

. . . so that suddenly Xenia was standing, screaming, a hoarse yell filled with startled pain, and Dodgson was on his feet beside her lunging for Lelia. Billie reached instinctively across the table to restrain him but there was no need, Eduardo had her; he'd appeared out of nowhere in the crowd behind her and had one of her arms while the man in the white Stetson hat had the other; they were dragging her back, and she could see the muscle in Eduardo's jaw twitch and thought, He'd like to kill her and I don't blame him, and Lelia was yelling something as they pulled her away but at first the crowd was yelling too and she couldn't hear. And then she did hear; she could see the twisted gash of mouth and the head whipping back and forth and back and forth.

"I *own* you!"

DODGSON

. . . he heard and thought, No, this is not possible; I made love to that woman and she can't be that thing they are dragging screaming away through all the astonished snapshot faces staring at us, at her, at me. Can't be.

LELIA

"No. It's over! I'm all right. I'm all right now."

At least they were away from the fucking gawkers, the faceless meaningless crowd, the rubberneckers—out on the street away from them.

"I'm all right!"

"The fuck you are," said the smaller one, the one without the hat, but she'd remember him; his hands were hurting her where he gripped her arm, so she said it again and again until they believed her—*I'm all right . . . out of control . . . sorry, sorry . . .* and finally the one with the hat let up and then the puking little cocksucker on the other side of her, though he still stood staring like he'd like to kick her teeth in but she was doing the kicking now, while the other one, the cowboy, began to move away, still stood staring, scared, hating her, and she couldn't let him see what hate was really like because the wind was blowing and all her life had led to this, to this moment, and the little man's mouth was good only for sneering and sucking cock and she wondered if he went down on Dodgson too, the little fuckface bastard.

I'm all right. I'm sorry. Really. I'll go away now, all right? I swear I will. I'll go.

He released her.

She started to walk.

Then so did he.

And in a moment she found the shadow.

She waited in the shadow between two houses. The winds, the dogs began to howl again.

This is what I have come to do, she thought. I have come for this. And they will not deny me.

She waited in the shadow. She lit cigarette after cigarette and watched the night drain slowly away like wave upon wave of cold seawater moving down the tideline, watched the people in the courtyard drift off like leaves upon the tide.

The havoc winds were unrelenting.

Men and women passed her but most did not see her standing there in the shadow and those that did and who recognized her leaned and whispered but did not stop. They had better not stop.

Her patience was a living thing inside her.

The man in the hat walked by. She watched him from the shadow.

She peered around the corner. The bar was closing now. The crowd was a thin milling crescent.

She didn't need to wonder if they were gone. She knew they were there. The hounds could smell them; the winds bore their scent on the low broad tide of blood. She hugged the shadows.

She lit a cigarette. Then lit another and another and another. Four of them burning. She bundled them together.

This time she would . . .

She moved from the shadow into the dim light.

This time she would . . .

She walked toward them easily, quietly. Unnoticed. The remains of the crowd gently parting.

This time she would . . .
     . . . *claim him* . . .
     . . . *put out their fucking* eyes.

DODGSON

. . . they sat inside at the bar because there was room there now and the terrace was too public after what had happened. They were joking with Xenia, who was still pretty shaken but whose sense of humor had returned enough to allow her to wonder who would be first to ask her if she'd cut herself shaving. Fingering the Band-Aid on her chin.

All but Billie had their backs to the door and she must have come gliding up behind them like a ghost. It was still poor Xenia she was after—*was it just that kiss she'd seen? that one small gesture?*—because all at once they saw Billie's sudden look of fear and by the time he turned to see she'd put a handful of cigarettes into Xenia's face—she was going for the eyes— but Xenia jerked away and he saw them sink into her cheek as though it were butter, the smoke and flesh bubbling up liquid like teardrops.

And then he was on her with Eduardo and Danny, and Michelle was clawing air to get at her, Billie still recoiling, and Danny reached out and hit her openhanded in the face while Dodgson and Eduardo grappled for the hands that were clawing toward the women, a wild wiry strength lashing out for them. She was tossing her head and spitting, eyes shot red, head whipping up and down, back and forth, and she didn't even seem to feel Danny hit her except that the mouth began to froth and drool, white froth flying off the bared clenched teeth, spraying them all as her body jerked and slammed against them.

Then somehow they got her to the door. He heard Eduardo

screaming "Damn it! goddamm it!" and Xenia, who seemed to
be gasping and moaning and sobbing all at once, and worst of
all he heard her, Lelia, growling and snapping at them, the
growl set deep in her throat, her voice as deep as a man's, a big
man's if you could believe it was human at all and not some
animal, and the teeth snapped shut and the spittle flying at him.
He felt her fingernails rake his forehead as she reached for him,
and as he looked into her eyes he saw something reaching for
him in there too and he turned away as though afraid he'd turn
to stone while they propelled her out the door back onto the
terrace. And he thought *Who is she?* who is she?

The eyes had not been human.

And then suddenly he was afraid, more afraid than he'd ever
been in his life because they were pushing her back and he
could tell it was coming, he could feel it, *see* it even with his
back to them, as though it had to be. He turned and knew he
was right and that she could see it too.

The hand clawed out for him, the eyes pleaded—no, they
commanded him to help her, yet he was frozen there, unable to
do anything but watch her driven back between Danny and
Eduardo and then watch Eduardo let her go, as though he
sensed the danger as well now, a danger that was more than her
own physical peril but was immutable and final for all of them.

For a moment it seemed as though all that would happen
from this time forward stretched out before him in one clear
terrifying vista, and he yelled *No!* and Billie was yelling too
behind him, but it was too late now as he'd somehow known
it would be; it was going to happen and nothing and no one
would dare to stop it happening.

Lelia smiled.

He saw Danny take her one step backward. And then she
was falling and Danny was reaching for her, realizing finally,
a look of anguish on his face—that strange mad smile on
hers—lurching wildly toward her and nearly falling too. They
heard the *crack* that was loud as a gunshot in the still night air

as she fell the three steps down, the crack of her neck snapping at the impact, saw the mouth blurt blood and foam into the astonished crowd, the head lolling slowly to the side so that he could see the bloody spill growing fast like an inkstain behind it, spreading, the eyes flickering once and then settling into something cold and composed and utterly, monstrously empty.

For a moment no one moved.

A man in the crowd reached down for her wrist and someone beside him darted back as though he'd stepped into a nest of spiders, her blood speckling his trouser leg. Then everyone was shouting.

Dodgson looked down at the one taking her pulse. It was the big man, the Frenchman. His eyes nearly as blank as hers.

"Dead," he said. And shrugged.

Danny looked frantic.

"Easy," said Dodgson.

"I didn't . . . I didn't know . . ."

"Nobody knew," he lied. "Easy."

Eduardo was behind them. "I've walked these stairs a thousand times," he said. "And I never saw it coming. It's not your fault."

"I killed her."

"She killed herself," Eduardo said. And then more mildly, "It was an accident." Dodgson saw he was shaking. He turned and went back inside to Xenia.

He felt Billie come up beside him. He moved away from her down the steps.

The Frenchman stepped back, staring at him.

Dodgson looked down into her blood-splattered face.

"Damn you," he said.

The wide red mouth yawned open.

GEOLOGICAL NOTE

At 4:55 Saturday morning, approximately two hours following the death of Lelia Narkisos on the steps of the Harlequin Bar in Mykonos, an earthquake off the volatile coast of Santorini measuring 6.5 on the Richter scale sent homes, hotels and tavernas tumbling down the cliffside into the sea. It failed to activate the island's volcanic core.

Seas were high all day throughout the Cyclades to the north and as far south as Crete. Because of the early hour few people were about and only eleven casualties and thirty-three injuries were reported. But because it was Saturday and the day before Easter on the Greek Orthodox calendar—the most important holy day of the year—the event was variously interpreted.

Among the local ministry, some said it perfectly symbolized the resurrection of Christ—the death occurring on the final day of fasting with rebirth scheduled quite appropriately for the following day. Others, who saw it more in terms of human tragedy, speculated darkly that Christ had abandoned his followers and would not in fact arise at all that year.

So that there were pessimists on the one side and optimists on the other.

The Church itself refused to comment except to say that seismic events and cosmic events were not the same thing at all, and to warn its parishioners against magic and medievalism.

TREMORS

When the seas began to rise Orville and Betty Dunworth were smack in the middle of the Aegean, and it was questionable whether the thirty-four-foot cruiser *Balthazar* was up to it. By 10:00 A.M. Orville was pretty frightened.

He stood on the fly bridge scanning the dials, alert to disaster—checking temperature, oil pressure, rpm's, like a doctor hooked up to his own private cardiograph and waiting for his heart to stop. Nobody'd told him the Aegean could get this bad. Sure, they'd warned about *meltemi* winds in July and August but this was only March for Christs sake and the swells were lifting her up god knows how high in the air and slamming her down with a tilt and a crash and a grinding sound that was frankly scaring the shit out of him.

Dockside *Balthazar* had felt big and new, secure. She didn't now. She felt like a sixteen-footer. And sounded a hundred years old.

Exactly how he felt.

They'd overloaded her for one thing. Fuel and water tanks full and gear enough to last them their entire two-month vacation in the islands. Enough for *six* months actually. The goddamn beautiful scenic Greek islands. It was Betty's idea, naturally. What in hell was wrong with Florida, anyway? He'd be sipping a daiquiri by now.

He squinted through the dripping fiberglass and saw the biggest one yet come rolling toward him, a sliding solid wall of water. He braced and prayed. This was no damn business for a retired optometrist. Just get me through this one, he thought. Just this.

111

The wave lifted her high and he felt the sickness rise in his stomach, not from the buck and roll so much as the fear. For one roller-coaster moment he felt weightless, felt the hull beneath him slide and shift, and then the sharp swift crack that seemed to grind at his bones, that stunned him like a blow to the head.

Where the hell was Betty?

Damn that woman! Not that she'd do him any good up here. But he could use the company. Somebody to yell at, anyway. He was in a trough now, starting to lift again. It wouldn't be as bad as the last one. *Couldn't be*.

"Betty!"

He'd tried to raise somebody on the one hundred-watt ship-to-shore but all he got was Greeks. He couldn't understand a word of it. He was all alone out here.

"Betty!"

"Coming, dear!"

She moved up unsteadily beside him. He nudged her away. He didn't want her crowding him. He meant his glance to be reassuring but from the look of her it wasn't. A handsome sixty-year-old woman with the body of a forty-year-old and now, the face of a scared old crone of a hundred fifty-five.

"Is it getting any better, dear?"

"Not much. No chance to make Santorini now. Mykonos isn't far, though." He tried for a hearty tone and failed completely.

"But we were going to do Mykonos at the *end* of the trip, dear."

"Jesus Christ, Betty! We'll be lucky to make it at all, for god's sake!"

He was screaming now into the wind.

"What?"

"Never mind."

She patted his arm. "Don't worry. Mykonos will be fine." *Crash. Roll*. His stomach took a leap.

It better be fine. It better be.

. . . Linda McRae and Will Sandler were going to get off the

island when the storm hit, to spend the last three days of their
vacation in Crete. Now they rethought that idea. With one day
wasted and so little time left it was hardly worth it. They
couldn't afford to fly. And the long shipboard journey would
only give them about a day, hardly enough even to see
Knossos. So they decided to stay on in Mykonos where it was
cheaper, anyway, living out of backpacks and camping at
Paradise Beach, and where they knew they'd be having a good
time. Which was what they'd come all the way from Forest
Hills to do in the first place.

That and dump their parents.

It wasn't easy, being sixteen and in love, despite what you
saw on TV. You had to sneak around for one thing. You made
it in cars and behind bushes at the country club and at friends'
houses when their parents weren't home. And when you
couldn't make it, it *killed* you.

They'd managed to fix that here.

Neatly too. Coming away on vacation without either Linda's
parents or Will's knowing that the other guy's kid was going.
Luckily the McRaes and the Sandlers didn't talk. Luckily they
hated one another.

The old *Romeo and Juliet* business, thought Will, had its
points.

It was a nowhere beach day because of the storm so they'd
hiked to the old monastery, which was pretty boring.

Linda killed a ladybug.

And that was about the height of their day.

Unless you counted the evergreen. That was kind of neat.
Who'd expect to find an evergreen tree in Greece?

Linda broke a branch off that.

She was a big strong girl, Linda. Athletic. Blonde.

And Will guessed she just liked to break things.

. . . *he cursed her and cursed her*. Cursed the day he'd
married her, cursed the pretty oval face and the bright black
eyes, the slim figure, the flirtatious smile. At heart she was a
village girl and would always be. When what was wanted was

a city girl. Or better yet, a tourist girl. A blonde, maybe. Yes, a blonde from England or Sweden or California.

And now of course she was pregnant. A year after now she'd be pregnant again. That was the way with village girls. And in five years or maybe less, he thought, slim lovely Daphne Mavrodopolous will be fat the way they all are fat and the eyes will not smile for me anymore, but only for the children.

Five years after _that_ she'd have a mustache.

I have never seen a tourist girl, he thought, with a mustache.

Kostas Mavrodopolous watched his eighteen-year-old wife clean the tables of his waterfront taverna with a damp cloth until he could not stand to watch anymore and stared out angrily over the rough dark waters.

Today, because of the seas, there would be even fewer tourists than usual.

He was twenty-two years old.

He had only just learned he was about to be a father.

So far, his taverna had not caught on. Only in July and August, when everyone in Mykonos made money, did he make money.

His wife was happy. She sang as she worked. She was going to have a baby and all the women were happy for her. For the village girl.

Two years now he had tried, and still he had nothing.

He could think of only one thing that would comfort him. Tonight, after closing, after the chairs were stacked and the tables tucked away, he would go to the bars, where she could not follow. Tonight and however many nights it took thereafter. It would help nothing. He would find no answer to his problems there. But it was something.

He would find himself a tourist girl.

SANTORINI WINE

Among those present on the island of Santorini when the earthquake hit was Tasos Katsimbalis.

Koonelee Tasos, industrialist, landowner, importer and rabbit thief had arrived the day before in order to supervise the loading of crates of Santorini wine worth 2.2 million American dollars, bound for New York on the Greek freighter *Herakles*. Absences due the forthcoming Easter holiday had caused delays and half the crates remained to be loaded when the quake hit at 4:55 that morning.

The crates survived.

Tasos did not.

He had chosen a hotel overlooking the bay. From the terrace it was possible to watch the *Herakles* far below. At 4:55, like nearly everyone else on the island, he was asleep, having sampled three glasses of the local product. Wine made Tasos sleepy. He had been reading a book, a good book though rather long and difficult—Sir James Frazer's *The Golden Bough*. It lay open on his lap when a four-foot slab of concrete from the floor above fell sideways onto his chest, cutting him nearly in half, and it plummeted down beside him when an entire quarter-section of the bedroom slid screeching down the mountain.

JORDAN THAYER CHASE

ATHENS

He finally made the phone call to Elaine from his hotel room in Athens Saturday night. It was ten o'clock, Holy Saturday. In another two hours it would be Easter.

The line was good for a change.

"Jordan! My god! Are you all right?"

He could hear the concern and relief in her voice and wished he hadn't waited so long.

"A little cold," he said. "Otherwise I'm fine."

The cold was more like flu. He'd been gobbling aspirin and what passed for vitamin C here, a dissolvable pill like an Alka-Seltzer that tasted like some evil orange Kool-Aid. But the fever held on.

"You're in Athens?"

"Yes. You have the number on the pad there by the phone."

"I know. I tried to call you."

"I got the message. I'm sorry."

There was a pause on her end of the line. The wire crackled.

"Jordan, what are you *doing* there?"

Good question.

"I'm on my way to Mykonos. Soon as the holiday's over. It's silly to try to travel now. The whole country's traveling. And Tasos is right—Greeks board a boat as though it were the last one going anywhere and get off as though it were sinking."

"You've seen Tasos?"

"A couple days ago, yes. He's well, sends you his love."

"So what's going on in Mykonos?"

"I'm meeting someone there. Business. I'll call when I have an address for you. I'm sorry to keep you waiting like this. I really am."

"It's been *days*, Jordan."

"I'm sorry, honestly. Things just got . . . out of hand here."

He had the feeling she was reading between the lines, gathering more than he was telling. He couldn't help that. There was another long pause from her end.

He wished he could read her but he couldn't now. The ability was fickle—it came and went. The overseas line didn't help any either.

When she spoke again though her voice was softer, more composed.

"Your Ampcomp people are making me crazy. They call here twice a day."

He smiled. "Hold them off awhile, will you?"

"I will."

"I miss you, Elaine."

"I miss you too. You know I do."

"I'll phone as soon as I get to Mykonos. Promise."

"You're not an easy man, Jordan. You know that."

"I know."

"So promise me something else then."

"What."

"Promise me you won't do anything . . . that isn't business . . . without telling me."

He laughed. "Like what? Take a lover?"

"Don't play games, Jordan. I'm serious."

"I know. I promise. I love you."

"I love you too. Take care of that cold. You sound terrible."

"I will."

"I love you."

He hung up and leaned back on the bed. His head pounded.

He sat up and took two more aspirin and skimmed though the International *Herald Tribune*.

His stocks were mostly up and that was nice.

Mount St. Helens seemed set to erupt again, and geologists were pulling their study teams out of there.

In France they were still stalling after nine full months on the execution of a major Iranian terrorist whose photo stared out at Chase balefully. The government was fearful of reprisals. An editorial in the paper accused them of cowardice.

And the Italians seemed to have found themselves a brand-new miracle. In Porto Ercole the figure of a madonna kept appearing in the bole of a cypress tree.

He folded the paper and put it aside. Maybe a walk, he thought. To clear my head. Fresh air.

He walked slowly up to the *plaka*, the old town. It was nearly deserted. Normally this time of night it would be churning with hustlers, vendors, bouzouki players, tourists, but with most of the taverns and shops closed up for the holiday the American kid on the corner with the guitar and the rotten nose— to Chase it looked like skin cancer—was getting no action at all and sat there in his dirty jeans strumming introspectively.

He headed for the little church at Kadathineaon and Sotiros streets.

A line of Greeks—families—moved slowly ahead of him.

He passed through the wrought-iron gates. There were twenty people or so in the courtyard outside the church, waiting. He stood beneath the trees and could see inside through the open door to where they were lighting votive candles and talking, a small, cheerful little crowd, the icons and altar behind them.

Candlelight threw a glow into the courtyard. Beside him a woman fingered her rosary. Men held firecrackers and sparklers. A teenage girl came around and handed each of them a long thin candle.

It was nearly twelve.

The crowd began to file out of the church.

They filled the courtyard. There was quiet conversation and laughter. Most everyone was smiling. To Chase it looked more like a picnic or the Fourth of July than a religious occasion. It was hard to remember that this was the most important day on the Orthodox Calendar, but that was the way with the Church in Greece. It was never somber. Even the priests drank and sinned.

He knew that the early Church Fathers had grafted their holy day onto the pagan Festival of Adonis, who had died for the love of a goddess and was reborn again each spring. In ancient times, a very cheerful occasion. Here, at least, it still was.

The priest took the dais now. He was singing. The crowd grew quieter.

The candlelight in the trees, the soft, Eastern-sounding music—it was very pleasant here. He was glad he'd come.

And now the priest raised his arms and shouted, *"Hristos Anesti!"* Christ is Risen!

Church bells began to peal from near and far away throughout the city. From balconies of homes above him sparklers and skyrockets flared. Beyond the gate fireworks exploded.

In the courtyard they lit their candles, passing the flame candle to candle. The man beside him lit Chase's for him and then embraced him, kissed him on the cheek. Chase kissed him back. A little woman with a gold tooth turned from her family and kissed him too, warm and welcoming. He found himself smiling, stooping to return the kisses of her little boy and girl as well.

In a while people began to drift away, many of them, Chase knew, to break their fast with the bloodred eggs that symbolized the resurrection and rebirth and to drink some wine. Others returned to the church. Another service would begin soon now.

He stood beneath the trees. He could smell incense thick on the night air, and gunpowder.

On an impulse he went inside.

He walked to where the votive candles were burning and placed his own, burned low, among them.

As he took his hand away it guttered out.

And he thought, *Tasos*.

He saw a crumbling mountainside. A harbor. A man falling amidst a shower of debris.

He felt a moment of warning, of terrible design.

Then emptiness.

He began to cry.

Faces turned to him in sympathy, in concern, but no one moved to interfere with him. He stood and watched the others place their candles next to his through a growing film of tears.

Then suddenly he felt like a stranger there and walked away.

In the morning he had the details from Tasos's wife. It had been swift, anyway. There was that much.

He told her on the phone why he would not be able to make the funeral, heard the silence at the other end of the line and knew she did not understand.

For the second time in twenty-four hours he called Elaine.

LELIA

MYKONOS

The box in which she lay felt thin as paper.

She sat up slowly, felt a soft fleshy rending from the cold gray shell beneath her like the petals of a flower blossoming outward from the bud.

She gazed across the room at the altar and the icons. They were poor and worn with age.

The flowers had no scent.

She looked down at the vault of flesh.

She waited.

DODGSON

MYKONOS

"You knew, of course, that she was pregnant?"

"What?"

The police lieutenant nodded, tapping the desk with his pencil. Even at noon the station was dingy, airless and dark.

"Two months pregnant. Long before you knew her, though, correct?"

He thought of her as he'd seen her the day before, lying in a plain wooden coffin in the tiny church, a lily in her hand. Someone had placed a fifty-drachma piece over her lips. *For Charon*, Xenia said. *It is the custom*.

The mortician's art had failed him. The face did not look peaceful. Even in death she frightened him.

It was impossible to believe she'd been carrying a baby.

Something gentle in all that violence.

"Yes. That's correct."

The policeman shrugged. "Do not let it concern you."

Lieutenant Manolakas looked nervous. Dodgson wondered why. He'd questioned them early Saturday morning just after the accident and then again that afternoon. He'd been completely controlled and actually quite decent—only asking them not to leave the island for a few days in case he needed more from them. He took statements from all of them and from the other witnesses. All quite calmly. So what was bothering him now?

"Pregnant," said Dodgson. "God. I didn't know."

"Of course not. Many things, I think, you didn't know." He sighed and wiped his forehead. "Many things I don't know."

He glanced at Billie and could see that she read anxiety in the man too.

"Like what?"

"Like . . . let me begin for you." He sighed again, shuffling some papers at his desk.

"First, we trace the Canadian passport, correct? She has no family left in Quebec. Mother, father, both are dead. But her father is clearly Greek and Narkisos is not a common name, so we look for family here. We find a cousin in Athens, but he does not know her. Wants nothing to do with her. Says, bury her.

"But there is more in our records on Miss Narkisos. This one, she is a bad one I think."

Billie's grip tightened on his arm.

It felt good to have her there. It was well past dawn Saturday morning when they'd gone back to his room and made love for the first time, in a kind of mutual frenzy at first, throwing off the fear and blood and violence, but then it had changed, become infinitely sweeter and far more special, a quiet commingling of them both that was passionate but concerned too, and afterward that was what had remained, the passion and the concern, and he knew she had touched him in a way no other woman had ever touched him, not even Margot.

"What do you mean?" he asked.

"She has been in Greece almost two months according to her passport. February in Athens there was a disturbance in a bar. Her name was taken down, but she was not arrested. It appears she assaulted . . . forgive me, how do you say *putana*?"

"Prostitute," said Dodgson.

"Prostitute. The woman's face, her jaw, she broke it. Also one rib, and the woman had to go to hospital. But this woman is also a bad one so Miss Narkisos is not arrested. Okay.

"A month later in Ios a German tourist complains that she steals his money. This is the beginning of March and we look for her, but she is already off the island. We do not know where. Still we look. And we think she go to Santorini next because more money is stolen there, this time from a Swedish girl Miss Narkisos rooms with a few days. But we cannot be sure it is her. And again, when we begin to look she is already gone off the island. But she assaults this girl too. Hurts her badly."

"My god," said Billie.

"Yes, it's true. I believe it is not good to know this one for long. But there is more. And worse. For *me* worse, anyway."

He paused. He was sweating. Anger and embarrassment seemed to vie for possession of the man. He threw up his hands.

"She is gone!"

"Gone?"

"The box, the coffin is there. But Miss Narkisos is gone."

His mind couldn't wrap around it at first. "How . . . ?"

"Let me explain. This morning we intend to bury her. There is nothing to be learned from the body, there is no one to claim her. So we would bury her. I tell two men, I say go to the church, inform the *papas*, the priest. Fine. They are gone maybe a minute when the priest is *here*. In my office. A good man, a very pious man, very responsible—and now he is crazy. Because he heard nothing last night, nothing, yet this morning the box is empty. The body is gone."

"But where . . . ?"

"We do not know. My people are searching now. This is very bad for me, you understand."

"Of course, but . . ."

"To care for the dead . . . properly . . . is a most sacred duty. The *papas* is disgraced, I am disgraced. And you must all account for your whereabouts last night. You can do that?"

"Of course we can."

"Good. Good for you. Not so good for me. I don't understand it. Who would *do* such a thing?"

"I don't know."

He wondered what to tell Danny, who was still so shaken that Dodgson didn't even like to mention Lelia in front of him. He guessed they'd all discovered something about themselves on the steps of the Harlequin that night that they didn't really like.

Lelia could do that to you.

Billie tugged at his arm.

"Let's go," she said. "I want a swim in the ocean very much right now. Is that all right, Lieutenant?"

He nodded. "I will take your statements later, after dinner, if we have still not found her by then. You do not seem like body snatchers to me. But please be careful, though. The seas are very high today. The earthquake, it changes the weather."

"We will."

"I will let you know when we find the body."

"Thanks."

"Don't worry."

They walked out into the midday heat. They turned into the narrow streets off the harbor.

He thought about standing in the dimly lit church yesterday morning, Xenia and Billie beside him.

Good-bye, Lelia, he'd murmured.

He recalled now, strangely, that he'd said that once before.

He'd been early.

THE SUMMONS

Shortly after midnight on Holy Saturday, while Jordan Thayer Chase made his sad way home from the church in Athens, while Lelia Narkisos lay in her well-made wooden box, while Billie Durant and Robert Dodgson made love the second time that night, Gerard Sadlier lay in his tent at the campground off Paradise Beach, dreaming.

• • •

He had gone through a door and it was the wrong door but he was unable to go back, and now it was night upon the mountain, and he was Chosen.

He climbed through a throng of people. All of whom were his subjects.

Some were small, weak—human clutter that blocked his way, that tested his will and resolve.

Others were huge, even bigger than he was, and from these he received a passionate, proud obedience. His slaves. They pushed the others aside for him as he passed with no concern for bloodied bodies or broken limbs. Yet he sensed a vivid danger from them too. Should he show the slightest weakness they would crush him.

A beautiful woman with long blonde hair approached him. Like all the other women she was naked. *Don't you know me?* she said. He reached out and recognized her by the heavy ripe weight of her breasts. Then he gestured, *follow me*.

He knew her.

She was his victim. His sacrifice to the Other.

At the top of the mountain lay a bowl of fruit, still on the vine, surrounded by white flowers. He tasted it. It was sweet, rich, flowing with nectar.

The woman lifted the white robe off his shoulders while he peeled the pearlike fruit and tasted it.

He turned to her naked, his penis erect and throbbing. He thrust her to her knees. She opened her mouth, ready to take him inside.

He was the true Son. All this night to be treated as the Living God.

Her mouth closed over him. The men bowed. The women gnashed their teeth and slathered with lust.

The dream shifted.

He stood before a woman dressed all in black.

He knew her face. And knew he had no power over her. Quite the contrary.

The woman held a knife like the ones that shepherds carry, with a curved sharp blade. She swung it in a slow reaping motion down across his body as she told him what it was he had to do, and he nodded.

The dream shifted.

He became a common laborer, digging with a spade.

The dream shifted.

He was back atop the dark looming mountain, his cock thrust deep into the throat of the first woman, while behind him stood the Other, dressed in black, reaping.

A cry of adoration burst from all those gathered there.

The world went to its knees before him.

Sucking him. Sucking him dry.

He woke with an erection and the sense that he was not quite well, an ache in his bones like the flu.

He could not clear away the images of the dream. In every other dream he could remember the images had faded quickly. These grew clearer. He looked around at the tents on the hillside and they all seemed unfamiliar, distant, strange. Superimposed over all of them was the mountain, the woman in black, the dream.

When at last Dulac awoke and crawled from his tent Sadlier sat in front of his campfire feeding it twigs one by one and staring into the flame, at the flickering image of himself in flowing white, at an immense obeisant crowd, at the breasts he could see through the veil of black.

Dulac was annoyed.

That great dumb hulking Sadlier had not even bothered to start the coffee.

"You might have thought of us for once," he said.

Sadlier said nothing.

"Prick." He squatted before the fire, rubbing his hands to warm them.

"The woman," Sadlier muttered. "The one who died."

"Yes. What about her?"

The rasp in Sadlier's voice surprised him. Was he ill?

"We'll get her."

"What?"

"Get her."

"Go back to sleep, Gerard."

"No. You don't understand."

"No, I don't. Go back to sleep. I'll wake you later. With some coffee."

He watched him turn away from the fire. It seemed to Dulac that his eyes were not focusing properly. He opened his mouth as though to speak and the lips hung slack for a moment, gleaming wet. It was not like Sadlier to be sloppy. Filthy, yes, but not sloppy.

Then he did speak and Dulac thought, of course, he's still asleep. He's talking in his sleep. Either that or crazy. Because what he said was, *She's alive.*

Dulac merely looked at him.

He said it again, with force this time and leaning close.

"She's alive! She'll give us *everything*!"

His eyes were red, his face perspiring. His breath smelled horrible.

Dulac had not seen him this way since Pakistan.

Since they'd killed Henri.

He'd realized, then, that it was not over the hashish that they'd killed a man but simply because they had the opportunity and the reason. He'd seen that on Sadlier's face then and he saw something much like it now.

He sighed. "What do you want from me, Gerard?"

The thin lips parted in a smile.

Ah, yes, thought Dulac. Sadlier stared and smiled, and Dulac knew that look very, very well.

And he thought, We're in for it now.

PART THREE

PERSEPHONE

"Oh, what a wicked thing it is for flesh
To be the tomb of flesh, for the body's craving
To fatten on the body of another . . ."

— **Ovid**, *Metamorphoses*

THE ISLAND

THE FIRST DAY

The harbor woke.

Fishermen stepped from caïque to caïque, each to his own, checking traps and nets in the first red glow of sunrise, then ambled to the dockside café and waited for the owner to organize and prepare his good thick coffee.

They smoked and watched the waves. The sea was less tortured today. On this side of the island, at least, they'd get some fishing done.

A pelican woke—a brisk flurry of pinfeathers. Its bright red eye caught something moving along its back, an insect. Its long snakelike neck turned the head ninety degrees and its orange-yellow bill plucked the bug from its feathers. Then it began to preen. A fisherman from the café doused the pelican with a bucket of water. The bird was used to this. It dipped its head, acknowledging him.

Cats prowled the narrow strip of sand in front of the café and dipped beneath the hulls of boats blocked and awaiting repair, their noses twitching to the scent of decay. A pair of mongrel pups raced across the square, faced each other and began to play.

The morning was warm and breezy.

The flower man woke beneath a wall of snapshots, all pictures of himself—his basket on his shoulder, grinning into Polaroids, Nikons, Kodaks.

Kostas Mavrodopolous' pregnant wife Daphne threw open the

turquoise louvered shutters to their bedroom and looked out upon the bed of red and yellow flowers. She turned and smiled upon her sleeping husband.

At the Sunset Bar on the other side of town a starved tabby cat hopelessly stalked a sea gull perched upon the rocks by the shore. Inside the bar its owner Georgio selected tapes for the evening, Vangelis and Irene Papas—one less item to deal with later, allowing him time on the beach today with the French girls he was meeting this afternoon.

In the shop two doors down, the town carpenter moved his sawhorses out to the concrete ledge by the sea. It would cut down on the sawdust in the shop, and there were many orders for repairs and refinishings and new chairs and tables now that tourist season was beginning.

Across the island at Paradise Beach the campground still slept. There had been a party the night before and with no one around to enforce the four o'clock curfew the taverna had stayed open till dawn. So there was no one yet awake to see that the waves were still high on this side of the island, the winds still strong.

Two kilometers from the main beach, in a damp sea cave brushed by the waves at high tide, the body of Lelia Narkisos lay naked and rotting, faceup, in a shallow pool of stagnant water.

Crabs had found her face and body. Her eyes, lips, ears and nose were gone. So were most of her internal organs. What was left was white and bloated and lay with legs crossed together at the ankles and arms spread wide, like a Christ crucified and left to the mercy of the sea.

In front of the cave the water was deep and crystal-clear in most weather, but today it boiled with sea-life—with crabs and fishes who could see that over the narrow lip of rock there was death nearby, and good feeding.

By midafternoon the dockside cafés were bustling. Two cruise ships were anchored in the harbor, one full of middle-aged

Germans and the other, retired Americans. Always pragmatists, shop owners who had previously piped out rock 'n' roll into the square now switched to gay bouzouki to encourage the older tourists' purchases of sailor caps, shawls, jewelry, liquor and painted china.

When the *Nais* docked around four it brought with it by far the largest group of tourists that season—mostly kids making their first stop on the islands out of Piraeus.

The cafés switched to rock 'n' roll again.

No particular notice was taken of a tall, muscular American businessman in a lightweight summer suit who got off the boat carrying a single large leather shoulder bag and a briefcase. He was conspicuous only to the old Greek woman who had rooms to let back near the windmills, and who knew a good bet for a reliable quiet tenant who would pay a slightly inflated price when she saw one.

Jordan Thayer Chase stepped off the *Nais* at just about the time that Gerard Sadlier, Ruth and Dulac awoke at their campsite at Paradise Beach, not very far at all from where Billie Durant, Robert Dodgson, Michelle Favre and Danny Hicks lay on their beach mats tanning in the sun.

The day drew on to disgorge its night.

At 5:00 Billie Durant turned off her shower and peered through the pebble-glass bathroom window.

She felt she was being watched.

There was nobody in the bedroom and the front door was securely locked. Not even Dodgson had a key.

She went back to her shower, uneasy.

Michelle Favre and Danny Hicks were walking past a rack of color postcards near the Montparnasse when each of them felt someone walking directly behind them, practically touching their elbows.

They stopped and turned at exactly the same time.

There was nobody there.

At 5:45 Xenia Milioris napped in her bedroom. She dreamed

that someone came into her room off the porch through the glass double doors and went through her pocketbook. The dream was very vivid.

So much so that when she awoke the first thing she did was reach for her pocketbook.

It was impossible to know exactly how much money had been in the change purse because it had been four days since she'd been to the bank. And then there were the tips.

But she estimated that 3200 drachmas, the equivalent of about forty American dollars, was gone.

She tried to recall the dream that now, it seemed, was not a dream at all, to recollect the shape of the intruder. Male or female? Short or tall?

She couldn't remember.

She showered and dressed. The room was hot and steamy. She opened the glass doors to the porch and looked outside. By the railing she saw a small pile of charred paper. The bottom paper had not burned away entirely.

It was a fifty-drachma note.

It was probably the harsh brown soap but the burns on her face started aching badly.

JORDAN THAYER CHASE

He still felt terrible. The cold hadn't gone away.

He walked down past the Remezzo through the gauntlet of expensive stores. Elaine would have liked the shopping. In the windows he saw fox and mink and sable, one-of-a-kind gold and silver jewelry, dresses with Rome and Paris labels. Even the window-shoppers were chic, the men out of *GQ*, the women out of *Vogue* and *Elle*, all of them young.

He barely noticed them.

He was looking for something. Someone.

I'll know you when I find you, he thought.

And then what?

It was only around seven and he'd already showered and shaved, changed clothes and hit the streets. The room in Little Venice was fine. Spacious, clean and private. Its windows overlooked the sea, jutted out right above it. At high tide the water would rise to five or six feet up the foundation of the building—he could see the waterline. Outside of the real Venice he'd never seen anything like it. Lying on his bed he'd be able to watch the sundown.

According to the landlady one other room was tenanted, and that was three floors up. He assumed that price had something to do with that. The room was expensive. He knew he could do better on price, but he liked sunsets.

And now there was about an hour to this one—and instead of sitting in his room enjoying it over a bottle of wine or finding a little taverna by the sea where he could get something to eat he was roaming the streets, psychic antennae turned up to high. He'd have liked that bottle of wine, in memory of Tasos.

He walked past the Harlequin and saw a young Greek woman there, smoking a cigarette, alone on the terrace. It was still very early for the bars. It came to him that the woman worked there.

There were bandages on her cheek.

The woman looked hard and angry.

He felt something from her. Not what he was looking for but something. He decided she'd be one to watch.

He walked through the narrowing streets to the harbor.

He was hungry. He walked across the square to the little snack stand and ordered a souvlaki—five smallish pieces of meat on a skewer, topped with a thick slice of bread. He tasted the meat. It was pork. It was nearly impossible to find a lamb kabob these days.

He walked back across the harbor and stopped in front of a thirty-four-foot cruiser, painted white and nearly new. The *Balthazar*. A woman of sixty or so was sitting on the deck sipping a drink. Her blouse was a floral print, a very cheap material for a woman with so much boat under her. American, he thought. There was another deck chair beside her but at the moment it was empty.

Her distress signal was loud and clear.

Chase winced. He didn't like coming across something like this but every so often he did. Troubles with her husband. Lurid doubts about her marriage. Sometimes you felt it from a friend. The friend could be smiling but inside he was screaming. It happened. And then what did you do? *Hi. I see you're having some trouble here.*

No, you shut up and let it go if possible. At least here he could just keep walking.

He was passing the overseas telephone office when a man walked by.

Every alarm system in his body started shrieking.

Middle to late twenties, Chase guessed. Long blond hair, small dark eyes. A sharp one. His clothing Indian and ratty. Built like a steamroller.

The man had just done something shocking.

He tried to focus, to make it out, but his reading of the man was incomplete, jumbled, a cataract of sliding, twisting emotions. He read pleasure, expectation, lust, and at the same time death and despair and some sick, perverted sexual energy that seemed to inform all the rest of it like a kind of twisted superego, as though in some way it were not even part of him.

The man was . . . *contaminated.*

Chase followed him.

Waves of feeling thrashed off him like snakes writhing. Chase felt sure he was insane, but something more than that too. The man's intensity staggered him. Broken thoughts flew off him like sparks, like pieces of a shattered, exploded building.

He rubbed his temples. The headache had come suddenly and it was not his cold.

He felt pain, horror and a wallowing in death, in blood. He stopped and turned away, trying to end the welter of impressions pouring over him, a physical pain now throughout his body. *"Stop!"* he said aloud, fingers pressed to his eyes. A teenage girl with a backpack glanced at him as though he were crazy.

The man turned a corner, out of sight. *But not out of mind.*

The pressure continued. Images hit him like hammers.

A dead, bloated female body. Dragging it. Bending over it. Open pale blue eyes. The face unrecognizable. Hands on damp cold thighs. Then another woman—this one alive. Dragging her too. The woman screaming. Then the corpse again, his hands on her cold breasts. His mouth going down . . .

Jesus!

He turned and ran. Away from the man. Back through the streets, back to his room.

And it was only when he'd opened the bottle of wine and stood sweating in the sunset by his open window that he remembered the Greek girl with the angry face on the steps of the Harlequin Bar. The man was a killer. She was a victim.

Somehow they were connected.

CHILDREN SHOULDN'T PLAY WITH DEAD THINGS

Linda McRae was roaming the sparsely wooded hillside above the campsite gathering sticks and twigs for their fire when she saw the woman in a copse of trees.

She had just rolled over a promising-looking log but it was all rotted underneath; there were maggots under there, dirty-looking pale white things. So she stomped them. And then got mad at herself.

Because look what she'd done to her sandals.

Revulsion and the fact that she'd just killed something again made her almost want to cry. She didn't know why she had the urge to stomp on things, to break things. She wasn't a bad person. It just happened. Will said she was angry at her parents and that was why. Sure she was angry. But so was Will, and you didn't see him smashing stuff all the time.

She scraped her sandals in the sandy earth.

Then she looked up, and there was a woman.

A really lovely woman, dressed all in white, in some white flowing thing, and it was almost perfect, the woman standing on the hillside amidst all these tender young trees, a picture-book image of some beautiful Greek goddess, so beautiful it made her catch her breath for a moment. She wished Will were here to see her. She wished she had a camera. She wished . . .

The woman smiled at her.

The smile was so . . . *physical!* Like a push!

It jolted her. She dropped the load of twigs and sticks she was carrying. And then felt foolish. She knew she was blushing.

The woman laughed.

And that was better, because then Linda could laugh too and it wasn't so embarrassing to be blushing anymore. Probably the woman was used to reactions like that, as lovely as she was. Maybe she got them all the time.

The woman nodded. *Come on up.*

They were leaving tomorrow. She didn't really need to make new friends but it was hard to resist her, an older woman that drop-dead gorgeous who seemed at least passingly interested in her—and what could she do now anyway, after staring and then dropping the wood and everything, just ignore her?

"Hi," she said. And walked up the hillside.

The woman did a sort of half turn, still looking at her, and Linda could almost see the soft outlines of her body through the flowing white material. And she *did* look like a goddess standing there, like something out of a movie, and she resolved to tell her that, no matter how embarrassing, as soon as she got up there, even if it did sound kind of funny, because seeing her so lovely was making her heart pound and bringing tears to her eyes, it was that moving, she was actually almost crying again, just like before.

She wondered for a moment why that should be.

She hadn't hurt anything.

Will was damn near ready to call out the troops when he saw her coming down the hill.

By then he had the fire going. Just a small fire, because fires on the beach were illegal. But he was going to need some more wood.

And along she comes, empty-handed.

Sometimes it was hard being patient with her. She could be incredibly cranky sometimes, or else she'd just forget things, like birthdays or even dates they'd arranged, and it made him wonder just how committed she was. He was sure he loved her. He wasn't sure how much, but he was sure he did. And the *how much* part only got to be a problem at times like this.

Not a stick of wood. Not a twig.

He looked up at the sky. It would be dark soon. And it looked as though if he didn't go get some wood himself there wasn't going to be any. What had she been doing up there? Women could be an intense pain sometimes; they really could.

He got to his feet and walked toward her.

"So where's the *firewood,* Lin?"

No answer.

And what the hell was she smiling about? Maybe she'd been toking on a joint up there.

Great, he thought. Smile. Meantime there's a real good fish down here waiting to be somebody's dinner.

"Hey, what'd you do, break an arm or something?"

Then he got closer and realized it wasn't a smile at all. Her lips were pulled back, yes, but something was wrong. It looked more like she'd been crying.

All at once he wasn't mad at her anymore.

"Hey, hon. You okay?"

And he thought for a moment that she was going to pass him by without even saying anything, which would have been weird even for moody Linda, and he just had time for a glimpse of a woman in white way up ahead of them on the hill, when Linda turned to him and he saw that she hadn't come totally empty-handed, not entirely, that she had one short stubby stick in her hand, a stick with a sharp, pointed end to it—and had no time to scream at all but only gurgled and looked at her face bathed in tears, pink tears because of the blood from the crushed bloody dome of her skull as she drove the stick into his neck just above his Adam's apple. And he realized what was wrong with her.

Then a moment later he was dead too.

SADLIER

She stood before him naked, her skin glowing in the dim flickering light of his candle.

He made no attempt to reconcile her presence there with the sprawl of rotting flesh and bone that lay between them on the floor of the cave. They were one and the same and yet they were not. The high reek of decay did not faze him. He was aware of a faint odor, of a running slime beneath his sandaled feet. But the corpse meant nothing to him. He did not even remember bringing it there. Certainly not what he'd done to it afterward.

She spoke to him. The lush wide mouth seemed to move just a split second *behind* the words:

"Say what you want."

He said nothing, only stood there, yet she nodded.

"It's yours," she said. And he understood her to mean, *but not for free*.

She told him her price.

And he agreed.

For what he asked the price was very small indeed. Her lips moved again, the voice just barely preceding it. It rolled with resonance inside him.

"Do that," she said, "then come back to me."

He nodded, backed away, his erection grinding at the thin loose trousers.

"I will make you *new*."

He saw the cave wall sweating.

Suddenly she was gone.

He saw crabs swarming over the body, carrying away bits of flesh between their pincers, scuttling all around, blue-black and shining in the candlelight.

Cupping his hand to the flame he moved quickly to the far side of the cave, heard shells crack beneath his feet, ran up the goat path to the top of the hill.

The moon was bright. He paused there, breathing heavily. He blew out the candle. He saw the moon glinting on the waves, the bright white clouds overhead.

Beside him, she turned and smiled. She was naked as before.

He watched as she drew herself up and the muscles of her calves and shoulders pulled back off bare white bone, the smile the long wide grimace of a skull, the muzzle of an animal. She dove down and out like a graceful, slow-flying bird into the sea.

Nothing disturbed the water.

He turned, cold, and walked back to the campground to do what he had promised.

JORDAN THAYER CHASE

The woman's glance appraised him and did not appear to find him wanting.

It was 11:30 and the Harlequin was crowded, so all he could get from the waitress, the Greek woman, was a fugue of drink orders, faces of customers, and a kind of general struggle against running down—so that when this one stared so openly he decided to pursue it for a while. Maybe he could learn something.

She was beautiful. Thick red hair. Light blue eyes. Spectacular.

Only twice in their sixteen years together had he been unfaithful to Elaine. Once in the year before their marriage. He saw that now as a last-ditch attempt to cut the growing ties to her and continue going it alone, which up to then was all he knew. And he thanked god it had failed. The second time was recent and aberrant and very, very brief, and beyond itself meant nothing—certainly nothing to what he felt for Elaine— and the wild bitter memory of that was nearly faded now. It would never happen again. He was secure in that.

Though this one could tempt the saints.

He was flattered, really.

Miraculously, the seat beside her had just opened up. He took it and ordered a drink.

He could guess a few things about her. The glance was just a little too open, as though she was undressing him with her eyes—an obnoxious male gesture that was slightly less offensive in a woman perhaps because it was less familiar. The smile

142

had a calculated sardonic quality that was like a challenge. The tough-girl pose. I've been around, said the smile. And I'm still here. Care to find out why?

Beyond that he couldn't read her. Nothing more than what she gave him on the surface. If she were drunk or nearly so that might account for it. Or maybe he'd just hit a blind spot again.

"I'm not supposed to do this," she said.

The music was loud but her voice cut through it easily. Chase practically had to shout.

"Do what?"

She tilted her drink.

"Liquor. Cigarettes. Have you got one?"

He fished one out of his pocket, lit it for her. Her eyes held on his while she drew up the flame. Her eyes were an amazing color.

There was something familiar about her.

"Have we met?"

She exhaled deeply and shook her head. "I don't think so. Unless you go to Paris."

He did, but not often. Then he realized. "You're a model."

"How'd you guess?"

"Psychic," he said.

"Sure, you are." She coughed. "Damn things."

"You're not supposed to smoke?"

"No. Or drink. Lungs are shot, heart's shot. Doctor says they'll kill me."

"At your age?"

"I'm afraid so. Had my first heart attack a year ago. I think it was a year ago."

"Tough life, being a model."

"Tougher than you think."

"But you're not from Paris."

"Sure I am. Oh, you mean originally? No."

"Where? I can't place the accent."

"You're not supposed to." Her voice had gone bored and expressionless. She tossed her long red hair.

"Look," she said. "This place is too loud. I know another

place. It's just opening tonight. Want to go and try to find it with me?"

"Try to?"

"I know the general area. But not where it is exactly. I just got in today and the streets are pretty confusing."

He hesitated. He looked for the barmaid. She was outside hustling drinks. It didn't look like there'd be much letup for a while.

He'd come back later. The woman intrigued him.

He examined his motives. Yes, that was all it was. That was as far as it went.

He still couldn't read her.

"Let's go."

They moved out the door, down through the crowd in front of the terrace, into the streets.

"They built this to confuse pirates, you know that?"

Chase said he didn't.

"Sure. The idea was that the locals would know exactly where they were going but nobody else would. Gave them a head start against invaders. They're still the only ones who know where they're going as far as I can see."

"Are we lost yet?"

"Not yet."

"You in a hurry?"

"No."

"Slow down, then, will you?"

She had a good ten years on him and they were going uphill into town. The going wasn't hard but his cold had cut his wind down.

She eased the pace a little but still stayed three or four steps ahead of him. He didn't want to complain again. But he wondered if this had been a good idea.

She kept turning corners. As though she knew exactly where she were going. He'd turn a corner after her, and there would be another one.

He didn't know if she was lost, but he was.

Hell, it's a small town, he thought. They'd come out someplace he knew eventually.

She kept talking. *This looks familiar. No, that's not right. Maybe here.* He heard a note of steadily increasing anxiety in her voice, but it was strange—he couldn't *read* anxiety.

He knew by now that she wasn't drunk. Usually, if he tried, he could penetrate to some level, and anxiety—any strong emotional state—only made it that much easier.

But she was utterly closed off to him.

He had blind spots, sure. And never knew why or when he'd have them. But almost always there was *something*.

And where had he seen her before?

Somewhere.

Those eyes. Nearly the same color as . . .

"Here we go."

She moved confidently out ahead of him.

The Greeks turned in early. Some of the streets were brightly lit and others completely dark. This one was dark.

He narrowly avoided hitting his head on the projected rail of a balcony. In the distance he heard the bass thump of rock 'n' roll. So there was definitely a bar nearby. But it was hard to tell in which direction. He was tiring.

The whitewashed walls all began to look the same to him, as did the closed, shuttered stores and markets. Vines and flowers brushed his hair. His shoes sounded loud on the fieldstone walk. The night was warm. He was perspiring.

The music came and went, chimerical. She turned another corner.

It occurred to him that he didn't even know what her name was.

"Of course you do, Mr. Chase."

Startled, he turned the corner.

The street was empty.

Yet now he felt her there, nearby and all around him. He *read* her.

The full weight and force of her. Alien and frightful.

All she'd concealed from him.

BILLIE

She was getting very close to Dodgson. Very quickly.

It was always somewhat dangerous with a man, but with this one it was probably more so than usual. A writer who said he'd never write again. Suppose they stayed together. *What in the world would they live on?* She had to laugh.

Why was she so happy?

Because she was happy—listening to him in the shower singing tunelessly, waiting to make love to him again. She lay across his bed and closed her eyes and let the fantasy come. He'd walk out of the shower and see her there. He'd drop the towel and lean over. She knew exactly how he'd smell, of plain soap and that Aussie shampoo, the stuff with papaya. She imagined his hands on her, very firm and gentle.

There came a time when you simply had to close your eyes and jump, didn't you. When you had to have a certain courage.

She recalled her mother dying, riddled with cancer. She had always been very close to her mother. And on this day, the day before she died, Billie had been taking it badly. The end was so close now. Her mother had awakened and looked at her and then reached over and patted her arm.

I'm doing this alone, she said. *You can't go with me.*

Her mother had known about courage.

And she wondered how her mother would have felt about her involvement with Robert. She'd known about the hospital in Spain and the rape. And she'd looked on, saddened, Billie thought, as she cut herself off from men, saddened but understanding.

She thought she knew what her mum would say.

He's a nice man, isn't he? Well, you're your mother's daughter, dear. And you need a man.

She closed her eyes and saw them making love and felt her nipples tighten. Her eyes snapped open.

I know what, she thought.

She got off the bed. She unbuttoned the checkered blouse and pulled off her jeans.

Underneath she wore a filmy beige bra and matching bikini briefs. Thus far, Robert had seen neither of them. She looked into the mirror. With the tan, there was almost the illusion of nakedness. I'm never going to look any better, she thought. Dodgson, I've got a little treat for you. You'd better appreciate this because my ego's showing.

She hopped back into bed.

Cover or no cover?

She felt like a cinema director laying out the properties.

No covers. And a little stretch to tighten up the tummy. She laughed aloud. *Really*, Billie.

I'm not certain Mum would approve of this at all.

She heard the shower go off and Dodgson humming, drying himself. Any moment now.

She wondered if she was blushing.

"Billie?"

He opened the bathroom door and stood there. She couldn't help laughing. The expression on his face—perfect! Then he laughed too.

"I think I've died and gone to heaven."

He dropped the towel, sat on the edge of the bed, and kissed her. His hair was still very wet when she put her hands into it.

"You look lovely," he said. "I almost hate to take them off."

"Don't then, for a little while."

"Okay." He kissed her again. "For a little while."

She pulled him down to her mouth, to her neck, while his hands moved lightly over her breasts down to her belly and over the side of her panties to the fine gold down of her inner thigh, teasing her—then back over her hips and butt and up to pluck and roll the nipple under the thin material. His hands were smooth and felt wonderful to her, urgent and masculine yet thoughtful, considerate of all the textures of her body, the sleek tight surfaces of muscle here, the tender softness there, of all the weights and hollows.

She felt herself flush, heat rising quickly and steadily. She pulled the panties off and was open to him.

And now he moved down over her, his mouth tracing a tingling line of fire from her breastbone over her ribs and belly down inside her until his tongue found its target and she began to sweat in earnest, shuddering, until the small pitchfork jabs of fire became one long burning that seemed to go on and on, so that when he rose over her grinning his cheeks and chin were slick with her and as he entered her, she was half again her normal size . . .

. . . and when it was over, inexplicably, she was crying.

The look on his face questioned her—what? why? but she could scarcely tell him, she scarcely knew herself. It had just happened, out of control, automatic, timed to her release. Let go, she thought. If you have to, babble.

"You see this?" she said. "You see what a wreck you've made me? You know what you're doing to me? Because I don't, dammit!" And she was laughing now as well.

"I see it. And whatever it is, you're doing it to me too, Billie."

"Am I?"

"Yes."

"Really?"

"Really. And you'll keep on doing it too, I think."

"Dodgson, don't leave me, okay? I didn't want to say that. I promised myself I wouldn't say that. But don't."

"I won't."

"You didn't count on this, did you?"

"No."

"Neither did I. I thought it was years and years away."

"It was. We just grew up fast together. That's all."

He hugged her very tightly.

"And what if you leave me?" he said.

"Fat chance. Dodgson, you should live so long."

Later his voice was drowsy.

"You've still got the bra on," he said.

"I know. You can take it . . . if you want you can take it . . ."

And smiling, she fell asleep.

In her sleep she felt a sudden cold.

It awakened her.

It wasn't Dodgson. He still lay asleep beside her and his body was warm.

The cold surrounded her. Like a damp mist.

She felt it everywhere—on her breasts, her thighs, her face. She touched her stomach. She wasn't sweating. She wasn't sick. It wasn't a cold sweat. She looked at the window.

It was open.

Perhaps that's it, she thought. Though she felt no breeze.

She got up and went to the window and closed the shutters.

The cold seemed to follow her.

Wake him up, she thought.

And then urgently she thought, *No, don't.*

She climbed back into bed. Trembling, she pulled up the covers. She moved close to him.

A few minutes later the feeling passed.

Was it fever?

Exhausted, she fell asleep again.

SADLIER

He crested the hill where their camp lay and saw them in the glow of the fire, Dulac on one side and Ruth on the other. Ruth strummed the battered old guitar and they passed a bottle of wine. From the way Dulac thrust the wine at him Sadlier knew he was drunk.

"Finish it," he said. The voice was slurred. "We have another."

Sadlier accepted the bottle, tilted it back, drained it and tossed it away. He stood behind Dulac and watched him uncork the bottle of red.

Ruth continued strumming. She was a terrible guitar player. Sadlier rolled up his sleeves.

There was little point in waiting.

"Adieu mes amis," he said.

His hands moved down to the sides of Dulac's head. His knees bent forward to brace the body. His powerful arms and shoulders flexed and twisted, snapping the head around to the side with a sound like green wood breaking. He released the body and Dulac fell toward the fire.

Ruth's guitar chord hung in the air. She opened her mouth to scream. He reached through the fire and pulled her toward him, into the fire, facedown, and held her there until her legs stopped twitching and he could no longer stand the billowing smoke. He pushed her aside.

Her hair was almost gone. The eyes boiled in their sockets. A small twig poked through the blackened upper lip.

His hands were badly burned. In his excitement he barely felt them.

Dulac was bleeding from the eyes, nose and mouth. Sadlier hoisted him up on his shoulder. He dropped to one knee and threw Ruth's body over the other shoulder. They weren't particularly heavy. Like starved children. Unmindful that someone might see him from another campsite he walked down the hill.

For Sadlier their bodies were sacks of gold, jewels, precious metals.

His purchase into eternity.

BILLIE

When she woke this time she was frightened.

Something had touched her.

Something had touched her *there* and it rocketed her out of her pit of dreams as though doused with ice-cold water—and perhaps it was a dream, it had to be a dream, she was sure of it, but the touch was cold, so cold and so private and foul that she couldn't sleep, couldn't think of sleeping. She sat with him in bed and waited for the sunrise. It felt safe to do that. It did not feel safe to dream.

Because dream or not she'd felt it slip inside her, and its touch was cruel and evil.

SADLIER

Her gown was black and made of illusion. Sadlier knew that now. It didn't matter.

He dumped them down in front of her, near the black and crawling thing on the floor and near the other two, the teenage boy and girl, and did not wonder how they came to be there, knew only that she had gathered them, and saw that the crabs had begun to find them too as they would now find Ruth and Dulac. He didn't care. She was everything to him now.

She motioned him outside ahead of her.

She walked halfway up the goat path before she pushed him to his knees and roughly turned him around. There was power in her hands, great power. He could not have resisted her.

She parted her gown to reveal a small perfect breast, a wide pale nipple. He took it in his mouth. He sucked and tasted blood.

He swallowed it greedy as a child.

She pushed him back. Behind her the night surf thundered.

She stepped up to him and straddled him and parted the gown still further. She pressed herself against him. Her flesh was cold to his hands but inside of her his tongue found a blazing, scorching heart.

Again he tasted blood. Old blood, dead blood. Raw and ripe.

Suddenly it poured over him.

He lapped at her like a dog. She pushed him down.

She tore away his shirt and smiling, leaned over him, pressed her body to him, her smile broadening as she felt him wet inside his trousers.

152

"Close your eyes if you want," she said, her voice like a silk glove.

He kept them open.

So that it was like watching a snake, or perhaps a wolf or a bird of prey, because she drew back slowly, he could feel the hard muscles coil, and then when it came it was sudden, faster than he could possibly have imagined it would be.

For a moment the wide blue eyes seemed to float before him, blotting out the stars.

Then the mouth flew open and the head struck down as she tore at his neck and shoulder, blood pulsing out over both of them as she ripped at him and bolted his flesh, head darting forward and then jerking back as she swallowed, and the last thing he saw as a living man was the look of ecstasy on her face, and knew that it matched his own.

DODGSON

THE SECOND DAY

"What is this, Malibu?"

They stood on the hilltop over Paradise Beach. They'd had to walk there. In the harbor at Plati Yialos the waves were choppy and none of the ferries were running. Yet here it was more than choppy. This was surf! Where normally it was placid as a lake.

The weather had gone strange again.

"You ready?"

Dodgson grinned. "Guess so."

"You tell anybody you went bodysurfing in Greece, they'd never believe you."

Danny led the way down. It was the first time since Lelia's death that he seemed himself again. Michelle, he knew, had been working on him. Breakfast this morning was nearly the same kind of boisterous affair they'd known in Crete. And now they had this weird, magical beach day—high waves and a clear, cloudless sky. You could hope it would complete his recovery.

He touched Billie's hand.

"Want me to carry that now?" He pointed to the small portable easel and shoulder bag containing her pad, books and materials.

"I'm fine."

She's quiet today, he thought—subdued, introspective. He wondered if anything was bothering her. He knew she was basically happy. With him, with the two of them together. He supposed that if and when she wanted to tell him about it, she would.

They spread out their mats and anchored them against the wind with clothes and sandals, stripped down and ran to the water.

There were half a dozen people out there already beyond the sandbar. The waves were high—six-foot curls, some of them. They were breaking far from shore and that was good, because the sandbar was infested with sea urchins. But you wouldn't get near that now.

He'd never heard Michelle whoop before.

But she was whooping now, running out ahead of them, leaping into the whitecaps. The undertow tugged at his ankles. It drifted to the left, but without the power the size of the waves would suggest. It wouldn't be bad.

They really had a perfect day for this.

He grabbed Billie's hand and ran. Ahead of them Danny tackled Michelle and they disappeared into the foam, came up laughing and sputtering.

In a little while they were out far enough so that you could catch a wave and ride it, but they were bunched too close together. Danny and Michelle would shoot right over his head.

"We'd better spread out," he said.

Danny nodded.

Billie squeezed his hand.

"Us too?"

"A little. No farther than this."

She smiled. "Good. Because I'm really sort of awful at this."

"It's easy. All you do is float. When the wave comes along you flatten out and try to swim with it, just below the curl, until it catches you. Then you just go with it."

He looked over his shoulder. Two waves back he saw a big one building.

"Go over these next two and wait for the next."

On Billie the water was just chest-high. He watched her push off the bottom and bob over the crest.

"Hey, Dodgson!"

It was Danny. He'd seen the wave.

"You ready?"

"I'm ready."

He reached over and squeezed Billie's hand. He stood at three-quarter profile to the wave and watched it build. It was going to be big and powerful.

The second one passed them.

"Okay. Get ready to hop right into it and start swimming. The same time I do. Swim hard so it doesn't pass you by."

She looked doubtful. "You're sure about this?"

"You're going to love it."

He let go of her hand. He saw Michelle and Danny catch it behind them to the right, pushed off with his feet and swam like hell, then felt the velocity envelop him and shoot him forward so that there was no need to swim anymore, he'd caught it just right—and there was a moment when the ride was smooth and exhilarating, and then another when it was rocky, jarring, but just as good, and then he was in white water and the wave was churning sand all over him. His knees hit bottom. He twisted over on his buttocks and let it carry him along the sand awhile and then stood up.

Billie was ten feet behind him to the right. She was grinning.

"Again, please!"

"Can do."

Michelle and Danny were about three feet apart, five feet up the beach. She lay there like some kind of *Playboy* foldout, smiling, while Danny crawled over on his hands and knees and flung himself on her. She screamed with laughter. They rolled in the surf, kissing, hugging, biting. Then Danny stopped abruptly, kneeled, looked up at them and spit sand off his tongue.

Dodgson turned to Billie.

"He'll be fine," said Dodgson.

Some waves were good and some were very good, and they kept at it until Billie and Michelle were exhausted. Then there were just the two of them out there and the big waves kept breaking.

There's maybe three or four left in me, he thought, then it's quits. He didn't want to quit. He felt like a kid again.

But Danny looked tired too.

They went out farther so they could catch the waves earlier for a longer, smoother ride. If they stood on tiptoe now their chins just cleared the water. It gave them just enough height to push off strong for the big ones, they ones they wanted to ride, and to bob up easily over the others. The tow was pulling them down the beach some, but not much. He could see Michelle on a beach mat and Billie sketching a few yards over to the right.

Danny was just in shouting distance, maybe twenty-five feet away.

Dodgson saw a good one building.

He watched it over his shoulder, prepared to make his move. His muscles tensed and he enjoyed the feeling—it had been a while since he'd had a good workout. He watched it rise.

His timing was excellent now. Practice had sharpened him. He waited for the moment. He felt the sucking sensation at his legs and the push at his shoulders and went with it. The biggest one so far.

Everything was right. His balance perfect, his position perfect—and he was flying along just under the curl, a weightless feeling, flying along in a line straight as a bullet, yet it hadn't even begun to break yet, wouldn't for a while; he was riding this one high.

• • •

And then something sucked him under.

He swallowed water. The wave continued barreling along ahead of him while something pulled him to deep water. It had his ankle. He kicked at it, thinking *shark*. He felt no impact and no pain either but he'd heard about shark attacks and shock could do that to you: there wasn't any pain till later.

Maybe his foot was gone already.

Panic flared through him.

He kicked again. Struck nothing.

The wave he was riding crashed to shore, a muted thunder. Something still pulled him back, pulled him hard, and to Dodgson it suddenly felt like a . . . like a goddamn human hand, adjusting its grip, closing tighter, dragging at him.

Faster.

That was impossible. *Danny?*

He struggled to turn and gulped more water. He was losing strength. He opened his eyes to the stinging, swirling sea, turned and looked around.

As suddenly as she'd taken him, she let him go.

He saw a woman, naked, turning just as he opened his eyes so that all he saw was her swimming away from him, stroking fast toward the surface—and he gave her no time at all, with his strength going and the water in him he just started climbing, hand over hand, kicking, scissoring, looking up at the bowl of sunlight shining through the waves and feeling the pressure in his ears, straining to pull himself up until finally he broke the surface. He gasped and coughed, trying to take in the air and coughing it right back out again, his body slack, drained.

And he wasn't out of trouble. He could breathe now. But she'd dragged him far. Something inside him measured the distance to shore against his remaining strength and he knew he could never swim it.

And now the undertow had gotten stronger, much stronger, as though she somehow carried the current out along with her as she swam away and drew him out, *she was after him still,* and though he knew that was nonsense the thought, the image of her pulling along tides and currents and riptides was there; he couldn't shake it.

He turned and saw a wave.

It was not a huge wave. But maybe.

He saw another one behind it. It was bigger but much too far away and he'd forgotten how cold the water was, he'd forgotten about hypothermia and he'd been out a long time now without a break, and what strength she hadn't drained from him the water was swiftly taking.

If it wasn't this wave it wouldn't be any.

He waited. He wasn't even sure he had the strength to get the position right, or to get to it fast enough. It had to be right. If the position was off the wave would roll over him and he'd be left there. He'd drown there. Go down maybe before the other one even hit him. Don't panic, he thought. Control.

He waited and watched the wave.

And for a moment wondered where she was.

If she'd even been there at all.

Then the wave was on him.

He flattened, started stroking. His arms felt heavy.

There was a sickening moment of equilibrium when the push of the wave and the pull of the undertow were at nearly equal force, leaving him nowhere, and he thought the wave would pass him. His arms pumped desperately. He thought he screamed.

Then it caught him. He was in an even, gentle rolling. But it had to get him a long, long way so he kept on swimming as hard as he could, torturing his arms and legs and lungs to do more for him while he fought to get ahead of it once and for all—and then he was ahead, had only to brace and flatten and hold his position, yet that took everything he had, just to keep going, eyes closed and teeth grinding, until the wave deposited him like a dying swollen thing in the shallow sand a yard or so behind the sandbar.

He saw Danny first.

"What'd you do out there, sport?" said Danny. "Find a mermaid?"

JORDAN THAYER CHASE

His instincts all told him to leave, to run.

He'd run last night.

That was twice in as many days. Once from the man and once from the woman. If she was a woman.

The man was sick, crazy, probably homicidal—and somehow he was connected to her; he was sure of that. But he was nothing next to the woman.

The woman was pure fear.

Something had slithered out of the shadows last night that had made him think of demons. Lost, not knowing where he was, he'd run through the streets unerringly like some blind terrified mole instinctively finding his burrow.

He remembered his vision at the *tholos* tomb in Mykene.

He wondered which had scared him more.

Delos. That was where he'd resolve all this.

It was frustrating. There was an urge to get it over with, to *see*. But now he had another day on his hands.

The Delos run was canceled because of high winds and rough seas. He'd attempted to bribe his way over but none of the fishermen were buying. Their boats were their livelihood. No rich American tourist was going to scuttle one. You couldn't blame them.

But what was he supposed to do now? Sit here and drink all day? It was tempting but it was a bad idea.

He wasn't much for the beach.

At breakfast he read the paper, in which the only item even vaguely of interest was that a pimp had been murdered at

Stonehenge, of all places—the French were still holding their nice little terrorist amid much debate, cowardly as ever—and then he talked to the waiter.

The waiter said he was in luck because there was a festival at San Stefanos today, just a short ride out of town. A cab could take him there. It sounded as good to Chase as anything else.

The cabbie quoted him a price that was much too high but Chase thought, what the hell.

They drove through the back part of town into the hills. The land was greener here and more rugged. He saw patches of farmland, vineyards, the cruel cutback of the vines set in circles on the cleared earth like so many crowns of thorns, barely sprouting. There were a few whitewashed houses. Then long stretches of bare rock open to erosion and the winds.

"Is just up here," said the cabbie. "You like it, I promise."

They turned up a narrow dirt road. He could see the church in the distance. It was set on a hill, with a long expanse of green grass and shade trees between it and a ruin of some sort. Along the grass people were dancing in small groups of seven or eight, bouzouki music playing on their tape decks. They sat under trees eating bread, cheese, salad, and drinking wine. There were donkeys tethered near the ruin, and a horse.

He got out of the cab.

"You will return from here no problem. Someone will give you a ride. Maybe on a donkey, no?"

Chase hoped not.

"What's the church?"

"Is the Church of the Virgin Mary Evagedistria. Two churches, see? Old one." He pointed to the ruin. "And new one. Is Easter Week. Is good festival. You have a very good time."

"Thanks."

Chase tasted dust as he drove away.

Over on the grass a group of teenagers danced around the base of a tree. An old man sat sipping a bottle of wine. The man saw Chase approach and offered him the bottle. Chase smiled and declined. He made his way over to the new church, crossed himself, and stepped inside.

There was nothing impressive here. The usual icons. The heavy smell of incense. It was made out of ugly new red brick. He dropped a coin into the poor box and left, walked back across the grass to the old church past where the younger children played and past the donkeys and walked inside.

That was better.

What surprised him was that it was still in use.

It had obviously been burned, you could tell by the buckled, blackened walls and the makeshift roof, just planks of wood badly fitted together. Compared to the new church it was tiny, about twenty square feet. But there was still a worn, water-stained red carpet leading to the altar and a few small icons to the Virgin, looking lonely and poor against the faded, streaked white walls. There were even some candles burning.

Maybe the old folks prefer it, thought Chase. I do.

He walked around back. There was a cemetery there. Man-size boxes of cement, mortar and wood lying above ground, each with a little window displaying preferred wines, tobaccos and photos of the deceased.

In the Greek Church they buried the dead for only three years, then dug them up and put them in boxes. Tasos had told him once that it was simply a matter of space, that Greece was small and there was just no room to bury the dead. You could stack boxes. But Chase thought it probably had something to do with resurrection too, or at least it had in the beginning.

By the side of the building, close to where the children were playing, a repository had crumbled open.

He saw skulls and thighbones, bleached and old and brittle-looking.

It shocked him slightly: that no one had bothered to seal it up again. And that the children were allowed to play there.

Death. It was always very visible in Greece.

He remembered when Tasos's mother died—the keening, wailing women, the slumped silence from the men. For a week the men went unshaven, and everywhere they walked they walked slowly, as though bearing some heavy weight, as though inconsolable. And perhaps they were. But it was also very public. It honored the dead by identifying their mourners. The women wept. The men were stony.

A week later the men shaved again and went about their business and the women stopped their wailing in the night. The ritual was over. Yet even then the women would dress all in black and the men wore their arm bands—you could still tell who the mourners were—and it lasted for forty days at least, Tasos said, and if a woman had lost a child or a husband she might wear black forever.

Visible and public. Like the windows in the coffins.

He walked back to the trees. A pretty teenage girl offered him a glass of wine and a slice of feta. He took the feta and refused the wine politely.

He had a sudden vision of Elaine dressed all in black, veiled, holding a bouquet of flowers like a bride.

He shook it off.

It was getting warmer now and the wind seemed to be dying down. Tomorrow, maybe, he'd get to Delos. He hoped so. Whatever this was, he needed it to be over with. He was much too interested, lately, in death and coffins.

He walked to the road. He stood there staring at the drifting clouds.

In a little while a Jeep came by and they motioned him in back. He climbed in.

There were two empty cases of wine back there with him and as they drove to town he gazed abstractedly at the symbols etched in the wood without realizing, at first, exactly what he was seeing, only listening to the rattle of the bottles and the roar of the old Jeep's engine.

A circle, a wolf's head, and a grinning skull.

The symbols were ancient but here was clear indication that they were still in use. It didn't surprise him. The symbols of the threefold goddess—Selene/Artemis/Hecate.

The moon, the hunt, and the dead.

Chase smiled.

The wine, of course, was from Delos.

It was her island.

AT NOON . . .

. . . Daphne Mavrodopolous, two months pregnant, saw the most beautiful woman she'd ever seen pass their taverna holding a naked infant child draped only in the hem of her long white dress.

She did not know whether to be enchanted or concerned— such a very young child should not be exposed to the noonday sun. Yet the woman seemed to know what she was doing. She looked so purposeful, so controlled and aristocratic.

She called inside to Kostas. She wanted him to see this. Kostas had been gloomy lately. She knew he worried about money and the baby. Perhaps it would help him to see this lovely new mother and her child.

He didn't answer right away so she ran inside to get him. She found him sitting by the bar, idly polishing a glass, and told him to hurry. Then she dashed outside again.

Just in time to see the woman disappear into Vassiliadis's wall like smoke through a window screen.

She fainted. Kostas, behind her, was barely able to catch her. He brought her inside into the shade . . .

AT TWO O'CLOCK . . .

. . . Orville Dunworth sat on the deck of the *Balthazar* drinking a vodka martini. Betty had been out shopping all day—she still was—and the deck was cluttered with souvenirs, most of them wrapped in brown paper. Hats, T-shirts, canvas and wicker bags, jewelry. She had a list and ticked off the names with a pencil. Their daughter, her husband, their four grandchildren, and six or seven friends. If they stayed much longer she'd break him.

But the weather wasn't clearing.

They'd had one calm day since docking when they could have gone on to another island, but they'd only just arrived then—and who'd have thought the seas would get so high again so quickly? So they'd stayed. Spending money.

Mykonos wasn't cheap. Not with Betty around.

One good thing. There were an awful lot of great-looking women.

Like that one now, holding the baby.

Awfully small baby. The woman was a knockout, though, an absolute stunner. You could bet you wouldn't catch her out shopping for sailor caps and T-shirts with windmills on them. Not on your life.

One of these days he'd like to sail over to Paradise or Super Paradise, one of those nude beaches. He wondered what Betty would say about that.

He was surprised when the women stopped in front of the *Balthazar* and looked her over, inspected her, like she knew a little something about boats. Surprised and happy. God! if he were only ten years younger! No, if he were *alone* and without Betty. You never knew about younger women these days. He knew older, scruffier types than himself who'd managed it. He might have had a shot. The boat impressed her, that was certain.

Well, he'd tip his hat to her anyway. Might as well be friendly.

She looked at him and smiled. And it was funny but the baby seemed to smile too, at exactly the same time she did.

Cute.

He grinned at them. She nodded and moved away.

It was only then that he realized what was really strange. That baby. That tiny little baby.

That baby had a lot more teeth than he did.

AND AT FOUR O'CLOCK . . .

. . . Eduardo Maria Santos returned home from the pharmacy with a bottle of aspirin for his headache, walked into the bathroom, and found someone who simply wasn't there writing across his mirror.

The lipstick had been left by Xenia years ago. He'd forgotten it was even in his cabinet.

The writer had almost finished when he came through the door and saw the tube of bright lipstick clatter into the sink. Minus the "o" in his name the message read

YOU TOO, EDUARD

He got out of there, fast.

DODGSON

They sat on the Harlequin's terrace together comparing notes.

They sounded a little insane.

And he wondered if they all could feel what he was feeling, a cold drift up the backbone, as though she were right beside them.

"It's Lelia," he said.

They looked at him.

"Come on, Robert," said Danny. "You saw her. Drachmas over the eyeballs, remember?"

"I know. It's crazy. But I swear it's her. I know it's her."

"She's *dead* for Chrissake!"

A man in a light summer suit was sitting across from them. Dodgson wondered if he could hear. He decided he didn't much care.

"Wait. Let's think it through. Look at the possibilities. They haven't found the body. So? There are instances of people . . . reviving, aren't there?"

"Unh-unh," said Eduardo. "Won't wash. That's fine for somebody tugging at your ankle and for Xenia's money. But you forget. I *saw* that goddamn lipstick and there was *nobody home. Not a fucking soul.*"

"He's right," said Billie. "You can't explain what happened in bed to me that way either. Either I was . . ."

"Mass delusion?" said Michelle.

Billie nodded, then went on. "Either I was manufacturing it somehow out of my own paranoia, or else it was . . ."

"What? It was what?" She'd never seen Danny so defensive. "Are you trying to tell me we're *haunted?*"

And that was when the man at the table across from them leaned over and said *"Yes, I believe you are"*.

Dodgson jumped.

Then he had a look at him. He looked like a businessman on a holiday. A successful businessman. Good suit but a little formal, slightly out of place here. A clear strong voice and steady eyes. And serious as hell.

Who *was* this guy?

"Jordan Thayer Chase," the man said to Dodgson.

"And I may be able to help you. On the other hand, don't bet on it."

The man smiled.

He was the only one who did.

BILLIE

"Can you accept the notion that people can be psychic? Can know things that are normally hidden?"

"I guess so," said Dodgson. "Telepathy, at least."

"That's part of it. But you'll have to go one better. You'll have to consider that it's possible to see things that haven't even happened yet—sometimes very vaguely and sometimes quite clearly—and know that they *will* happen, like it or not. Know that they *have* to happen."

He looked at each of them in turn.

"I don't know about that," said Dodgson.

"I do," said Jordan Chase. "That's the point."

Billie liked him. She was going by instinct but she liked him right away. There was something real and straightforward about the man, despite the insanity he was confirming—and something *humane* as well. He acted as if he cared, though they'd only just met. She believed he did.

"The first thing you'd better tell me," he said, "is who she is."

"Wait a minute, hold on."

Danny's having an awful lot of trouble with this, she thought.

"Hold on a second. Nothing's happened to us—to me and Michelle. Why's that?"

"You sure?" asked Dodgson.

"Nothing that I can remember."

He glanced at Michelle. She shrugged.

"Nothing," said Danny. "Nothing at all"

"It will," said Jordan Chase quietly. *"You killed her."*

Danny's face went white.

"How in hell . . . who talked to you?"

"It's written all over you. Think of me as one of the few around who reads the writing."

"The police. They told you."

"No. I haven't spoken to them."

"Bullshit. How do I know that?"

"You don't. You'll just have to trust me. Look, if I were here to con you, would I check in with the police beforehand? Does that make sense?"

"You're telling me we got ghosts here?"

"I don't know what you've got. I don't know what she is."

"I trust him, Danny," said Michelle.

"I do too,"said Billie.

Eduardo and Xenia nodded.

"So far," said Xenia.

"Okay," said Dodgson, "for now you've got our vote of confidence."

Chase smiled. "Good. But I've got to be straight with you. I know this thing *I've* got and how it works, basically, and I think I know at least part of what's going on here. But I can't say I've got the answers for you. Far from it. There's a lot you'll have to fill me in on. Which brings me back to my first question. Who is she?"

"Was she," said Danny.

"A woman I met in Crete," said Dodgson. "Lelia Narkisos."

The man went rigid.

"Who?"

"Her name is Lelia Narkisos. We met in Crete, in Matala, and I—"

"Excuse me."

He got up suddenly and rushed inside the bar.

He's going to be sick, thought Billie.

He *knows* her!

She took Dodgson's hand. Xenia lit a cigarette. The wind gusted through the narrow street.

They sat silent until he returned.

"Sorry," he said. He sat down.

"You know her," said Dodgson.

"Yes, I do. In Canada, we met at a party—it was months ago. Three months, four months, I don't know. Both of us . . . we were strangers there. And I . . ." He shook his head. "And I think I met her again, last night. She wasn't . . . the same. Her hair was red. Her face and body . . . entirely different. But I should have known . . . the eyes. I should have known those eyes. I thought I'd know them anywhere."

He stopped. He sat there, thinking, and then a moment later she could see something dawn on him. For the very first time he scared her.

"I wonder if it's her," he said. "Maybe. Maybe it's been her out there all the time, drawing me, getting me here.

"My god. I think it's me she wants."

Dodgson shook his head. "Then you'd better think again," he said. "Looks to me like it's all of us."

For a moment Chase seemed puzzled. Then he nodded. "You'll have to tell me everything." he said.

They did.

By the time it was over it was early evening, and Chase sighed and leaned back in his seat.

"Well, one thing's clear," he said. "You'd all better get off the island as fast as possible."

"Fine with me," said Danny.

"There's a ferry tomorrow at four o'clock," said Xenia. "Also a plane direct to Athens at ten."

"Be on it. All of you."

"We work here," said Xenia. "Eduardo and I have work here, homes here."

"Leave them. Leave them for now. You can come back when all this . . . when this is over."

"What about you?" said Dodgson.

To Billie, Chase suddenly looked very old.

"How much do any of you know about Delos?" he asked.

"The birthplace of Apollo and Artemis," said Xenia. "A very holy place once, in ancient times. Now it's mostly ruins."

"I'm supposed to go there."

"You're *supposed* to go there?" asked Danny.

"That's right."

"Is this really the time to play tourist?"

Chase smiled. "Sight-seeing has nothing to do with it. Believe me, Delos is still a holy spot. It always will be, priests or no priests. It's like the Valley of Kings or Easter Island or Stonehenge—a place where there's *power*, real power, something that leaks right out of the ground. In a place like that every bell in hell goes off for somebody like me, but anybody is likely to feel something."

He looked at Danny. "You don't believe it? Try a few. I can give you a list. Try the valley of central Mexico, some of the ancient ruins there. Go to Tlaxcala and I warn you you can *feel* what it was like to be part of an entire culture gone visionary or crazy or both, where all your gods had fangs and claws and names like Eater of Filth or Lord of the Flayed and wore belts of human phalluses.

"I don't know what causes them but they're not in short supply anywhere on the earth—I tripped over one in the woods north of Cape Elizabeth once, another in a dingy little apartment building in lower Manhattan—but Greece has a whole lot more than its share. I just left one. Mykene. And I swear to you, it *sings*.

"Something there got me here to Delos. I'm hoping it'll get me back again."

Dodgson nodded. "You think this has something to do with . . . our problem?"

"Yes I do. I don't know what."

"And you're going to try to end it."

"I'm going to do what I think I'm supposed to do. Maybe that'll end it."

"And if not?"

"I suspect you'll know if I haven't." He stood up.

"I'm going to need some sleep," he said. "Let me suggest that none of you stay alone tonight. I don't want to alarm you but I suggest that very strongly."

"He doesn't want to alarm us," said Danny.

Dodgson ignored him. "And you?"

"I'll be fine. But the rest of you take care of one another. I'll meet you at the port tomorrow morning at, say, eight o'clock?"

"All right."

"Good night," he said. He waved to them over his shoulder.

The wind was still up and Billie shivered.

"I wonder what he did to her," she whispered to Dodgson.

He finished his drink. "Probably nothing," he said. "With Lelia you didn't have to."

She thought he knew better.

TOURIST GIRLS

Kostas was angry, and a little drunk.

These damn American girls kept too much to their own. He'd been in the bar two hours and was getting tired of the words *No, thank you.* The best of them, the dark-haired woman in the corner with the halter top, was surrounded by three men at all times—Americans, like she was. He couldn't get near her. The rest huddled together like sheep.

Why did you come to Greece and not want to meet Greeks? What was wrong with them?

TK's was closing soon. Apart from the old gnarled fisherman who just sat there with his Metaxa three-star he was the only Greek in the place. The old man had been drunk when Kostas arrived. He still was. The old man was the only one in the bar who looked more foolish than Kostas.

The old man had hungry eyes.

Hungry for what? One of these *putanas*?

Maybe for the old days, he thought; for bouzouki.

The music was all American now, or Europop, and Kostas did not dance. Beautiful women all around him, dancing, touching, sweating, and he was blessed with a pregnant wife and no sense of rhythm. The god of his fathers was no damn god of mercy. At least the fisherman—his name was Theodoro—could dance the old dances, the *hasapiko*, the *kalamatianos*, if given a chance. He'd seen him.

He hoped the old man would not get the opportunity tonight. He could bear just so much humiliation.

But there! god*damm*it!

• • •

He checked his watch—a Bulova. It was almost two o'clock. It had been Bowie or Madonna all night long and here it was the last dance, probably, and they gave the old bastard a *serviko*! He knew it! The last indignity was to have to watch this drunken old lecherous fool. To hell with it! To hell with the god of his fathers!

Just look at him!

Girls all around all of a sudden. American girls, who like to play at being Greek but do not fuck Greeks, *do you girls*. Don't worry, old man. You're safe tonight. Nine or ten of them around, and now the music's too fast for the old *malaka* and the women are doing the *hora* or the Mexican Hat Dance or some damn thing, paying him no attention at all as he tries to teach them. Drunk! All of them drunk!

He thought they had no pride.

A Greek has pride.

He drank the last of his seven-star and ordered another. The waitress told him it was last call. He shrugged. Of course it was. The waitress put his drink in front of him and he gave her an appraisal. Not bad. He actually *liked* fat thighs. So long as they were not too fat.

The woman who walked through the door, however, did not have fat thighs.

The woman was sleek and elegant.

She took one look at the children cavorting with the drunken old man and nearly walked out again. Then she saw Kostas.

And he could not believe it. He had made the woman pause. *He!* Kostas! He felt himself blush with pleasure.

But now he must do something.

He smiled.

It was not much to do.

Shit!

To his surprise she smiled back. *She's not even drunk!* he thought. I would bet on it!

She inclined her head, motioning him toward the door.

He did not even finish his Metaxa. He slid off the chair and was beside her in an instant.

She was taller than he was. He was a little dismayed. But no matter.

He held the door for her, and from behind he had a chance to look at her. Her dress was black, some sheer, thin material, cut almost to the waist in back, and wide at her long graceful neck. She was thin, yes, but her legs were wonderful—and her ass! He would have killed his sister for that ass! Just to hold it between his hands and whisper to it in the night . . .

He could think of nothing to say that was not completely stupid so he said nothing.

She smiled at him again.

What a mouth! What eyes!

His pulse was racing.

"Let's walk, shall we?" she said.

A good idea—he had to sober up for her. The cool night air would help. He would walk firmly, breathe deeply. A longish walk, perhaps. Romantic, by the sea. Though of course that was up to her.

"Yes," he said.

They walked silently up to the windmills. He watched her look down to the rocks below. The moon made the water sparkle.

Yes, he knew she would like the sea.

"Down there," she said.

"Yes . . . it's nice."

He wished his English were better.

They started down. Her shoes were not made for climbing. But she was very surefooted, as sure as a donkey—better than he was because of the brandy.

Halfway down he had a wonderful idea.

He would have her there, on the rocks.

He could barely contain his pleasure at the notion. Yes! His business might fail, his wife might give birth to a hundred squalling *malakas*, get fat and grow a beard as well as a mustache for all he cared. Just give him this woman, this night, here by the sea in the shadows of the windmills of Mykonos, and he would rejoice the rest of his life.

It was almost as though she'd read his mind.

"Want to go down to the rocks?"

"Oh yes. Very much."

"Good," she said. And she grabbed his arm.

And her fingers were strong as a vise as she hauled him out in front of her and held him there a moment over the drop. He whimpered once. Then she shoved him out away from her, down to the rocks below.

He fell and did not die.

He lay there, spine cracked, brain leaking—and through blood-filled eyes saw her leap from where she stood twenty feet above him and land like a leaf within inches of his thighs and then reach down with the long, long nails he had not noticed before but which glittered now in the moonlight and saw her tear him open and break apart his chest with her elbows askew like a hunter setting his trap.

Then he saw nothing.

He felt no pain.

Perhaps, he thought, it was the Metaxa.

BILLIE

They walked home past the Sunset Bar, the windmills in the distance. Water slapped at the rocks beside them. The waves were still high. They had to wait for one to break over the concrete platform where the carpenter used his sawhorses during the day. They watched it recede, then they splashed across the platform to the higher ground behind the Caprice. They walked toward Spiro's past the little stretch of sandy beach that was now almost entirely under water. The moon passed behind a cloud. It was very dark.

She could barely make out the little boat in dry dock there. Until the cloud passed by.

And then she saw the eyes.

Watching them from beneath the boat hull.

Watching them from behind the piled-up tables and chairs of the darkened open-air restaurant ahead.

Cats.

Dozen of cats.

She stopped. She clutched Dodgson's arm.

She felt his puzzlement, then felt it turn to awareness.

The eyes stared. Neither moved nor shifted. She could see the huddled bodies.

And she thought what a dozen cats could do all at once, because she knew what one could do; she felt it again very vividly.

Ten pounds of claws and teeth and speed and hard muscle that had ripped at her like some mad, otherworldly weapon . . .

"Dodgson . . ."

"Billie, she can't command the animals."

Can't she?

Go back, she thought.

She turned. But now there were more behind her.

She shuddered; it gripped her and continued, turned to a trembling that was uncontrollable and had nothing at all to do with ocean breezes.

"Walk," he said. "Go slowly."

She held back. He tugged her forward, gently.

The eyes followed them, rippling reflected light as though in a prism.

They passed the boat. The eyes followed.

Nothing moved.

The blood hammered in her face, her head.

They moved through the tables and chairs, the stillness of the empty restaurant like a single sentient claw poised and waiting for the first show of panic. She felt the wildness of them. Cats just inches away. Cats no one had ever tamed. They walked in the shallow stillness of their own breathing.

Past them.

• • •

They did not look back.

So they could not see the bodies that scampered into full moonlight along the path they had taken, that stopped and continued to watch them with a concentration normally reserved, in their species, for smaller animals. For prey.

DODGSON

Take care of one another, Chase had said and this was the way to do it.

The first time had lasted a good long time and now he was ready again, still slick with sweat from before and from their bodies pressed close together in the warm Mykonian night. There was affirmation here and security, a poignant sense of life, and he felt it could continue this way throughout the night, their last night on the island, until they exhausted each other and maybe slept a little.

Then she poisoned it.

He was inside her, moving slowing in the warm depths of her, watching the face he loved now move through a kind of fabulous agony of pleasure, the tiny cobweb lines at the eyes etched more deeply by the drawn muscles of her mouth, a gleaming hint of moisture in them, watching the breast flesh tremble, her shoulder muscles lengthen as she reached for him.

When suddenly she changed beneath him.

The eyes flashed open.

They were blue. Pale blue.

The broad open lines of her face shifted, narrowed.

On her pillow the hair grew and darkened.

He felt a cringing horror. The wide mouth grinned and the lips were Lelia's. He began to tremble.

The soulless eyes stared up at him.

Insane.

He closed his own eyes and tried to feel her, just feel her, and she felt the same—Billie, not Lelia.

Yet when he opened them again Lelia's face leered up at him, superimposed like a double image in a photograph. He saw the narrow hips beneath him, the pale wide nipples, the smaller breasts, the self-inflicted marks across her belly.

"What's wrong?"

It was Billie's voice but Lelia's too, the first one worried, the second mocking him and dripping with venom.

What's wrong, asshole?

He felt himself shrivel inside her.

He wanted to hammer her, destroy her, filled with anger that she could do this and afraid of her too.

He pulled away. He sat shaking, fighting for control.

He had almost hit her, pounded at her. The way you'd destroy a snake.

"What's wrong?"

It was Billie. Wholly her now.

"Lelia." He felt a kind of vertigo, felt himself falling. "You were Lelia."

"I . . . ?"

"You were."

Green eyes again, a blessed green. Wide with disbelief.

"I'm not crazy."

"No."

He saw her try to believe him, to understand.

"It's just that I . . . felt nothing."

And then he saw her grasp what she'd done to them.

"No! She can't *do* that! Not *here*! Not here too!"

"She did it, Billie."

"Noooooooo!"

It was a howl of pain and despair that raced across his spine, chilling him. Her tears came suddenly and hard.

"It's not fair!"

"I know."

He held her.

"We did *nothing* . . ."

"I know, I know."

He continued holding her, rocking her, and the tears subsided a little.

"So long ago," she said. "It seems so long ago. We did nothing to her. But that first night in Matala. I knew it. I knew something . . . even then."

"So did I, maybe. But not like this."

"No, never. Not like this."

She began to cry again and he held her sobbing against his shoulder, the tears warm against him, until she stopped.

"That man. Jordan Chase. Can he help us?"

"I don't know."

"And if we leave tomorrow, can she follow us?"

He had no answer for that.

"I can't lose you, Robert. Not now. Don't let me lose you."

"You won't. I promise."

The promise was empty. He fought back tears of his own now.

She drew herself up, wiped her eyes.

He could still almost feel Lelia's hands on him.

"Keep her out of here," she said. It was like a spell, like magic. An incantation. And then she said, "Hold me. Hold me."

A murmur in the shapeless, alien night.

JORDAN THAYER CHASE

"Elaine?"

"Yes?"

"It's not a good line."

"I know."

"I just wanted to say . . ."

"What? I can't hear you, Jordan."

"I just wanted to say I love you."

"What?"

"I love you, Elaine."

"I love *you*. I hate this goddamn line, though."

"Yes."

"Where are you—still in Mykonos?"

"Still in Mykonos, yes."

"For a while yet?"

"A little while."

"Come back soon, Jordan. Will you? Please?"

"Yes."

"You promise?"

"Yes."

"I miss you."

"I miss you."

"What?"

"I said I miss *you*."

"Soon, Jordan. Okay? All right?"

"Yes. Soon."

It was less than an hour before dawn, that time when most

people die who are going to die, when the temperatures of men and of the earth sink lowest, that Chase leaned sleepless out his window to gaze at the sea and saw Lelia Narkisos standing naked in the water, holding out to him a tiny bundle of likewise naked flesh that screeched and writhed in her hands while she smiled and then moved just the slightest bit away from him so that the writhing bundle, the baby, became his own maggot-white dripping severed head.

PART FOUR

HECATE

"I don't want to hold the key
To some ghostly mansion
Where souls are set free."

—Gordon Lightfoot

MELTEMI

THE THIRD DAY

"We're *stuck* here!" said Danny.

It was nine-thirty in the morning and no planes were flying to or out of Mykonos, and the word at the tourist office was that no ferries were running either. *Meltemi*, the travel agent said, the high, gale-force winds that periodically boiled the Aegean. And he sympathized because no one could remember when one had struck so early in the season, or so hard.

Perhaps tomorrow, he said, and went back to pushing whatever paper there is to attend to in a travel agency when no one is able to travel.

So Danny turned to the rest of them and uttered what they all were thinking in the same flat astonished voice any one of them might have used.

"We're stuck here!"

When the silence was over, when all the dire glances had been exchanged, Jordan Chase said, *There are seven of us. From this moment on we stay together.*

It was, in its way, a declaration of war.

SHELTER FROM THE STORM

They sat encased in misted glass in the restaurant by the harbor listening to the patter of the rain and the howling wind, watching the boats toss and roll. The restaurant was crowded. Nobody else had much to do either.

"Tell me about it, Chase," said Eduardo. "What's it like?"

Chase seemed to listen inside himself for a moment. He smiled.

"Sometimes it's actually kind of fun. I've . . . eavesdropped, I guess you'd call it, on some funny things. Ever wonder what goes through a lawyer's mind when he tells you he's billing you for one hundred eighty hours of his time? I can tell you.

"Then sometimes it's damn depressing. You hear the most godawful things. Cruelty, pettiness, the most incredible stupidity . . .

"But then you get a real intuition, a *knowing*, and it can be one of the most exciting things in the world. Because you get it first. Before everybody else. To see things before the event, before the turn of the wheel . . . though that can be unsettling too. I knew about the Iranian hostage situation, for instance—when was it? '78?—almost a week before it happened. A company of mine was based there."

"What did you do?" asked Michelle.

"Nothing. Not very much. That's just it. Sometimes there's not much you *can* do. You know the story about Cassandra in the *Iliad*? Well, Apollo fell in love with her and gave her the gift of prophecy. Then he turned against her when she refused

186

his love. So since he couldn't take the gift back, he decided to make it useless to her. He arranged it so that nobody would ever believe her. So she'd always *know* when disaster was coming and be completely unable to avert it.

"What could I have done? Called the White House? *Uh, Mr. President, there's this rich crackpot on the phone* . . . And then later, when I'm right, what do I tell the CIA?"

"No, I just got my own company out of there and let it go at that."

"You're rich, huh?" said Danny.

"That's one of the benefits, yes."

"Me too. Fat lot of good it does me. Maybe we could whistle 'Taxi' and hire us a liner. Get us out of here."

Chase shook his head. "I've tried every boat on the island. I've called Athens. Nobody's willing to buck the *meltemi*. 'As soon as it's over' is the best they can do."

"Can you get any handle on Lelia now?" asked Dodgson. "On what she's doing?"

"On what she *is*?" said Eduardo.

"No to the first question. You get blind spots. Nothing you can do about it. It's frustrating, like having just a single thumb instead of two. You can catch a ball, sure, but what you *can't* do is swing the goddamn bat and hit the thing.

"As to the second, I don't know. I know something's happening here. I've felt it all through Greece. Like something's . . . *changing*, or about to change. You've been here before, Dodgson. Xenia and Eduardo, you live here. You notice how things seem to have . . . decayed so rapidly? Just three years ago Greece was a really *good* place, content, really happy."

Xenia shrugged. "Everyone made money. Is not so now."

"That's part of it. But there's a lethargy about the place too. People don't seem to care. Things fall apart and don't get repaired. Terrorists waltz into airports, shoot a few people, waltz right out again. A lot of the values are going—the openness to new ideas, to people, the really deep respect for what was good about the old ways, the *hospitality*."

"*Filokseneea!*" said Xenia.

"That's right. *Filokseneea*. This country's ripe for some kind of . . . renewal. And I'm wondering, what if we're in the middle of that?"

"What do you mean?" asked Dodgson.

"I don't think it's any accident that we're just across from Delos. In ancient times, remember, it was *the* power spot, the place you'd look to for any kind of regeneration or renewal, be it spiritual or physical. The doctors, for instance, were the best and most learned in Greece. I feel something happening out there. I feel it even as we sit talking here. I've never been to that island but I bet I could almost describe it to you. I feel something *growing*, some power surge. Something.

"And maybe Lelia's tapped into that somehow. Something about this time and this place. I don't know."

The wind had torn a small boat loose in the harbor. A plastic tarp careened around the corner.

"What happened between the two of you?" asked Billie. "Do you mind saying?"

Chase sighed. "An affair. I'm sure you'd guessed as much. Very brief and very nasty. I'd really rather not . . . go into it."

He and Dodgson gazed across the table at each other.

"She was something, wasn't she?" said Dodgson.

"Yes, she was."

Despite all the people the restaurant was quiet. Maybe it was the weather but there was a heaviness about the place, Billie thought, a feeling of expectation.

"How about some wine?" said Danny.

"It's pretty early. But sure. Why not," said Dodgson.

They ordered. The waiter brought the wine, uncorked the bottle, placed a cash-register stub under their ashtray along with the breakfast stubs, nodded and walked away.

The rain was falling steadily now in gray windblown sheets, obscuring their view of the harbor. It was dark where they sat.

Michelle sighed. "So what do we do now?"

"I think we ought to do exactly what we're doing," said Chase. "The more people around us, the better. I think we have to expect anything from her, absolutely anything. And she'd probably want to separate us if possible. It would make things easier for her."

"And tonight?"

"Same thing. We stay together. There's plenty of room at my place, though some of us will have to sleep on the floor."

"Fine," said Dodgson.

"After lunch we'll check you and Danny, Michelle and Billie out of their rooms and settle up the bills." He turned to Eduardo. "I presume you and Xenia are already packed?"

"I'm ready."

Xenia nodded.

"Good. Then the same thing applies. We all go to each place together and pick up what we need. From here on in, we're a family."

"Okay," said Eduardo. "All that is going to take maybe an hour or two. What are we going to do the rest of the time? We can't just sit here all day, drinking."

"Why not?" said Danny.

"At some point I tend to fall down."

"Do it moderately, then," said Chase. "Order Nescafé. Whatever. But I like crowds at the moment. I like them very much."

"So do I," said Billie.

"Let's stay till the rain lets up a bit," said Dodgson. "Then we can start getting the bags and bringing them over to your place. One question, though."

"What's that?"

"What if it's the same thing tomorrow? What if we *still* can't get out of here?"

"I don't know," said Chase. "I guess we handle that when we get to it."

There was a silence as they thought about that for a moment. Then Danny raised his glass.

"To good company," he said.

He drained it.

PARADISE

The first they took were a pair of campers, young men surf-casting for their breakfast and too busy to notice the figures moving toward them through the fog until there was only time to turn and recognize, as in a nightmare, the sharp stick skewering the neck of the teenage boy, the trailing entrails of the Greek, the charred black face of the thin young woman dressed in rags—time only for that before the big man with the open, festering shoulder wound sunk his fingers into the eyes and mouth of the nearer one and pulled him down into the foaming sea, breaking his neck as he fell, while the others moved over his friend with open, hungry mouths.

The big man watched them die.

Then, later, watched them slowly rise.

There had been six of them. So that now there were eight.

They moved through the morning mist and afternoon rain, scattering along the shoreline and up through the rocks and down to the beach, wading into the sea, separating and coming together, moving toward town.

The next were brother and sister, twins, Germans, eighteen years old, handsome blonds. It was raining by then, a light drizzle. They had strung up a line between a pair of trees so the rainwater could rinse out their clothes. The boy was naked. Everything he owned except a pair of socks was on the line already. The girl wore a white cotton blouse. She was hanging up her brother's socks when the line went down and a girl no older than she appeared and pulled her onto the sand, clawing at her.

Her brother tried to run. But they were much too close by then, a horrible proximity of pale, reaching hands. He tried to run in one direction and then the other, and then sank to his knees and cried. And watched his sister die before they got to him.

The old Greek fisherman sat in a boat anchored twenty feet offshore. He was checking his traps, which unfortunately for Lelia were not empty. So that in his distraction with the traps it was a simple thing for the twins to wade out to him and overturn his boat, then hold him under. The last things he saw were three molting crabs peering out at him from inside a trap he would never live to harvest. One was a very good size.

The fisherman made eleven.

The rain fell hard and people stayed indoors. But even so there were stragglers and their ranks slowly swelled—and those few Greeks who lived along the way and noticed the slow-moving group of *tourista*s trudging into the wind along the distant shore were accustomed to seeing strange foolish things from these foreigners, who stayed out all night and slept all day, who took the sun on their fair skin, who treated dogs like children and their children, sometimes, like dogs. They thought nothing of it.

They thought nothing, either, of the woman who walked alone well behind the rest, who seemed to drift in and out of focus in the shifting wind and rain. Except, perhaps, some of the men who saw her. Even at a distance the supple poise and strength of her was visible beneath the flowing white garment. Even at a distance she was desirable.

To some she looked like a goddess.

DODGSON

They walked the now-familiar maze of streets back to Chase's room in Little Venice. It was eight o'clock, nearly sunset and turning cooler. The rain had stopped but the seas were still high. There was still no getting off the island.

Dodgson was tired. The tension, the inactivity, the wine—all of them had made him yearn for sleep, for oblivion.

But she likes it when we sleep, he thought. No can do.

They waited while Chase fumbled with the key, then opened the door. All their gear was inside. The spacious room looked cluttered now.

"I'd like to shave," said Chase.

"Me too," said Eduardo. He stroked his chin.

"I imagine we all want showers, don't we?" Billie looked from one woman to the other, and Michelle and Xenia nodded.

"Ladies first, then," said Chase. He sat down heavily in the chair by the window.

Dodgson felt uneasy. "How much privacy do you need?"

"None," said Xenia. She answered for all of them.

"Suppose we double up, then. It'll be faster—and safer."

Xenia shrugged. "Come on, Eduardo."

She pulled off her shirt and jeans and dropped them to the floor, flung a towel over her shoulder and marched naked into the bathroom. In a moment they heard the water running.

"How's your supply of hot water?" asked Eduardo.

"Good. Very good."

"Terrific." He stripped and followed Xenia inside and shut the door.

The room had two beds. Billie and Dodgson sat on the one nearest Chase by the window. Danny took the straight-back chair—probably trying to stay awake, thought Dodgson. Michelle was digging through her suitcase, looking for something.

Dodgson watched Chase stare out the window. The man looked older than he had this morning. The five o'clock shadow almost succeeded in making him look seedy. He wondered what Chase wasn't telling them.

"Something out there?"

"No. I was just . . . remembering."

"Remembering what?"

He didn't answer and Dodgson didn't push him.

Billie nestled up under his shoulder. She felt warm and comfortable.

He noticed that the beds had been made while they were out. He wondered what the landlady had thought of all the sudden luggage.

"When this is over," said Billie, "what are you going to do?"

He sighed. "Well, I've had enough of Greece. You?"

"Quite enough."

"I think I'd like to go home for a while. Care to see the States?"

"I haven't the money."

"I do."

She looked surprised, then she smiled.

"Thank you, Robert. I'll . . . definitely think on it."

"Think hard."

"I will."

Her hand brushed lightly across his cheek.

"Got it!" said Michelle.

She held up a thin-handled safety razor. "I thought I'd lost it."

She plopped down hard on the bed across from them.

"*Merde!*" she said. "I am exhausted!"

Dodgson suddenly saw her eyes change, saw them go down to the bed. For the moment she looked like a fighter who'd been punched too hard. He followed her gaze. He saw something move. Then she screamed.

Suddenly she was on the floor, scrambling toward them on her hands and knees. Dodgson started toward her. Danny was on his feet already. He heard the water go off in the bathroom.

She was still screaming when she fell into Billie's arms and Danny came around behind her.

"What? What *is* it?"

"The bed," said Dodgson.

He remembered thinking that the landlady hadn't done such a good job over there, that the covers were more rumpled than on the one they were sitting on, but he'd thought nothing of it and now . . .

. . . they were *writhing*.

Something moving beneath the covers.

Michelle was crying, hysterical. The bathroom door flew open and there was Eduardo, naked, dripping, Xenia peering out over his shoulder.

"What . . . ?"

Chase got out of his chair. He stepped toward the bed. Dodgson didn't like it.

"Chase . . ."

"It's all right."

"It's not all right. Be careful."

He reached for the corner end of the bed sheet. Flung it, leapt back.

Michelle screamed again. Billie too.

The bed hissed at them.

It swarmed with snakes.

They were gray and brown and red and Dodgson recognized them, the dark markings along the back. Vipers. Fifty of them, maybe more, sliding over one another, tongues tasting the air, flicking, searching for body heat. Fifty, and any one could kill.

They began to slide off the bed.

It looked like it was melting.

"Get out!" he screamed. Chase flung the door open. Eduardo and Xenia ran naked from the bathroom. They crowded toward the door. Across the cold concrete floor snakes hissed angrily. They continued to fall off the bed—a hideous heavy sliding, falling sound behind him. Then Chase and Eduardo and Xenia were through the door, and then Michelle and Billie, and finally Danny, kicking at one that darted near him, screeching in raw panic.

And then it was as though a wind came up around him, a huge dense burst of air.

The door slammed shut.

He heard them shouting his name and pounding on the door as he pulled at it but it was as though it were cemented shut. He turned and saw snakes pouring off the bed, winding through the room, seeking, the hot steamy bathroom full of them already—but they were coming toward him too. He heard the agitated hissing, the slide of muscular flesh against concrete.

He picked up the chair by the window.

One of them was winding its way up the chair leg and he flicked at it with the back of his hand, screaming, until it fell away. He threw the chair through the window. The glass exploded outward. The chair fell back inside, into what was already a pool of snakes ahead of him, and he hurled himself through the window in what was undoubtedly the single best dive of his life.

He saw the waves beneath him and was grateful, for once, for the storm—the waves were high and he wouldn't crash to the rocks below. Then they churned and parted.

He saw her reach for him.

Lelia. Arms spread wide dripping kelp and seaweed, naked breasts bobbing on the surface, face and hair streaming, gleaming with water and starlight.

He plunged down into her, into the waves.

The cold water shocked him. He closed his eyes, praying.

He pulled out of the dive to the surface. He looked for her.

"*Lelia*," he gasped.

She was gone.

They were dragging him out of the sea.

"I saw her," said Danny.

"You did?"

"She was there all right. I was just coming round the corner. We heard glass breaking. She went down with you. You fell right into her arms."

"Jesus."

"You all right, buddy?"

"I think so."

Danny lifted him to his feet.

"Come on," said Eduardo. "My house. Hurry, I'm *freezing*."

Chase stripped off his shirt and gave it to him. Danny gave his to Xenia.

Billie grabbed hold of Dodgson. One or both of them were trembling.

They followed Eduardo. It wasn't far. They turned two corners and they were there.

They went inside. This time they left the door wide open.

The place was a mess. Eduardo had thrown himself together in a hurry.

Nobody sat down.

Eduardo pulled on a pair of pants and handed a pair to Xenia. He got shirts for them out of a drawer and gave back Chase's and Danny's.

While they were dressing Dodgson looked at Michelle. She was still burrowed deep in Danny's shoulder. He caught Danny's eye, looked at him questioningly and then glanced at Michelle. Danny nodded. Good. She'd be all right, then.

Chase's eyes were fixed on the doorway. And that was okay too.

"What now?" said Eduardo. "I mean, what's left? What's *safe*?"

"Nothing," said Chase.

"What?"

"Nothing. Nothing's safe. We stay and watch and wait. If she wants us she'll find us, and I don't think there's much we can do to stop her."

"Great."

"I'm sorry."

Xenia buttoned her shirt and rolled up the cuffs of Eduardo's pants. They almost but not quite suited her.

"I could use a drink," said Danny. "Got anything?"

"Sure." He went to the closet and pulled out a liter bottle.

"Scotch! You're a genius, Eduardo."

They passed it around. Nobody refused.

"You should get out of those wet clothes," Eduardo said to Dodgson. "I've got some that should fit you."

"Thanks."

He found a pair of linen trousers and a large pullover sweater. Dodgson stripped and put them on. Michelle passed him the bottle, summoned up a smile for him. Just a small smile but it was good to see. He felt a moment of impotent fury. These were all good people. They didn't deserve this. None of them did.

"*Listen,*" said Chase.

For a moment he heard nothing. He looked at Xenia and she shrugged, as puzzled as he was. Then he did hear something, far off in the distance.

They huddled in the doorway.

The wind had died outside and the night was warmer. The weather was truly strange, he thought, changing from moment to moment. He'd never seen anything like it.

He listened.

Voices. Shouting. And something else—a kind of crackling sound, like static on a telephone line.

Women wailing. Screaming.

"What is it?" whispered Billie.

"I don't know."

"Whatever it is, it's big," said Danny.

He was right. It was far away but clearly there were many voices, sometimes one alone and sometimes many together, rising and falling. And underneath them that other sound.

A breeze wafted past them. Then all was still again.

It felt eerie standing there, listening to some human chaos far away from them yet remembering what had just gone on in Chase's room. The night felt thick with a terrible potential.

Anything could happen. Anything.

He felt Billie's arm draw tight around his waist. A light breeze blew up again.

"*There,?*" said Chase. "Smell it?" He took a breath.

"*Fire.*"

They heard footsteps, someone running in their direction. They flinched as a group of men came tearing around the corner.

Xenia ran into the street.

"*Tee enay? Tee enay afthoh?*"

One of the men whirled at her. The others kept going toward the harbor. His face was contorted with fear. "*Fotia!*" he shouted. He spit the word at her. "*Bar Harlequin! Eji pandoo fotia. Ohla! Pandoo!*"

He turned, stumbling, and ran on after the others.

"What is it?" asked Billie. "What'd he say?"

"Chase is right. He says there is fire at the Harlequin. Fire everywhere!"

"She's burning it," said Dodgson.

They could smell it clearly now. Billie clutched his arm.

"But we're okay up here, aren't we? Listen. It's far away."

He did listen and she was right, it *was* far away. But not so far as before, he thought. Not quite. *No. She'll burn the whole damn island*.

What do you want, Lelia? What do you want?

"I don't think so," he said.

He looked at Chase. His eyes seemed to mirror his own. He read a cold fine wariness there.

"I don't think we're safe anywhere here," said Dodgson.

Chase nodded. "I agree," he said. "I think she's proved that. Nobody's safe on this island. But have a look at that."

He pointed out to sea, to the ocean glimmering in the distance.

It was smooth as glass.

And Dodgson realized that for some time now there had been virtually no wind.

"We could leave! Get the hell out of here!" said Danny.

"Unless that blow starts up again," said Eduardo.

"Jesus, it's worth a try."

"Is it?" said Chase.

"Of course it is!"

"You know what the nearest island is, don't you?"

"Sure. It's . . ."

"That's right," said Chase. His smile was bitter, and Dodgson saw the sadness play across his face as gently and distinctly as someone closing the eyes of a dead man.

"The nearest island is Delos."

He watched him. They all did. He didn't move. It seemed to Dodgson that he was inside himself again, listening. A moment passed. Distant voices howled like lost souls, like the damned.

Finally he sighed.

"I can't tell you a thing. Nothing at all. I'm not surprised. All I see is fire.

"It's possible, I suppose. It's possible that Delos is where we'll escape to. But I doubt it. Quite the contrary. I think that's where we'll find her. Really find her."

"We've *already* found her," said Danny. "Or she's found us. I mean, what were those things in your room, Chase, party invitations?"

"Maybe. Something like that."

"Come *on*, Chase. The fucking island is burning up! Jesus, let's try it!"

"I have a boat," said Xenia. "We can do it. I *know* we can. It takes twenty minutes to get there. Even if the seas go high again we can make it if we have just ten minutes of calm. That's all we need. Ten minutes. Please, come on."

"All right," Chase said calmly.

He looked at Dodgson, then at Billie. The others started off toward the harbor.

"You're sure?" asked Dodgson.

"Not at all. But your friend Danny's right. This place is a known quantity. We know she can get at us here. There—who can tell what'll happen?"

"You're not convincing me."

There was more than bitterness in the smile now; it was more like pain. He shrugged and turned, and began walking after the others. Billie and Dodgson followed.

"It's me who needs convincing," he said.

"What do you mean?"

"I ought to have told you."

He spoke so softly they could barely hear him. He was talking to himself now, thought Dodgson, leaning forward as he walked, shoulders hunched against some unseen wind.

"I think I'm supposed to die there," he said.

They stopped for a moment, staring at him. And then kept walking.

SIEGE OF A SMALL ISLAND

The fire had three points of origin, all more or less along the harbor.

The biggest blaze was at the Harlequin. It had already spread to the adjoining buildings before anyone noticed there were two more fires—one at the travel agency at Taxi Square and the other at the far end of the harbor at the City Lights Disco. These two were confined, mostly, to interiors—the buildings in Mykonos were built like bunkers—but they added to the confusion, billowing smoke out over the town and sending locals and tourists alike scurrying out into the streets.

The Harlequin was an inferno, however; the genuine article. How it began was a mystery. Whoever might have had information on that—waitress, patrons, bartender—had all been trapped inside.

There was little to do. With limited water for such an emergency and no organized fire department the strategy was merely to wait until the fires burned out and hope for as little damage as possible. But the fact that there were *three* fires and not just one sent a wave of panic through the town. Somewhere out there a madman was among them, and any store, home or taverna might be next. Businesses were abandoned as people flooded through the streets to the open expanse dockside. Some stood guarding their homes with ancient rifles. Some just gawked at the flames.

Boats pulled out of the harbor hoping for safety at sea, their owners highly aware of the vulnerability of their craft to sparks from the Harlequin. There was no order to this, and in the darkness there were quite a few near-collisions, with the bow of the sixty-foot British Chris Craft *Ruby Lee* actually broadsiding the fifty-four-foot Striker *Holy Moses* just out of port.

Orville and Betty Dunworth had been enjoying a late dinner at Kostas'—if not each other's company—when news of the fire reached them. They hurriedly abandoned their kabobs and *tzadziki* and headed for the *Balthazar*. Orville had never quite mastered the drachma so he dropped a handful of bills on the table, imagining it was more than enough and cursing the damn fool Greeks who seemed willing to let their town burn down around them.

Where he came from you protected property.

"If anything happens to that cruiser," he told Betty, "I'll kill them."

The following events—and word of them—added immensely to the town's prevailing mood of fear and chaos:

Back by the windmills on the far side of town a pair of goats and a donkey were found eviscerated in a field, parts of them scattered through the scrubby grass and across the low fieldstone fence. A blond teenage boy and a dark teenage girl were seen walking away from the field close up by a reliable witness, a grandmother of twelve, who said that even in the dark she could see that the back of the girl's head seemed to be matted with dried blood.

• • •

At the overseas telephone office near the City Lights Disco, Kostas Mavrodopolous, who had been missing for over a day and whose wife, it was well known, was worried sick about him, ambled by the flower man, who for once was without his basket, and when the flower man tried to stop and talk to him Kostas turned and hissed like a cat, his head at an angle so that the neck looked broken, dried blood all across the front of his fancy shirt, his eyes covered by a thin, lusterless, cloudy film. The flower man had lived through two world wars and knew a dead man when he saw one, and as far as he was concerned Kostas was completely dead, and walking.

Eight locals and a tourist watched as a naked young man and a half-naked girl who was obviously his twin walked slowly past the burning tourist office at Taxi Square, each of them holding and eating what appeared to be a large piece of charred meat. The girl ate with only one hand. According to three of those nearest to her, including the tourist, the other hand was holding in the gray-white coils of her viscera.

A lovely young woman holding a naked infant child was seen walking *into the fire* at the Harlequin well after the doorway was already a white-hot sheet of flame.

Two old women, sisters, were discovered lying dead side by side on a street to the rear of the Sunset Bar by a passing neighbor, who recognized them immediately and went for help. By the time he returned both bodies were gone, yet the street was literally awash with blood.

Dodgson's group saw some of this too, though they didn't know what it was exactly.

They were headed for the boat, two streets down from the Harlequin so that they could see the glow in the sky where it was burning and hear timbers pop like gunfire. People were racing past them back up into the town or down to the dock. They saw frightened, anguished faces, heard screaming, crying.

The town was coming apart.

They passed a fancy boutique and stepped carefully because the plate-glass window was out, shattered in the street. Inside the store, shadowy, slow-moving figures seemed inexplicably to be tearing all the arms and legs off the mannequins, stumbling through a rubble of torn, scattered clothing.

At the kiosk dockside the boy who sold cigarettes lay facedown in a pool of blood.

Out on the street two middle-aged women were fighting, one of them a Greek and the other a tourist woman wearing a floral print dress. They fought silently, grunting, in deadly earnest. The Greek appeared to be winning. But Chase seemed to see a great open wound at the base of her neck just before she shifted position, struggling.

"They're crazy!" said Xenia.

They reached the dock. He watched her untie the boat. He saw that her hands were shaking.

She had company.

Orville and Betty Dunworth climbed aboard the *Balthazar* and saw that it was just about the last boat of any size left docked there. Betty went below to deposit her shopping bags while Orville climbed to the fly bridge to start her up, cursing the other owners who'd left him a goddamn fucking obstacle course to get through, all of them anchored out there like a crowded checkerboard, just out of range of the sparks and debris from the fire.

He'd head through and beyond them. He was taking no risks.

She started up instantly with that lovely familiar roar he liked so much—to him the sound of power and cold hard cash. Oh, not a whole immense amount of cash by the world's standards these days. But enough. Enough so he was proud of her, and proud of the way she showed him off.

He checked the instruments and everything was fine, so he hit the lights fore and aft and carefully headed out. Running lights dotted the sea like fireflies. Over the sound of the motor he heard Betty rattling around below.

What in hell was the woman doing down there? She should be up here watching this, he thought, watching him maneuver through this bobbing checkerboard here, graceful as a swan.

Noisy old fuck, Betty was. Always had been. Always yap, yap, yap—always talking. And clumsy. Forever dropping something. It sounded like she'd dropped something now, in fact. One less present for her flit grandson or that wimpy, whiny little friend of hers, Dorothy. Well, fine.

Nice cruiser, he thought, as he steered past the big handsome Owens. In his lights he caught the makings of a party, young men with beer cans and tall drinks and a flash of young blond thigh. Pretty odd time for it, he thought. But hell, I wouldn't bitch. No party here.

He heard another crash below.

Damn that woman!

"Hey Betty!"

Jesus! What was she, drunk? They'd had about a half a glass each at dinner. Even Betty had more capacity than that. So what was she doing, nipping down below now? He wouldn't put it past her.

She starts going drunk on me and I swear I'll dump her, he thought.

He listened.

That was better. He heard her coming up the stairs.

Just let me slip by this Striker here and then we'll see what's what.

There was plenty of room but he cut it close anyway. Give 'em something to think about. He wasn't worried. The *Balthazar* handled like a Ferrari. He'd just set her bobbing a little.

He felt Betty's hand on his shoulder.

"Hold it," he said. "Just a second." *Then I'll have a little sniff of your goddamn breath*.

He described a neat curve around the Striker's bow. And that was the last of them. There was open sea ahead of him now.

The hand tightened on his shoulder.

Tightened a hell of a lot.

What the fuck?

He turned around.

It was Betty, all right.

And then again it wasn't.

She was missing an eye, for one thing. And she didn't seem to care much, either—just stood there grinning at him, her upper plate missing and the lower one askew. And behind her stood a man built like a truck and who had something very wrong with his neck and shoulder. And it was like one of those crazy funny-cars things in the circus because behind *him* were a bunch of kids coming out of the hold too, something wrong with every damn one of them, and behind *them* stood a woman. A beautiful woman. One he vaguely remembered seeing somewhere—and the whole insane tableau slipped like a worm inside his guts and scared him so bad that his bowels went and his urine and yet apart from that he couldn't move a muscle. Not even when Betty . . . *I loved you Betty . . .* not even when she raised the flare gun and pointed it into his open mouth.

And fired.

JORDAN THAYER CHASE

DELOS

He had dreamed this:

A mountain rising out of the sea, high and wild against the blue-black sky.

It was exactly that.

He could see ruins and fluted columns, a labyrinth of ruins, and a handful of shepherds' huts—but mostly it was the mountain, dominating everything. In the moonless starlit night it looked like an ancient craggy pyramid looming closer as the small boat sputtered through the waves.

He could feel the place feeling for him, trawling. Laving him like a cat with crisp pinprick waves of energy. He chain-smoked. He was frightened. Down to his soul he was frightened. He was sure he had reason to be.

He closed his eyes and for the first time he thought he knew who she was, and what his own role might be.

The mountain reached out to him, found him, flayed him gently.

DODGSON

"Did you know that the first Immortal was a woman?" Chase said.

Dodgson sat beside him in the prow of the boat, Billie on his left and Michelle, Danny and Eduardo behind them, with Xenia at the tiller steering toward the mountain.

In the starlight Chase looked preternaturally pale, his skin translucent.

"Gaea, her name was—Mother Earth. The Greeks called her the Daughter of Chaos. It's not unusual. In most civilizations, the first and oldest deity is a female, a goddess. The male seems to start almost as an afterthought, as a consort for the goddess. But the real power's with her, with Mother Earth. Mothers of Corn, of wheat or barley, that sort of thing.

"She's the very first step out of a system drenched in magic, with one foot still planted there. In times of drought, or when the crops were bad, it was magic the ancients went back to in order to get out of it. So they'd kill in the name of their goddess and sow the fields with blood. Sympathetic magic, like to like. Blood to feed the thirsty corn, corn to feed the people. Like to like.

"And guess who died, Dodgson?

"Men. A man. Some human stand-in for the consort of the Earth Mother. Always someone in pretty high standing in the community. If he was old and past it, the king. If not, if he was still too useful to let go or too shrewd to kill, his surrogate—some noble who would masquerade as king and even be treated as though he were king for a while.

"Thousands of years ago, the same thing happened here in Greece. Later, life got more civilized and people tried to forget about all that. You had the Golden Age—laws, citizenship, philosophy, mathematics, justice. But you were left with charming old stories about handsome young men who died for love of some goddess, of a Narcissus or an Adonis. It was a watered-down metaphor, but a memory of the real thing.

"They began in blood, these stories."

Dodgson looked at the mountain. Under different circumstances it might have been beautiful, he thought. Now it looked cold, blasted, as though despite the few shepherds' huts nothing could live there.

The waves were rising. There was nowhere else to go.

"You don't see what I'm getting at, exactly, do you?" said Chase.

"No. Not really."

"Remember we talked about Greece changing, decaying—being badly in need of renewal?"

Dodgson nodded. "Sure I do. Hell, the *world* could use refurbishing if you ask me."

"I agree. And for all I know something similar's going on elsewhere. Who's to say? But we're talking about here now. And the point is, renewal's the province of an Earth Goddess."

He pointed at the mountain. "Look at that," he said. "It's something like three hundred and seventy feet high, surrounded on every side by the ruins of the most venerated place in the ancient Greek world. The entire island consecrated to Apollo, the god of the sun. And to his sister, Artemis.

"It was venerated for a *reason*.

"I've been thinking about Lelia. Remember I said I thought she was drawing power from something?"

"Well, I've been doing a lot *more* thinking about Artemis.

"Because it wasn't really Artemis born there, not exactly. The goddess who *was* born there was much older, unnamed so far, but an earth goddess too, originally. Her myths are very ancient. There's even speculation that Apollo began, not as her brother, but as her consort.

"And then later she became particularized, what they call a tripartite figure. Her functions split. She was known as the Goddess with Three Aspects.

"So that as Selene she was goddess of the moon—the lighted, full moon—sort of a counterpart to her brother Apollo. Up until tonight, by the way, you notice we've had moonlight. And the moon is no negligible influence on the tides. Anyway, you've got Selene.

"But then as Artemis she's the Huntress, goddess of the hunt—of the hunt for *food*, Dodgson, not sport. For sustenance. And sustenance *is* renewal. Which is probably why she eventually became the most important of the three.

"Also of a kind of primitive ecology. She's protectoress of the animals as well. She commands them, informs their destinies.

"And as Artemis, she's also the patroness of childbirth.

"So. Tides and moonlight. Animals, hunts and childbirth. Beginning to sound at all familiar to you?"

Beside him Billie was silent, gripping his hand, listening close. He could hear the irregular chugging of the motor. His stomach lurched as they bottomed out of a high crested wave.

He said nothing.

"Then there's Hecate," Chase said. *"And believe me, Hecate is something else, my friend."*

Dodgson looked to the mountain. He could feel what was coming. There was an urgency, a fever to the man now, a fever in his voice.

"There's nothing like her in the entire pantheon, Dodgson. Greece is the cradle of humanism, after all. Of light and reason. There's very little left in its mythology that would really frighten anybody, that would hearken back to the old days. Very little except Hecate.

"What you've got here is a clear representation of the dark side of the ancient Mother figure. The death before rebirth, all the bloody sacrifice. Hecate was goddess of the *dark* of the moon. She was patroness of witches. Supposedly, the mother of Circe and Medea. Like a good, observant Mother she was said to walk the earth frequently, much more so than her brothers and sisters.

"And where did you find her? You found her in graveyards, or where three roads meet. People would leave sacrifices there—tethered-up dogs, or eggs or honey.

"She had an entourage.

"The dead. The dead were her entourage. She walked with them. She had the power to raise them up. Howling dogs announced her coming.

"You see what I'm saying, don't you? You see what kind of night we've got here?"

Dodgson nodded.

"Dark of the moon," he said.

The boat drew nearer.

He could see the dock now, empty. From here the ruins along the base of the mountain were a dark, shadowy maze.

"Get ready, Robert," said Xenia.

She threw him one of the lines. He stood up and glanced at Chase as they pulled up dockside. He wondered if the man had any plan at all. He saw him wince.

It's not cowardice, he thought. It's us.

I'd rather have ignorance, he thought. He feels responsible for us. He can barely control his own fear yet he feels our dependence on him. He's the only one of us with any equipment at all for this and it must be awful. I'd rather know nothing.

Despite the waves Xenia docked them neatly, barely scraping the dock. He stepped out and tied her off. The others followed.

Without the motor the night was terribly quiet. He found himself listening for wind but there was none.

There were supposed to be a handful of caretakers/shepherds

on the island. He wondered if any of them had heard them. In this kind of stillness they should have. It ought to have caused a stir. It was illegal to be here at night.

No one appeared.

"What now?" said Danny.

"Let's find someone," said Chase. He didn't seem optimistic.

They headed out through the broken city.

BILLIE

They walked along a broad, flat, dusty avenue past a row of pillars and broken pedestals, of porticoes overgrown with wild, tough grass. Low thorny growth scraped and pricked at her ankles.

Five marble lions crouched above them, luminous, features worn smooth by centuries of rainfall. There were empty pedestals for four more.

She clung to Dodgson's arm.

It wasn't fair, she thought.

She'd come so far with him in so short a time, forgotten her fears, learned to enjoy a man again. And now here she was, reduced to a miserable, insecure, frightened woman again, reduced by half from what she was only days ago. Walking through a city where everything was long dead.

It wasn't fair because they'd done nothing to deserve this, nothing commensurate with the revenge she'd already taken, much less what might lie ahead of them. Her death had been an accident. She'd brought it on herself. It was as though that greed she'd seen in Lelia from the start had flowered like some unwholesome, night-blooming thing into a monstrous gluttony that had nothing to motivate it beyond greed itself. She'd become a kind of feeding machine—feeding on the fear in them and their caring for one another.

Long ago while she was still a girl she'd given up believing in God and thus far the world had proved her out. The world was random and capricious in the extreme. But now she wondered bitterly about a different god or gods. Now, when her happiness with Dodgson should have been rising to its zenith all she could feel was fear for him and for herself, all she could do was tightly grip his arm—and she wondered about what Chase had said, if there were such things as gods, delighting in the torment of men and women. Vicious, cruel, rapacious gods.

"This way," murmured Chase.

They climbed a low stone fence and saw a small, one-story hut ahead of them.

Inside there were candles burning. Flickering through the tiny window.

In front of them Xenia was holding on to Eduardo, and Michelle to Danny, mirroring her and Dodgson.

The path was uneven and overgrown with weeds. She stumbled. Dodgson supported her. They scuffled along, unsure of their footing in the dark. Through his sweater she could feel dampness at his arm and waist, a light warm humidity.

The path narrowed. They crested a hill. Her eyes held to the candlelight in the window as though it were a lifeline. Her pupils contracted. The rest of the world darkened.

Michelle began to whimper.

"What is it?"

Billie could just see them. Two dark figures moving back and forth ahead of her, Michelle trying to pull away, Danny holding her gently back.

"It's okay . . . Michelle . . . it's okay . . ."

"No!"

". . . really, honest, I swear it's . . ."

"It's not. It's not! *No!*"

Then suddenly she was running, a shadow darting past her down the path. Billie saw Xenia turn around and there was fear in her eyes too. She turned from the candlelight and when her own eyes adjusted saw Michelle standing facing them, arms rigid at her sides.

"Michelle!" she said and started toward her.

"I won't go in there!"

It rang on the night air, hung there, echoed.

Snakes, Billie thought.

"I won't!"

"All right," said Danny, moving past her. "Okay. You don't have to. I'll stay here with you. We'll be fine. All right?"

He reached for her hand and she took it hungrily. She was crying. He turned to the others.

"We'll stay here. Okay?"

He'd addressed it to all of them but everyone knew that only Chase could answer it. So they waited. But Chase just shook his head. She thought he looked strained.

"I don't know . . . there's so much going on here. I . . . think so. I think it's all right. But be careful."

Danny nodded. "We'll stay right here on the path. That okay, Michelle?"

"Yes."

Billie looked at Chase. Why? she thought. *Why doesn't he know?*

If Chase was blind to the place she didn't think she wanted to go either. Not anymore.

She knew she didn't.

Why had no one come to the door?

Michelle's screaming had been enough to . . .

To wake the dead.

She was trembling. She supposed there was safety in numbers. She supposed they had to see.

They started forward. This time she kept her eyes off the lighted window. That had been a mistake. It could have been a bad one.

Pebbles danced out in front of her. She could feel the presence of Danny and Michelle behind them, watching, imagined their silent embrace.

They huddled together now. They moved up the hill. She let

go of Dodgson's arm. She wanted both hands free—just in case.

If only she could stop shivering.

They reached the door, old white painted wood. Chase knocked.

They waited. There was no answer.

He opened the door and they stepped inside.

She had time to register three small candles burning amid a shadowy jumble of tools, pots, pans, icons, clothing—and to realize that they were not alone but that someone was very near them, nearest to Xenia, when something shifted in the far corner of the room beyond the sputtering candles.

And she recognized her mother.

"Billie! Billie, come and help me; roll me over. It hurts, Billie! Please. Be a good girl."

The woman lay in bed, face ashen, and Billie remembered that she was crippled with cancer. How could she have forgotten? *"Yes, of course,"* she said and moved toward the bed. It was the bedsores, naturally, that were hurting her. Even the morphine wasn't much help anymore. She was always in pain now and would be till the end. The doctor had made that very clear.

"Billie, help me."

She wished the nurse were here. It was really very hard to move her all alone. Even at seventy-five pounds there was a curious heaviness about her. As though she were already dead. Dead weight, they called it. She didn't like to think that way but it was true. Besides, when she moved her alone she inevitably hurt her.

The withered hand reached out to her.

She moved closer to the bed, wondering why her movements should be so dreamlike, so slow, why her feet felt so heavy. Her mother was calling her.

"Billie . . ."

There was so much pain in her voice now. It had been a lovely voice once, rich and musical. Now it was all rasp and rattle. She would move her and then get her a glass of water. That would help some.

"Please, Billie . . ."

"Yes, Mother," she said but it was terribly hard to move, she actually had to struggle as though she were falling asleep on her feet—so she reached up for the gray, mottled claw of a hand, knowing that if she touched it first she could get there, could get across the distance to her, could help relieve the pain, her mother's pain, her poor dying mother *who had passed away five years ago in a little green valley in Derbyshire* . . .

The hand contracted, reached up . . .

DODGSON

. . . and Dodgson got up out of bed, he had his green-striped pajama bottoms on, and there was Margot wearing the tops, making breakfast in the kitchen.

Through the window he saw the East River. The morning sun was bright. He smelled ham and eggs frying and then as he shuffled closer, rubbing sleep from his eyes, the early-morning smell of her—teeth brushed, clean damp hair herbal-scented and drying.

"You're looking woolly this morning. Look what I'm making you."

The ham popped in the pan.

Dodgson yawned and reached for her. She danced away, waving the spatula, laughing. He tried to remember how it had been last night. One of their good nights, or bad? If it was bad then this was only making up to him. Otherwise it was nice. He wondered if he had to get to work later or if he'd finally finished the manuscript. He couldn't remember.

God! he must have done some pretty heavy drinking last

night. Probably that meant it hadn't been so great between them.

Well, never mind.

"Come here."

He reached for her again and she darted away toward the bedroom, giggling in that high, silly way of hers that he somehow dimly knew would later sound so much like the broken edge of insanity. But this was much earlier than that, wasn't it? This was the very early days of their relationship. So how could he . . . ?

The train of thought fell apart, unresolvable.

She stood in the doorway to their bedroom. He could see the rumpled sheets behind her. She lowered her head and smiled.

"Turn off the stove," she said.

He did. The dial felt oddly unsubstantial. For a moment the lights in the room seemed to flicker.

She unbuttoned the pajama top and let it fall off her shoulders. As always the sight of her naked aroused him. She was very pale. He could see the tiny light blue veins in her thighs and breasts, a delicate reminder of mortality.

He remembered he used to kid her about her New York pallor.

She began to back into the bedroom. Slowly he followed her. At the foot of the bed she stopped and sat down, leaned back on her elbows, spread her legs wide.

He moved closer.

She seemed to shimmer in front of him, to fall in and out of focus like a camera lens adjusting. This really was the king of hangovers, he thought. Can't remember, can't see.

So where was the headache?

What was going on?

He felt a thread of panic. Maybe he was sick or something, feverish.

He looked at her and it didn't make sense; she looked as though they'd already made love that morning, had *just* made love in fact, though he certainly didn't remember it. *Her skin was dripping wet.*

Sweat?

How could that be?

It glistened in her pubic hair, dripped down her arms and across her chest. And for a moment he saw the wide deep vertical slashes on the insides of both wrists, red as raw meat yet bloodless—and then he heard her laugh again, knew the laugh to be insane now as somewhere inside him he had always known, God help him, because *that* was his crime against her, would always be his crime, and lowered himself down to her pale white blue-veined flesh . . .

JORDAN THAYER CHASE

. . . Tasos was angry.

"You should have let me come, Chase. You are arrogant. I could have helped you."

"I know, Tasos."

"You are too proud."

They sat at the bar at Lycabettus as they had so many times before, sipping the Santorini wine that was going to make them a fortune—another fortune—and looking out over the city. The sky was clear and he could see all the way to the Acropolis, lit by huge klieg lights. Athens was only good at night, he thought.

He shook his head.

"It wasn't pride, Tasos. You get used to handling these things alone, that's all. I didn't want to involve you."

"*Involve* me?"

He stood up. His clothing flapped in the wind. And it was not the dapper gray three-piece suit he was wearing but rags, bloody rags, and Chase saw that his eyes had already sunk deep and turned a yellowish, reddish brown, the dry empty eyes of the long dead. His left arm was gone. From its stump maggots dropped to the table. A large piece of slate protruded from his collarbone.

"*This* is involved, isn't it?"

"She . . . ?"

"Yes, *she*! She did this to me!"

"Tasos, I . . ."

The thing before him seemed to stagger. He saw the twisted, broken angle to the legs. The sunken eyes stared balefully.

The waiter handed them their bill.

Tasos sat down again.

Nothing could have seemed more natural.

The ruddy tan was back. Tasos tugged at the tailored jacket and turned over the check, examining it.

"Not much," he said. "Considering."

"Tasos . . ."

"Think nothing of it, *fello*." He leaned in close. "I will pick up this check for both of us. *But I think you must take the next*. No?"

The lights of the city began to wink and flicker. Miles across from where they sat the Acropolis was melting, dripping, beginning to crumble under the glare of the klieg lights. Chase watched.

This too was her doing.

Chase began to struggle inside himself—not to get rid of the scene, but to augment it. He turned the lights higher. He felt them burn fiercely now.

He felt himself burn inside her.

"Yes," said Tasos.

The Erechtheum fell. Then the Parthenon.

The night faded. He was standing now, not sitting. The table was gone.

"Good," said Tasos distantly. "Much better."

"*Good*," said his afterimage.

The room burst into focus.

He saw Billie and Dodgson pale in the candlelight, both of them reaching out to something that wasn't there, sleepwalkers in that place he'd just returned from.

For a moment he wondered what she'd sent them.

Giving him Tasos had been a mistake. It was good to know she could make one.

Then he saw what had happened in the interim.

DODGSON

Someone was shaking him.

The bed, the room, the dead naked woman flew apart like shattered glass.

He was back inside the shepherds' hut and Chase had him by the shoulders, shaking him, hurting him.

"All right, all *right*!"

"Get Billie."

He saw her a few feet away, a strange little-girl sort of mannequin that was only half-familiar. He blinked hard and went to her. Images of Margot jumped and twisted as in a fun-house mirror. Then they were gone.

He shook her too timidly at first. Her pupils were widely dilated. She was very pale. He shook her harder, slapped her gently.

"Billie!"

She groaned. He slapped her again.

Her head fell forward. He felt her muscles go slack, then tighten.

"Rob. What . . . ?"

He saw Chase in the corner, using a lighter on a rolled-up newspaper—one of those three-color jobs, Greek.

"We're getting out of here. Come on."

There was something in the corner, some movement in the shadows, obscured from view by the heavy table. Something that seemed to feint forward and dart quickly side to side.

Chase had the paper burning brightly. He thrust it at the thing in the shadows as though he held a knife.

Dodgson moved her toward the door.

Then for one frozen moment he saw it, all of it. The face of the old ragged shepherd leering at Chase like a bloodstained mask as he lunged and pulled back, daunted by the fire. The figures behind him in the flickering shadows that crouched over the bodies on the floor—the still, dead faces of the bodies turned upward and wrenchingly familiar.

Xenia and Eduardo.

Shepherds sawing, slicing with the curved blades of shearing knives, intent, expert and mundane in that surrounding as though they were shearing sheep except that they were skinning, not shearing, and the skin they pulled away was thin and nearly transparent where it was not bright with blood.

It was peasants that had gotten her after all.

"Let's go! *Go!*" shouted Chase. He was backing away, waving sparks from the burning paper.

Even as Dodgson turned he vomited onto the earthen floor.

"Robert!"

Billie pulled him out.

He saw Chase toss the paper on the bed and slam the door.

The night air smelled suddenly clean.

Through the window he could see something flare inside. Good, he thought. Burn. Burn all of it.

They ran down the path under the blue-black starlit sky.

Danny and Michelle were exactly where they'd left them. They didn't need to be told—they ran in silence and it was only when they were past the row of lions and could see the smoke curl rising from the hut that they stopped and Danny asked after the others in a hushed, small voice that already knew the answer.

They sat silent behind a low stone wall, smoking, thinking.

A little time and distance had allowed him to be puzzled.

"Why did it stop them?" he asked Chase.

"What?"

"Your fire. Your newspaper. They had . . . they were
using *knives*."

Chase shrugged. "I'm not sure it did. The one, maybe. The
others . . . they were busy."

He remembered the figures bent low over the bodies,
remembered the tearing, cutting sounds.

"The fire was just reflexive," said Chase. "What you'd do
with animals."

He didn't understand.

"Dodgson, didn't you *see* them?"

"I . . . yes. For a moment, yes."

"They were *dead*. Every one of them. Not just Eduardo and
Xenia. All of them."

And Dodgson saw a change come over the man, as though
some far-off battle were raging and only Chase were witness to
it. The eyes were dreamy, lethargic—and pained.

Dodgson worried for him.

"Let's go for the boat," said Danny. "High seas or no. I
want off this island."

"Yes. *Please*," said Michelle.

"And go where?" said Dodgson.

Danny shook his head. "I don't care. Anywhere. Naxos."

"Naxos is miles."

"*I don't care, dammit!* A rock in the middle of the sea. I just
want out of here."

They looked at one another. Then they got up and headed
toward the dock.

It was empty.

They searched the water and Dodgson was the one who
spotted it bobbing over a whitecap a couple hundred yards
away, much too far to swim to. Xenia had tied the boat
securely. Now it was floating free.

There was no other boat in sight.

He took Billie's hand.

Danny and Michelle sat down on the dock, staring out to
sea. Jordan Chase paced the old rotting boards.

They were trapped again, he thought, just as on Mykonos. Chase had warned as much.

Only now the trap was smaller, tighter.

Tall as a mountain.

SADLIER/LELIA —THE MOUNTAIN

So many names for what he had been in that life before . . .

Smuggler. Rapist. Dope dealer. Murderer.

Even, long ago, tenor—in a boys' church choir in the slums of Paris.

There was no name for him now.

Now all he had ever been existed for him only as sand informs concrete, as wood informs fire. They were part of him but he was memoryless, transformed. She had done that.

Had he anything in his past to compare it to he would have been well pleased.

Alive he had been treacherous, cunning, casually cruel. But there were always hesitations, some measure of doubt. Now nothing existed between him and his desires but simple opportunity.

Already he had much of what he was promised. He took them fast and slow, easy and hard, some of them begging for death. And then he led them. He had known warm blood and cold inert flesh.

The world was black and fine.

And now he waited for another part of what was promised, a small part but infinitely desirable.

So that it was almost with recognition that he watched the blonde woman running below and grew bloated with the urge to take her.

• • •

She stood high above him at the top of the long sleep climb. Once there had been a temple here. Now there was only rubble and broken columns. She watched them scurry like rats through the maze of the city, past the House of the Trident and into the House of Masks. Her dogs began to howl. Cats lay small and cringing at her feet. She saw into each of them and held their tiny souls in the glove of her intense and ardent longing, as she would soon hold those below.

At every instant she was with them. Turning each corner, running, going nowhere. She felt how weak and small they were with their fear of the dead and their fear of her, only one of them with any strength at all—and she drew up out of her the infant that had died inside her and held it so it could see him, see what must be, and knew she would have to speak to this man before turning him loose to the vast, rich world of the dead.

The man was searching for her.

He was afraid, but he was man enough to search.

She saw the grim, firm set to his mouth and smiled.

The cats crept down the mountain. Vipers crawled over her breasts and shoulders. Her dogs howled.

She listened to the power in the marrow of her. It was old as the mountain, new as this clean, distillate hate. It flooded her with a cruel, supernal wine, with heartless song. In the wind she heard other, gentler voices, voices more amicable to man. But they commanded nothing. No earthly or unearthly creature. While she . . .

She watched the shepherds' hut burning. She fed her power to the charred, smoking bodies and rose them up.

The vipers hissed sweetly in her ear.

She released the Frenchman standing below her. He could go, move darkly down the mountain.

They all could go.

There were only two she wanted for herself, each for

despising and fearing the thing she had been and for their terror now.

Contempt was the very blood of her.

Deliciously, she felt it surging.

JORDAN THAYER CHASE

His head pounded; his skin felt so sensitive he felt he'd been burned along with those in the hut. He trudged wearily along with the others, feeling old, feeling betrayed by this thing that was no gift at all but a lie and a curse, which could not help them but would only allow him to sense more clearly when and how they would die there, and how horribly.

He felt the caress of a million daydreams, impressions, knowings, past and present.

He saw once again the serpent-fanged idol of the ancient *Mexica*, stared into its thousand wakeful eyes, alive again after a thousand years. He saw the dim mists of Avalon part to reveal a secret hiding place, which to all but Chase and those like him would remain hidden for centuries yet to come. He saw an unnamed spirit in a New England forest rise up against the locust encroachment of man and blast the earth barren, shrivel the lakes and streams, and in passing, explain to the ten-year-old boy that was Jordan Thayer Chase the bankrupt suicide of his father, a farmer who had seen all his land and holdings die before him, explain its terrible justice.

And he saw Lelia as he had first known her in Quebec, her pale soulless eyes, the eyes of the only other man or woman on earth he had ever met to possess his own terrible gift, his curse, his sight—he saw himself drowning on a bed of power with her, a bed of dreams, annihilated, exalted, his orgasm immense and frightening, saw himself put her in a taxi later,

saying, Yes, of course I'll call *and knowing he would not,
could not now that they had lived one night through in the
perilous whirlpool depths of each other, and saw in her eyes
that naturally she knew the lie and hated him for it, would hate
him forever for his cowardice.*

He saw these things and many others and they came like
ghosts to him, drew over his senses, a drifting fierce confusion.

Elaine, he thought.

He had no choice. He slipped into them.

DODGSON

They scrambled up through the narrow streets of the ancient
city.

Dodgson was watching Jordan Chase. He didn't like what he
saw. All of them were breathing hard and sweating but Chase
was moving like an old man now and even in the dark Dodgson
could see his pallor. When they glanced at each other there was
a feverish light in his eyes that made him wonder how firm a
hold Chase had on his sanity. He knew that look. He'd seen it
only minutes and years before. On Margot.

Still it was Chase who led them. He seemed somehow to
know the place—so that when he stepped over the guardrail
and into the ruin they followed, and found themselves standing
on a mosaic floor. Dodgson lit a match. He saw a god riding a
panther. The panther clawed the air and snarled.

"Apollo," said Billie. "I know this one."

"We'll rest," said Chase.

It seemed as good a place as any. There was one narrow
doorway but other than that it was closed off on all sides, open
only to the sky. The walls were high.

He hefted a rock. Perhaps it had been a piece of the building once. He felt a bit ridiculous. *David and Goliath,* he thought. Who are you kidding? But at least the rock was something. It imparted weight, substance, hardness. The illusion of security. Aside from Chase the others held them too.

He leaned against the wall facing the doorway and sank down into a crouch. Billie slid down next to him, leaned over and kissed him.

"I love you," she said.

"I love you, too."

Danny smiled. They had whispered but sound carried here. He didn't care. He didn't give a damn who heard him.

DUET

Lelia heard him.

From atop the mountain her fury boiled down like lava.

Chase didn't.

Leaning back against the wall he felt the blast of anger but had no idea as to its cause. It didn't matter. He knew where it came from.

It had been some time since the others had been wholly *in the world* for him.

He was aware of their proximity. They were bodies that moved along beside him. Familiar but somehow distant. He realized a certain responsibility to lead them. Occasionally to speak.

But his focus was with her, had been throughout the climb. He felt her intensely now.

He was amazed at how strong she'd become. He knew she was very much at home here.

She seemed to fill him completely.

He sensed other things, other voices, vague, undefined and insubstantial. Things with hooks and claws. Things that commanded, that blinded in a sudden white-hot glare. He knew they were important too but he could not hold them yet; he was too much with her.

He watched and listened. Filled, straining.

While she burned down at them.

While those she controlled crept down the mountain.

You will die here.

Her voice broke over him.

It was all too real, too powerful. Not a prediction but a curse. He felt a wave of nausea.

He tried to block it out, to concentrate on what was there, on the people around him, on the small colored tiles beneath his feet. Even on his heartbeat and the sound of his breathing.

All of you. I will suck you dry.

The tiles, he thought. Look at them. Something in them sounds the other voices.

Apollo. Brother, consort.

Show me.

He listened for them and dimly, they were there. And they were frightening too, unknown and immense as she was but more familiar, safer somehow—a kind of haven from some other time, another place. A rightness about them, a circle closing.

Louder now, commanding.

I will claw my name on your flesh.

He struggled with a flurry of images, to hold them and let them come.

A dark, dark room. Night. Stone.

Screeching.

Kneeling.

Mykene, and the crypt . . .

. . . and something hot and burning, hot enough to lay back the flesh of his eyelids in scorched, black cinders.

What?

I am very close to dying now, he thought. Very close. Let me see this first.

He reached. Fell short. Reached again—his breath coming in gasps, his body bathed in sweat.

He pulled at it, wrested it from the dark of the moon.

The earth went black and distant. The voices inside him were all, all there could ever be, her voice and the other and somewhere his own, screaming, crying for help and for a strength he could never, he thought, attain in any world under the sun.

Her vengeance moved down the mountain.

BILLIE

"Chase! Jesus, Chase, wake up!"

Dodgson was shaking him, slapping him.

One scream and then utter silence. What did he see?

Slapping him wasn't going to help.

"Stop it," she said.

Dodgson moved out of her way. She put her hand to his mouth and nose. He was barely breathing. His face had gone dead white; his eyes rolled in their sockets. The jaw muscles were clenched tight.

"Pry his mouth open," she told Dodgson. She turned to Danny and Michelle. "Get a stick. A strong one."

Dodgson had his mouth open. She felt for his tongue. It was curled toward the back of his mouth. She rolled it forward.

Danny tapped her on the shoulder and handed her a stick. She positioned it along the front teeth and back along the left line of molars.

"You can let go now," she told Dodgson.

The jaws clamped shut.

She felt his pulse. It was weak, but regular. His wrist was chilled and damp.

"We ought to have water," she said.

"I saw a jar back there," said Michelle. "What do you call it? An amphora. There ought to be rainwater inside."

"I just need something to wet him down with. Use Danny's shirt."

"Danny, go with her, okay?" said Dodgson. "Nobody wanders off alone."

"Right."

They moved toward the doorway.

"Hey guys?" said Dodgson.

They stopped and turned.

"Careful."

Danny smiled. "Just for you, Skip."

They waited.

The air was still. The footsteps faded. Dodgson slipped his arm around her waist.

She stroked Chase's face and ran her fingers through his thin straight hair, trying to bring him back to sensation. His breathing had a hollow sound to it, a subtle rattling. She'd check his tongue again in a minute.

Something moved in the brush.

They jumped.

A lizard scuttled across the tiles.

"Shit!" said Dodgson.

Danny and Michelle came back through the open doorway. Danny had his shirt off. He held it out to her. It was dripping wet.

"Thanks."

She moistened his lips, then began to mop his brow. She had

done this so often for her mother. The rattling sound had disappeared from his breathing. That meant his tongue was back in place again. She opened his shirtsleeves and ran the wet cloth over his wrists and forearms, rolled down his socks and swabbed his ankles.

Danny bent over her, watching.

"Any idea what happened?"

"No."

She ran the cloth over his face again, then opened his shirt and ran it around his neck. His muscles were very tense. He was taking an immense beating, an immense amount of strain. She watched the jaw muscles spasm. She wondered how old he was. She hoped his heart was in reasonably good shape. Right now it had better be.

Come on, she thought. We *need* you.

She thought she felt him relax a little. But he still had no color and his breathing was still shallow.

They heard dogs howling. Far away.

She looked at Dodgson. "You remember what he said?"

"I remember. *Dogs announce her coming.* I remember every word of it."

She removed the wet shirt. That's odd, she thought. She felt his forehead.

"Feel that," she said.

Dodgson put his hand to his forehead. Michelle touched his cheek.

"My god," said Dodgson.

"Fever," she said.

"He's burning up. When did this begin?"

"Just now."

She touched him again. "And I may be crazy," she said, "but it seems to me it's climbing. Climbing fast."

"Jesus," said Danny. "If this guy dies on us . . ."

"I know."

"What do we do?"

"There's nothing we can do. Only what I'm doing. And hope it breaks."

"So we're stuck here."

"I'm afraid so. We don't dare move him."

"Hell, I don't know where we'd go anyway," said Dodgson. "He's the one who'd know."

Michelle moved into Danny's arms. He hugged her tight.

Billie glanced at Dodgson. He was watching them, smiling a little. Feeling, probably, exactly what she was feeling—that it was good they had one another. That, at least.

Chase had nobody.

She touched his forehead.

The fever mounted.

JORDAN THAYER CHASE

He lay in a pit of fire and molten rock. The flesh of his hands, arms and legs melted, peeled back over sizzling, dripping fat and scorched muscle. He tried to rise. His mouth fell open in a howl of agony. Blisters filled and popped along his back, his loins, his chest. His lips and eyes burst. The muscles of his legs seared through and snapped. He fell into the pit, splashing liquid fire.

He lay quiet. It would last as long as it had to last.

He remembered Tasos's words.

He drank from the cup.

LELIA

She felt something stir below, sealed off from her, a blinding flame.

She felt no fear of him.

It was right that this should be so.

Still she prepared. She drew together all she had captured from the sleeping earth—the pull of the harvest moon, full in the springtime sky, the cruel mystery of its dark phase, studded with walking shadows.

She drew up the beasts, which were hers. And the dead, which were hers also.

She embraced them, drank their blood.

They stood bathed in hers.

LEGIONS

They heard a shuffling—like someone walking through thick mud—along the path, where there was no mud.

They heard rustling in the brush just beyond the entrance to the ruin.

Suddenly the illusion of security was gone, the illusion of hiding from her was gone.

They stood together and waited.

Dodgson felt resigned to it. Sooner or later they were going to have to face one another. He thought of the first time he had seen her, languid and beautiful in the sun. He thought there had never been any sense to it at all.

He clutched the stone in his hand and watched the door.

The rustling stopped.

Slogging sounds moved closer up the path.

And perhaps there was a moment then when they might have bolted out through the doorway and prolonged the inevitable. But nobody moved. Then Billie looked up over their heads to the top of the wall—some bright clear instinct made her look—and they heard her gasp. Dodgson felt her jerk away from him.

Her fear ran through them like an open wire.

They circled the top of the wall on all four sides, crouched like miniature gargoyles from another age altogether, eyes luminous, watching.

Dozens of them.

They saw the still, patient hunger. Noses twitching to the scent of fear, to the quick blood pumping.

Danny raised a rock.

"Don't," Dodgson whispered.

It would assure the cats' attack. The first aggressive move, the first sign of panic. For a moment they hung suspended there.

Danny lowered the rock. His eyes looked drunk, haunted.

Billie felt Dodgson's hand on her arm, pulling her gently, firmly, away from where Jordan Chase was lying, pulling her slowly toward the doorway. She was quivering. She felt choked, breathless.

Her nightmare opened out in front of her like the petals of some dark flower.

She knows me, she thought. Knows me well.

They backed toward the entrance.

The eyes watched. Depthless, calm, intent.

• • •

It was dreamlike and slow, as though the very air had thickened, like backing through mercury.

The slogging sounds behind them continued. Closer.

Chase moaned.

Not now, thought Dodgson. There's nothing we can do. They moved across the mosaic of the god who rode the panther, away from him.

He felt Chase *pull* at him.

Dodgson felt tied to all of them now by tough invisible strings, a chain of flesh—he felt Danny's strength and bulk beside him and Michelle's fast, whiplike frame next to Danny, and most of all Billie's thin soft flesh in his hand, flesh these claws could tear so easily and that had already known a tearing. He seemed to feel it tighten, coarsen, as though to protect itself.

He could almost feel the blood pulse beneath the skin.

I'm sorry, Chase, he thought. *Lie still.*

The entrance was only ten or twelve feet away.

He watched the watchers, eyes glowing against a field of stars, blazing through the moonless night.

Then Billie began to unravel.

He felt it before he heard it, a whimpering sound, welling up out of her like some black twisted thing she'd tried and failed to hold inside. Sounds like some small animal caught in the razor teeth of a trap.

He felt a dark flash of anger.

Lelia, you fucking coward. Get these away. Show yourself. To me.

The eyes watched them.

He smelled fear-sweat and something else, something he couldn't identify. Something sweet and cloying that bruised the clean night air.

Billie could barely move now. Barely see through a film of tears.

"Please," she said. Not knowing she would say it. Not

knowing she would utter a sound until it had escaped her—and then it was irrevocable.

It was like a signal.

Something moved atop the wall.

It slid down—a hiss of silken movement.

Strings snapped.

Dodgson felt them snap. He heard someone cry out. It could have been himself.

The cats poured off the wall.

They ran and at first there was a strange disorientation, adrenaline making him light-headed and dizzy as though he'd been in a car crash and they'd turned the car over and come up not knowing who was where, hanging there in some upside-down limbo while figures scurried out around him. Then he saw the door and knew his target. He heard yowling, snarling behind him, padded feet hitting the tiled mosaic like huge drops of rain.

He plunged toward the door, Billie at his side just behind him. Somehow Michelle had gotten there ahead of him and Danny . . .

. . . *where was Danny?*

Billie screamed. It cracked over him like a whip. He whirled.

The cat clung to her shoulders, wild-eyed, ears pulled low, mouth open wide and hissing. And there was Danny, there behind her, reaching for it, cursing. He saw him pull it off her, heard the shirt rip and saw blood fly as its claws pulled free and he tossed it back over his head against the wall. He heard it screech in pain.

. . . *and then they were close, too close.* He saw Danny turn.

Suddenly there were cats all over him.

Bodies tearing with teeth and claws, tight, muscular and dug-in deep as leeches in just that slim fraction of a second. Dodgson pushed Billie through the door. He could hear them ripping, tearing, while Danny struggled under the weight of them. Dodgson turned back for him. He heard himself screaming and some sound from Danny that he could not describe, and would never forget.

He saw Danny pound and kick while those that were not already on him circled, spitting, then leapt to find some open space on him, some space that was not already covered and bleeding, saw him fall back into a sea of writhing bodies that leapt off and back again as he fought. Dodgson moved forward, kicking, felt a grim delight as he heard one scream and felt its ribs crack, kicked another in the head and saw it fall away.

They were on Danny's arms and legs and up on his shoulders. Dodgson saw his knees buckle and saw him sink to the tiled floor as they swarmed, digging in with their forepaws and kicking with their strong back legs, tearing at him.

He kicked another one square in the face saw blood and spittle fly.

And then they discovered him too.

One launched itself at his head. He jerked away reflexively. A thin mangy tabby leapt onto his thigh, biting, claws sunk deep. He screamed and battered at it, broke its neck, flung it off. He felt Billie's hands on him, pulling him back, her fingers suddenly strong as talons.

He looked at Danny.

You could barely see him now.

He saw one bloody hand reach for the big black cat at his chest, grab it by the neck and pull. But he hadn't the strength to dislodge the animal. The arm thrashed uselessly. There were three at his neck, forepaws working, searching out the vein. His face was covered. Dodgson saw them biting.

Billie pulled.

For some reason the cats ignored him now. Some stared at him, others at something behind him.

He saw Michelle at his side, hands to her mouth, her eyes thin slits of loss and pain.

It was suicide to try to help him.

He spun her into his arms. He didn't want her to see any more of this. She hung there heavily, her body seeming to jump convulsively. He heard sobbing, terrible sounds.

He saw Billie gasp, saw her eyes go suddenly wide.

He looked at Danny.

They had found the jugular. Blood burst over the feeding bodies.

He grabbed Billie too and they stumbled out the doorway . . .

. . . into the arms of the black, slithering things outside whose flesh was steaming and oozed to the touch and filled him with nausea and horror . . .

. . . and he knew he was making sounds. He did not know what kind of sounds they were. Howls, screams, gibbering. He felt sanity take a leap and leave him stranded.

Fingers slid over his bare arms, cold, pustulated, gray-black liquid traces glistening in the starlight like the tracks of worms.

His mind shut off, staggered. His body went weak. He pushed at them, screaming, slapped at them like a hysterical girl.

In his mind he saw the burning hut, the torch. He smelled fire. Fire and the sweet high reek of burning flesh.

Fingers locked tightly on his arms.

They were suddenly all around him, groping, clutching.

He saw Billie break free and stumbled out beyond their reach. He felt a wild joy. Yes! Run!

He kicked, shoved, tore a blackened arm off his chest and spun the thing away from him.

"Michelle!"

He saw one come up behind her and wrap its filthy arms around her, saw the black mouth open wide as she struggled. Then Billie was behind her with a rock and she was pounding, pounding, until something broke inside its head and it fell away.

He felt arms slip over his waist, felt two more of them fumbling at each of his arms, their grip as slippery as his. He elbowed the one behind him over and over until it went down in a heap, then struck the one to his left with his fist, hit it low in the belly and felt his hand sink deep, the flesh parting, sink straight into a ripped-open tangle of guts through the charred shallow skin, and then it fell too. Only one was left.

He grabbed its slick flesh at the throat, filled with furious power now, a power close to madness, and he would have tossed it down the path away from him like a stinking sack of garbage except that he looked first into its wide, staring eyes.

And saw Xenia.

And in that moment as he hesitated it threw him down instead. He did not see the rock but only felt it crack hard against his skull.

Then there was only a whirling smoky blackness. And somewhere, far off, the lurid screams of women.

BILLIE

Billie recognized the big Frenchman instantly. And because he was familiar she thought he'd come to help them. So she went to him.

And then looked closer, deeper.

She saw what he was.

Just as the hand shot out sideways and slapped Michelle down.

She screamed as Michelle's cry of pain rang in her ears and the man advanced on her with a great lumbering lurch and crushed the breath out of her as he took her in his arms.

His hand tore down the back of her shirt and she felt the night air on her spine.

She fought, pummeled him with her fists, kicked him, curled her fingers into claws and went for his eyes. Then his hands were on her throat and he lifted her up and held her until there was no more struggle in her, until her throat and lungs were one great driving agony and she felt her eyes bulge, her tongue move outward through her lips, seeking passage. He dropped her.

She fell limp and choking, coughing spasmodically, help-less, as he tore the shirt away from her, as he tore the jeans down through the zipper and then split them along the crotch with his powerful hands, put his foot on her stomach and tore upward through the panties.

She saw none of it, only felt it—saw nothing but a darkness of asphyxia in which a yellow sunburst bloomed and faded. And when he pulled her to her feet again and lifted her by the armpits and shoved her against the cold stone wall she still could not see him, could only gasp for breath, muscles limp, racked with sickness and coughing, while she felt the cold unnatural hugeness of him abruptly enter her.

He took her pressed against the wall like a mounted butterfly—and when at last his own dry spasms began bit her below the collarbone and drank her blood like a suckling baby.

She looked down at him, the sunburst finally gone, the darkness gone, her vision clear again, and had one bright thought for Dodgson before the dead yellow eyes stared up and she saw his pallor and smelled his stench and something snapped inside her, rocketing her down to where nothing was dead and nothing gave her pain, where there was only a riveting silence.

SADLIER

He hoisted the dark one up on his shoulder, walked to the other and put his hand beneath her and lifted her to his side like a folded raincoat. He saw where the bruise already discolored the jaw of the dark-haired woman, relished the slack nudity of the other.

Like a hunter bearing his kill—though he was not to harm them further, not now—he walked through the ruins to where the great stone stairs led precipitously to the top of the mountain. Two cats followed at his heels. He ignored them.

The steps were many but he climbed them effortlessly.

Ahead he saw her outlined against the indigo sky, against star clusters thick as clouds. She was naked and her pale arm beckoned slowly, drifting out and back like a feather on currents of wind.

DODGSON

He woke alone.

The cats were gone.

The dead were dead.

They lay about him like broken rag dolls, even those he'd never touched, black limbs twisted under them. He couldn't look at them.

He couldn't look at Danny either. But he walked to where he lay and stood beside him staring at the wall, and moved only when he felt the tears start to come.

Chase lay where they'd left him, unharmed, still burning with fever. He had no time for him now.

Billie was out there somewhere, alive—he could almost feel her reach out to him in fear and pain. He knew she was alive because he knew why Lelia had taken her. To punish him. To leave him wondering, hoping. To make him follow.

It was not in Dodgson to abandon her. If only to help her arrive at some gentler death than Lelia would devise he had to follow.

He had seen what happened to Danny.

They had counted on Chase but Chase was useless now. He still felt sorry for the man. His turn would come.

He knew his own chances for survival.

He left the ruin.

He could guess where they'd be. On the mountain.

A beautiful place to die.

But I want to live, he thought. I want Billie.

He felt a rush of anger and it helped him. He had always thought anger and resignation were incompatible but they were not. He thought of the tragedy of Prometheus, chained to a rock, his body a feast for birds. Impotent, resigned, able to see his future—yet still raging. He understood that now.

Fuck you, Lelia, he thought. Don't expect me to come whining.

He stepped off the path and looked around. He found a broken tree limb, hefted it and liked its weight. It felt good—solid and gnarly. It was probably useless but what the hell. It might work better than shouting.

He found the path again and walked toward the mountain. At the base of the stone staircase he looked up and saw nothing but peaks and crags and stars.

He wondered if it was worth it to try to find an alternate route, something less exposed, something a little tricky. He guessed not. She'd had no trouble finding them thus far.

Might as well go on up in plain sight, he thought. Club in hand. Just like the ancient Greeks would do.

He swallowed and started climbing.

Call me Hero.

DARK OF THE MOON

She had watched from afar. The rape of the English girl had pleased her particularly.

And now he tossed them down. She saw the bruised, bloody bodies at her feet—and then she saw *into* them.

The French would be first to waken.

She directed him silently and watched while he tied her hands behind her back and trussed her feet together at the end of the long heavy anchor chain he'd taken off the *Balthazar*, now moored on the far side of the island. He worked quickly in fear of her displeasure.

As he finished the French girl opened her eyes. She cried, struggled against the ropes.

The ropes chafed her skin. If she continued she would bleed.

Her breasts tingled with anticipation.

And soon the English girl would waken too.

It was good that they both should see, each what would happen to the other.

She waited.

Soon the eyelids began to flutter; the face took on an expression of pain.

The face was remembering.

She saw where his teeth had torn her and the thin line of blood over one of her breasts, the stains on the inner thighs.

There was movement in the limbs. The eyes opened. She allowed them a moment to take her in—the perfect nudity, the radiant clear blue eyes that met the girl's own and vanquished them.

Her voice was thicker and deeper than Billie remembered. It almost seemed a ventriloquist's trick, as though it came less from inside her than from somewhere in the air around them.

Look, said the voice. *Look what I will do.*

Her fingernails were long, gleaming black.

Billie watched her draw them lightly over her thighs and stomach up to her small pale breasts, caressing them, then dig suddenly deeper and rake down, watched her tear long jagged troughs of red over her breasts to her belly, bloodless, tear wide at the stomach until she could see the gray-white folds of viscera. Then they moved to her face, reached up and clawed for the eyes and ripped them out.

She held one in each hand. Offered them to her. Then closed her hands and crushed them.

The wide luxurious lips parted in a smile.

The hands oozed liquid.

She screamed.

Suddenly Lelia was whole again.

The blue eyes blazed as before. The body was perfect and unharmed.

This is how you die, said the voice.

She walked to where Michelle lay cowering, her face muddy with tears, teeth bared and lips trembling in a half-mad grimace that distorted the delicate features.

She peered into the red-rimmed eyes.

And you, she said.

I have children, thought Michelle. *Children to return to, to teach, to learn from. I have a job I love and I have met a man I loved and I will meet others. There will be others.* She begged Danny forgiveness with all her heart but the will to live was strong, the remembered kindnesses, affections, friends and loves, physical loves—all so very strong. She had always been highly physical. It was one of the reasons that children responded to her, because they were physical too. And she remembered the small soft arms, tiny arms encircling her neck, the distinctive pungent-sweet smell of the very young; she could smell it even now. It was the smell of life, not death. She could not die. They could not kill her, not when there was so much to go back to, to go on to, so many good full years out ahead of her now . . .

She laughed as the French woman tried to crawl away. She tugged on the rope. The woman fell sobbing against a slab of rock, her feet pulled out from under her.

She bent low and stared, a cold amusement in her eyes.

You, said the voice. *I know what you like.*

She opened her mouth and leaned closer so Michelle could see.

Her world tilted, fell. Telescoped forever.

Lelia's tongue was gone.

In its place and gazing out at her was a small black hooded snake.

JORDAN THAYER CHASE

. . . the fires were a peaceful lapping water now of which he was a part, skin and blood and bone no longer, but liquid fire.

He swam to the god through a sea of flame, through the surfaces of suns, and the god toward him. The radiance of atoms imploded in him, while he exploded outward, and both were one. He felt the power rise inside him, the power he was born to wield far beyond the papier-mâché world of deals and stocks and money. He remembered that world but dimly—as a dreamer recalls the soft-edged constructs of a dream. The power lifted and filled him and soon would bid him rise, like Antaeus, renewed by the earth in this place where gods were born and died and then were born again . . .

BILLIE

Her screams went on and on . . .

Billie stood swaying, crying at the edge of the pit where they made her stand, weak, dizzy, in danger of falling herself—and she could see them writhing below as the big man lowered Michelle slowly down headfirst, dangling, spinning at the end of the anchor rope, could see because they'd thrown a torch down ahead of her to stir them up and so Michelle would be able to watch them slide toward her, gliding angrily along one another's backs to escape the burning torch, hissing on one another's flesh. And then would be able to watch them strike and strike . . .

. . . as they were doing now.

DODGSON

He heard the screams. *Billie?* Dodgson began to run.

The stairs were steep and there seemed to be hundreds of them. His breath came in short cold gasps. His lungs hurt and his feet felt heavy as lead. But the screams were shrill and final-sounding—wild, primitive. Someone was losing her mind up there. And dying. Both together.

Billie?

He couldn't tell.

He plunged ahead. He stumbled, hauled himself up and continued, his legs pushed almost to the limit. The breeze became a cold wind as he climbed. Still he sweated with exertion and fear. Clouds moved by, blotting out a patch of stars. The screams continued, rising higher, a torture in themselves.

Then they stopped abruptly.

His soul felt colder than the wind.

Bitch, he thought. He took a step. *Bitch*. The word became a cadence to him.

He ground his teeth together and plodded upward as though slogging through hip-deep snow.

He reached the top.

He heard the wind hiss over the mountain.

His legs trembled. His throat felt raw.

The trail wound over the peak from here but there were no more steps to climb, thank God, just a gentle incline to the summit. He could see nothing, no one, ahead of him.

He took a deep breath and started off at a slower pace. He thought it might pay to be careful now, to avoid tiring further. The screams had stopped in such a way that he knew instinctively whoever had uttered them was beyond his help. It came almost as a consolation to him. For someone terror had ended. For someone else, maybe not.

The trail narrowed to his left past a bold outcropping of rock. From where he stood the summit was almost at eye level. Another few feet and he'd see what was up there—and whatever was up there would be able to see him. He shifted the stick to his right hand, the outside hand.

He ducked behind the shelf of rock and waited. Listened.

At first there was nothing. Only the wind and his own raspy breathing.

And then the wind shifted.

He heard a sound that was familiar, very familiar, but completely out of place here—the silky abrasion of flesh on flesh. He heard strained breathing mingled with a stifled sobbing.

He knew the voice.

God damn them!

Anger warred with elation. Elation because she was alive up there and fury at this abuse to her. And then he heard Lelia's voice—soft, venomous, chanting.

Cunt. That's all you ever were to him. Cunt.

Timed to the fleshy rasping strokes.

He stood and looked.

She was standing on Billie's hands.

The huge body pumped at her. Long, punishing strokes that pushed her back cruelly over the bare rock.

Lelia's eyes glittered.

He climbed the rock. He made no attempt to hide from them.

He walked to where they were and Lelia saw him and smiled and stepped back. The big man was oblivious, intent only on

Billie. Billie's eyes were closed and that was good. This wasn't going to be pretty.

He spread his legs to even his stance and took the heavy stick in both hands and brought it down on the man's heaving ribs with all the force he had in him, heard them crack and the man shriek in pain, and when he raised it again he saw two bones pushing through the soft sluglike skin like the broken ribs of a wicker basket.

The man looked up at Lelia—it seemed in astonishment to Dodgson—and then rolled off Billie's body, and Dodgson brought the stick down across his face, caved in the front of the wide high forehead and the nose and saw teeth fly off like pebbles around him. And when he lifted it away he saw the face crushed completely—eyes askew in their sockets, mouth, nose and chin oozing a foul dark liquid.

The man rolled away and Dodgson twisted the stick around and clubbed him again between the legs this time, a sound like chopping wood. The man doubled over, vomiting thick bloody bile. The back of the neck looked good to Dodgson. He raised the stick and swung it down and heard the junction crack, saw the head slide off at an angle, limp, broken, hanging loose over his left shoulder.

The man crumbled and lay still.

For a moment he felt a ringing victory—he felt triumph.

Then he looked at Lelia and realized the man was nothing.

He saw her smiling and knew that this was just one more horror to put him through, nothing more. Like the cats and Danny, like Xenia. *Make him kill, yes.* It was part of the plan, part of some awful unknowable ceremony, some mad blood passage.

It was not nearly over between them. Not nearly.

Yet she didn't move toward him. She didn't speak.

He waited a moment. Then he knelt down to Billie.

She moaned, barely conscious.

The man had been immense. There was no way of knowing how badly she'd been damaged. He saw the blood on her thighs.

His rage was gone. He felt a chill pass over him.

He looked up. Lelia was gone.

And suddenly he heard dogs howling— back along the stairs and all across the summit of the mountain. Some distant, some nearer. All of them moving closer.

Not over.

JORDAN THAYER CHASE

The change was full and complete in him.

And it was not precisely Jordan Thayer Chase who rose off the tiled mosaic in the House of Masks and walked through the entranceway out through the winding paths of the city.

This new man glowed with a strange inner light. Her dogs shied away from him.

He sensed his way to her unerringly. He walked the long maze of streets and began to climb the processional steps up the mountain. Inside he felt the power of many suns in many times and places. They had worshipped power like this flowing out of stars a billion miles away, and they would again, many billions of miles away from that. As once they had here. And he knew what he had been sent to do if not what had sent him. That he would never know.

But the concept was old as time. The joining of the two—it was the figure of the universe.

Man and woman. Sister and brother. Moon and sun. Life and death.

And now one hard, rapacious woman as powerful as he had died and tapped a vein of purest fear. Not evil but fear—primal as the cave. Whether by accident, chance, or by the design of an anemic corrupted earth seeking to burst into violent life again she had found that vein and drunk deeply.

Now as always fear had its counterpart; death had its

counterpart. Each fell victim to the other. The circle closed again.

He walked the steps, a man no longer young, but felt no strain. The dogs yelped—scalded—and ran away from him.

In some hidden part of him was the knowledge that had been with him since the beginning—that he would die here. But as someone had told him once, in another life, in another world entirely, there were far worse places to do that. He stalked her up the mountain.

DODGSON

The dogs had scented them.

He pulled Billie under a shelf of rock so that at least they couldn't hit her from behind and then waited, holding tightly to the heavy stick, palms sweating into the smooth dry wood.

The baying stopped. They were near now. He could hear scuffling, paws scrabbling against bare rock.

There.

He could see eyes glowing in front of him and wished for fire. But there was no fire.

He screamed—ferociously, he hoped.

He darted out into them, swinging the stick wildly, sounding to himself like some great choking bear.

He hoped they wouldn't smell the fear on him.

They scattered.

He watched them lope across the mountain.

He went back to her. She was sitting up, staring at him. She said his name.

"Can you walk?"

She nodded.

They had to get away from here. Someplace he could defend. Someplace with just one entrance.

"You sure?"

"Yes."

"Okay." He slipped off his sweater and gave it to her. He looked at her, at the bruises and the blood, as she put it on. Something gave inside him. She saw it happen.

"Later," she said. "Tell me later."

"When we're out of this."

"Yes."

He gazed out into the night. He could see eyes glinting a few yards away.

"They're out there. Make lots of noise, all right?"

He squeezed her hand.

Then they were up and out, screaming, hollering, running around the side of the mountain while his eyes strained in the meager light to find some sort of break in the rock below, great dark shapes chasing after them, growling, snapping at them from behind and then bolting away as he turned and swung at them, hesitating and then coming back fast. He felt something grip his pants leg. It almost tripped him. He turned and kicked, felt himself connect and heard the big dog yelp.

She was ahead of him now and he ran after her, searching the mountainside. Down below on the far side of the mountain he saw a boat anchored in a tiny inlet—it barely had time to register. And then he saw a place a few feet down along a jagged wash. Some sort of hole. He called her.

She turned.

He saw the dog go after her, rushing past him, snarling. He moved fast, cracked it across the shoulder with the stick. The dog jumped and bounded away. He pulled her toward him and then down the few steps to the hole. She stumbled and they nearly went down the mountain. He caught himself and shoved her out ahead of him into the hole and then she was safe inside. He leapt after her.

Jaws clamped hard on his leg, on his calf just above the ankle.

He fell, reached forward to the edge of the hole and screamed, more in fear than in pain because there wasn't much pain yet, just the feeling of being drawn back, the unreal dreamlike agony of being hauled back by his own torn flesh from that place of safety. He saw her reach for him, the pale white palm of her hand.

Too far!

He whirled and slashed with the stick, caught the dog across the muzzle. Blood and spittle flew over him. He saw mad red-rimmed eyes. The dog yelped and let go. He tried to pull the leg up so he could crawl inside but the leg wouldn't go, something was wrong there—then he *did* feel pain, a rocket-burst of pain as a second pair of jaws replaced the first, came down *on the very same spot* and another dog hit him at the knee. He felt bone grind against bone. He screamed and struck out wildly.

He felt the hard-soft thud of contact once, twice, then three times and suddenly he was free again and his hand went out to her, and she'd angled herself out closer by then. Her grip was strong as he hauled himself toward her.

Then she screamed too.

The hand slid away, slowly, in slow motion, and he didn't understand, he couldn't hold on to it.

He saw pity and terror on her face, just for a moment—just for the slightest moment.

Then her face pulled back too and he strained and struggled to the edge of the hole and peered in, called her, and saw her sliding down, sliding away from him into the blackness in the depths of the mountain.

BILLIE

The walls were cold and wet, slick, smooth, and she could get no purchase with her fingers; she felt the fingernails break as she clawed the cool granite surface, as the hands drew her down and down into the damp-smelling darkness. They were Lelia's hands, she'd felt them before, she knew them, she was in some ancient cistern, going down forty feet or more while the smooth hard stone bruised and scraped at her, became colder, and she was dragged over wet slick steps cut into the living rock, cut thousands of years ago. With a cry of anger and despair she knew it to be her grave.

Hands jerked her around a corner and the dark sky blotted away entirely, so that now she plunged through a world of darkest night, and she turned and bent forward at the waist, not minding the bright stabs of pain as the steps bruised her hip and thigh. She swung hard with her fists at what dragged her, swung where the body should be, the face, the hands. There was nothing.

Nothing. The faint smell of ether. And the dragging.

She screamed his name. The walls gave back no echo. She heard the thing that was Lelia crooning to her:

Come. Come now.

She curled herself into a ball to cushion herself against the jolting—and then the stairs were gone and there was only a long, smooth slide, the walls around her as though the earth itself were bathed in a chilling sweat, and then that stopped too.

The hands released her.

She lay in a shallow pool of water, all around her a blinding, stifling darkness, and for a moment there was silence, just the faintest scraping sounds up ahead where she had come from— where Dodgson was—and then she felt the long black fingernails tear down through his sweater. She felt them on her breasts. Poised there.

Soft lips touched her neck.

She smelled the foul stench of her and remembered how it was supposed to end—the sudden rending—what she'd seen her do to herself a thousand nightmare years ago on the mountain.

DODGSON

He'd wished for fire.

He'd damn well got it.

He was halfway over the rim of the hole, trying to get to her, knowing the wounds in his leg made it impossible, when he felt a sudden heat and turned to see.

The figure came straight toward him, naked, streaming flame—long bright filaments of flame like a red-yellow swirling fog burning off into the air around him.

He walked through a raging holocaust.

A man. Or what had been a man. Something magnificent now and terrifying.

"Hecate!" The voice breathed crimson fire.

The dogs ran yapping away in confusion, ears flat, tails dragging.

Apollo, he thought.

Something he had made.

BILLIE

And Billie heard the hissing come from deep in Lelia's throat, felt her fingernails retract like cat claws, and saw the eyes light up with an inner glow, a liquid phosphorescence that moved from the eyes through the rest of her body like a flood tide surging; saw her crouched above her, hair standing on end, nipples long, erect, teeth bared in a wide feral snarl.

In the darkness of the cistern she was the only light.

She saw her muscles contract, tighten.

Then suddenly she moved, crawling up over Billie's body like some great pale spider. Up along the passageway to Dodgson and whatever called her name.

THE HUNTRESS

He had come to her.

She crept toward him through the cistern.

What she was informed her fully. In this she and Chase were alike now.

The others meant nothing. Not even Dodgson. She could not recall his name.

He was a vessel to carry the fear of her, from which the Other would drink, and change. No more.

She moved toward a convocation that had not been seen for over two thousand years on earth and which even then through all the ages before had been glimpsed only through veils of drunkenness, drugs and dreams in the raging minds of her initiate. A mummery of the drama that had made the world and continued to create it still in time, matter and space; that birthed new worlds even now billions of light-years away in the dissolute awakening of a great imploding star. Toward her dumb show she climbed, toward her Easter passion. The spider in the heart of the rock. The rock in the heart of the flame.

DODGSON

He fell back from the edge of the cistern as though a fist had slapped him down.

Such was the force of her.

Above him heat lightning crackled. He smelled ozone heavy on the atmosphere.

She emerged blue-black, drifting, luminous.

It wasn't Lelia.

The form was hers but the face, the eyes, the bearing—all had transmuted into something hard as steel yet delicate and light as air. He saw a grace she had never had in life, and saw that mixed with a great brute strength and something more. She was beautiful—unbelievably, perfectly beautiful—and terrorizing. As though changed to liquid stone—unnatural.

She looked at him, her head turning slowly.

The heartlessness of spiders. The tenderness of wolves.

His heart thudded massively in his chest. He closed his eyes, squeezed them tight. He could die under this gaze now.

She could kill at a glance.

He pressed hard against the rock face, his wounds, his pain forgotten.

He opened his eyes and she was staring into the column of flame that Dodgson knew was a man. A stutter of static electricity raced between them. Pale bolts of blue and yellow. Beside him the rock face glimmered.

She reached slowly deep inside her belly.

When her hands emerged again she held something writhing, crawling.

She held it aloft.

He heard a voice that was not a voice. He had the urge to scream. The rock face shuddered.

I give this to you.

He saw a child, tiny, covered with the blood and mucus of birthing, so small she could have held it in one hand—and it lived, it smiled. Its teeth were sharp and pointed. Its mouth drooled dark arterial blood.

Across from her the fires dimmed for a moment. He saw the man show suddenly through, the eyes of Jordan Thayer Chase blinking and flickering with a mute human sorrow.

Then the look was gone. The eyes blazed again, pools of roaring flame.

He saw the dead standing ranged about her. He saw Xenia. Danny.

She held the child out to them.

And you, she said.

She turned to Dodgson.

And to you.

He felt it like a curse.

Then her hands were empty.

He saw her smile and turn her hands out and over toward Chase in an age-old gesture of invitation, saw her step forward—a single step, yet firm, final—and then saw Chase move to where she stood and reach for her, take her in his arms, the real Chase now and not the thing cloaked in flames, the man, as naked as she was. She wrapped her arms around him and seemed to go softer suddenly. She opened her mouth to him.

He saw the lips pull back.

He saw teeth like the fangs of vipers.

"*No,*" he screamed, a warning lost in the rising wind, in thunder. Yet for an instant Chase looked at him, seemed to recognize him there against the rocks for the first time. His eyes were old and tired, knowing. In his face Dodgson read courage and inevitability.

Her head struck down.

The jugular broke. Suddenly they were bathed in blood.

He saw Chase's arms tighten swiftly behind her back and thought, *A reflex, a spasm,* but the strong arms pulled at her, pulled her down and the fire flared again as his blood spurted over them, sizzling. He saw his hips draw back—her teeth still deep in his neck, eyes ecstatic—and then plunge forward as he entered her.

She howled, tore her dripping mouth away from him and howled in rage, in pleasure and pain, struggled, clawed at him, but his arms held fast and he plunged at her again and again while the flames rose high around them, scorching the brush along the rock face, illuminating Dodgson trembling and holding tight and screaming into her screams like a single breath into a hurricane.

Above him lightning flashed too and suddenly he saw her flesh go white and transparent as the flesh of a maggot, saw the red and blue of veins and arteries, saw heart, lungs and larynx working, while her body thrashed and pounded him. He saw Chase rise up and dig hard and finally burst blindingly inside her in a bright red column of flame that filled her, burned her, scorched her. He heard her cry of joy ride brilliantly through the electric night sky.

And fell in a sudden blast of purest light.

AT SEA

Billie.

He had awakened to find himself lying in her arms. It was near dawn.

Beside her a bit of scrub was still burning.

Now the *Balthazar* tumbled through the waves.

The seas were relatively calm and that was good because Dodgson had little experience with boats. Billie sat next to him on the fly bridge, drinking whiskey from a paper cup. They'd found it below.

Along with a pair of bodies, male and female. Older people.

Billie shivered. Even with the blanket on she couldn't get rid of the lingering cold. Yet she couldn't bring herself to use the woman's clothing either. She'd taken some peroxide, iodine and bandages from the cupboard in the hold and she'd taken the blankets and whiskey. That was enough.

Morning dawned while they were still some minutes from shore, dawned bright and clear, a gleaming red glow on a glittering sea. In the distance they could see the town, the small squat whitewashed houses climbed the hill from the port in long, uneven rows. She thought of the zigzag maze of streets and wondered what they held now, what harvest the night had brought them. She'd been told the Greeks were resilient. She thought they had better be.

She finished the whiskey and came around behind him.

"Rob? It's over now, isn't it?"

She thought of the bodies lying below.

There were deep dark smudges under his eyes.

"Yes. It's over."

"What happened last night? What did you see?"

"I'm not sure," he said. "Give me a while. Then we'll talk about it. We'll figure it out together."

"All right."

She could see the tall masts of ships in the harbor.

Dodgson slowed their speed a little.

The world began in terror, she thought. She did not know why the notion should come to her now, staring out at the tranquil sea.

But all at once she knew she disagreed with him.

It wasn't over.

The knowledge came from inside her. Perhaps Jordan Chase would have a name for it but she did not. Nor did she know what it meant to her, good or bad.

All she knew was that inside her, faint as whispers, something stirred.

EPILOGUE

Two months later they sat in a café on the Boulevard St. Michel.

It was morning. Autumn was in the air. In a few more weeks it would be impossible to sit outdoors—was nearly that today. The good rich coffee warmed them.

Dodgson had his paper open.

He read the papers with uncommon interest these days. There were a couple of stories he was following.

First, the Greek government had finally fallen. Observers had been predicting it for months—what with the plan to falsely inflate the drachma to prohibit purchase of foreign imports failing as badly as it had—but now it had finally happened, and there was a great deal of scrambling for position. His interest in Greece had not abated. He was following the players as closely as the International *Herald Tribune* coverage would allow. There was one he liked. Interestingly enough, a woman.

In Washington State, Mount St. Helens had erupted again. A survey party was missing—among them, two prominent geologists and a nature writer with whom Dodgson had long ago had a brief acquaintance. But he watched this story less for news of the writer than because in one item printed the day after the mountain blew there was mention of an overnight crime wave in a nearby town. So far there had been no follow-up.

Here in Paris they had finally executed their Iranian terrorist. How nice that some people had balls again.

"Like an old married couple," said Billie. "You with your paper."

Dodgson smiled. He folded the paper and put it down.

"Old married couples go to Florida," he said. "Not Paris."

They had arrived two days ago, their first time back in Europe since Greece. Billie had just found a good art history research job beginning in New York next month and Dodgson was working on a book. So it was a good time to get away before the crunch started.

They had not even considered Greece.

"Anyhow," he said, "two months married is not *old* married. Old married is *eight* months married."

"Cynic."

He shook his head. "Not anymore. No way. Never."

Billie looked up at him over the rim of her coffee cup. He thought she looked very happy. He smiled.

"What are you so cheery about this morning? You look like you ate the canary."

She put down the cup.

"Just wondering," she said. "According to your logic. How much is two months pregnant?"

"That's new pregnant." He looked at her. "And you're kidding."

"No, I'm not."

"From . . . ?"

"That's right. Mykonos. I can almost pin the day down. I think it was our third or fourth time together."

"I'll be goddamned."

"Probably."

He leaned over the table and kissed her, squeezed her hand.

"Are you ready to be a working mother?"

"Are you?"

He laughed. "Sure. I think so. Why not?"

He kissed her again. And it was true. Initially at least he'd be home a lot more than she was. Writing with a kid in the house?

Absolutely.

And he could almost pin the day down himself then. If she said it was their third or fourth time together then he saw when it was, it had to be, they'd never been closer or more tender. It was the time she'd cried and asked him not to leave her and they were already afraid by then; they didn't know why or of what but it was already upon them, and he'd promised her he wouldn't and thought how far and fast they'd come together, and he said, *But what if you leave me?* He remembered her answer. *Dodgson, you should live so long.*

A breeze ruffled the paper.

The thought came to him unbidden. At first he considered it pretty strange—and then he didn't.

Because back there on the mountain Lelia had lifted up her child to him, and perhaps it wasn't a curse. Perhaps it was just a knowing of the way of things.

He thought, Thank you, Lelia.

There were still all kinds of renewal.

MASTERWORKS OF MODERN HORROR

_ 0-425-10533-4	**THE TALISMAN** Stephen King and Peter Straub	$5.50
_ 0-425-09726-9	**SHADOWLAND** Peter Straub	$4.95
_ 0-425-09725-0	**FLOATING DRAGON** Peter Straub	$5.50
_ 0-425-09760-9	**WHISPERS** Dean R. Koontz	$4.95
_ 0-425-09217-8	**STRANGERS** Dean R. Koontz	$4.95
_ 0-515-09251-7	**IN A PLACE DARK** **AND SECRET** Philip Finch	$3.95
_ 1-55773-113-6	**THE DAMNATION GAME** Clive Barker	$4.95